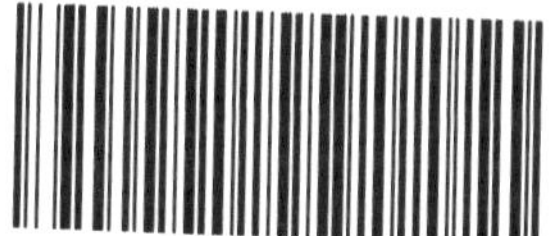

found

found

not quite a billionaire,
book three

rosalind james

Cover design by Robin Ludwig Design Inc.,
http://www.gobookcoverdesign.com/

Formatting by Dallas Hodge, Everything But The Book

synopsis

I'd lived my life on two principles: discipline and control. Until now.

There's that phrase, though. "How's that working out for you?" The answer, when it came to Hope Sinclair, was, "not so well." She might be little, she might be sweet, and she might be young, but if I'd thought she'd be compliant anywhere but in bed, I'd learned my lesson.

To keep her, I had to let her go. To hold her, I had to turn her loose. To have her in my life, I had to accept that she was nine thousand miles away in New Zealand, in my grandfather's house in Katikati, surrounded by the loving members of my Maori whanau and much too close to the not-so-loving ones.

All of that was killing me. On the other hand, I thought it might be working, so I was going to do it. No matter what.

author's note

For Rick,
who is nothing like Hemi.

other books from rosalind james

The Escape to New Zealand series

Reka and Hemi's story: JUST FOR YOU
Hannah and Drew's story: JUST THIS ONCE
Kate and Koti's story: JUST GOOD FRIENDS
Jenna and Finn's story: JUST FOR NOW
Emma and Nic's story: JUST FOR FUN
Ally and Nate's/Kristen and Liam's stories: JUST MY LUCK
Josie and Hugh's story: JUST NOT MINE
Hannah & Drew's story again/Reunion: JUST ONCE MORE
Faith & Will's story: JUST IN TIME
Nina & Iain's story: JUST STOP ME

The Not Quite a Billionaire series (Hope & Hemi's story)

FIERCE
FRACTURED
FOUND

The Paradise, Idaho series (Montlake Romance)

Zoe & Cal's story: CARRY ME HOME
Kayla & Luke's story: HOLD ME CLOSE
Rochelle & Travis's story: TURN ME LOOSE
Hailie & Jim's story: TAKE ME BACK

The Kincaids series

Mira and Gabe's story: WELCOME TO PARADISE
Desiree and Alec's story: NOTHING PERSONAL
Alyssa and Joe's story: ASKING FOR TROUBLE

table of contents

Contents May Shift During Flight	1
Not Desperate	5
How to Love	12
The Wages of Pride	21
The Sharp End	26
Inconvenient Emotions	33
Still Paying	43
No Cinderella	50
Rubbish at Negotiation	57
Same Old Story, Same Old Song	68
Whatever You Fancy	76
Feet to the Fire	87
Wairua	98
Coming and Going	107
Comparisons	115
Another Fabulous Growth Opportunity	122
Alpha Tendencies	128
Closer All The Time	136
Sweet Anticipation	143
Surprise Package	148
An Unexpected Visitor	159
Sixteen Going on Thirty	166
What We Have Now	174
A Woman's Heart	183

Mending the Broken	190
The Te Mana School of Negotiation	199
Mermaid Out of Water	210
How Forever Feels	222
Attitude Adjustments	232
Right Speech	243
Something That You Do	249
A Different View	258
Right Choice	268
Naked Ambition	275
Maori Mana	282
Threads of Silver	291
Threads of Gold	301
Acknowledgments	310
About The Author	313

contents may shift during flight

♡

Hope

It was raining on the day I ran away from home.

Well, storming, more like. Or let's tell it like it is. The gods had decided to dump every bit of their accumulated wrath on the southern Pacific, and I was smack in the middle of it. My doom was coming complete with driving rain, lightning, and turbulence that rocked the Air New Zealand Boeing 777 as if it were a crop duster.

Hemi had told me that the silver fern painted hopefully onto the tail of my deathtrap stood for new beginnings and rebirth. As I clutched the armrest and was grabbed painfully by my seatbelt and slammed back down again into the narrow Economy seat, it felt more like the end of everything. At least the end of the breakfast I'd forced down an hour earlier, when my life hadn't seemed about to end. When it had just seemed miserable.

I'd left my fiancé. I'd left my sister. I'd left *both* my homes: the we'll-call-it-a-one-bedroom-and-get-more-for-it Brooklyn apartment that had housed me for twenty-five years and my sister Karen for all her own sixteen, and the however-many-bedroom-I-can't-count-that-high penthouse on Central Park West where Karen and Hemi still lived. To come here. And, apparently, die. Along with my baby.

Did I mention I was pregnant? Well, I was. I'd run, and I'd taken Hemi's baby to New Zealand along with me, and he'd be furious, and so upset, and… I couldn't think about that now. I had enough to deal with at the moment. I couldn't imagine our baby was enjoying the ride, either.

Did eight-week fetuses get airsick? Probably not. But its mother sure was.

You see how I was trying to maintain. To be rational. To be normal. Not to be a hysterical, nauseated, overemotional, terrified wreck. And that—that moment right then, when I was climbing on top of it all, rising above, when we were either going to land or going to die, and nothing I could do would influence the outcome—that was when Sean, the formerly sweet, contented, chubby-cheeked toddler beside me, threw up into my lap.

One second, he was crying. The next, he made a strange choking sound, and then every bit of his breakfast was on my jeans.

"Oh, no," his mother, Moira, called out over his wails. She was clutching the baby for dear life, hanging on with both arms and the grip of a superhero. Or a mother. And if I was scared, how much more must she be? She'd been a cheerful, organized, ponytailed brunette twelve long hours ago, back in Los Angeles. Twelve hours after I'd taken off from New York. Back when I'd been a human.

"I'm so sorry," she said now. "I'll just . . ." She took a hasty hand off the baby even as I tried to tell her not to. I grabbed for him myself, and she reached for a cocktail napkin from her seatback pocket, thrust it at me, then resumed her death grip on Sean while I laid the flimsy square of paper on top of the mess on my leg and swallowed back hysteria along with my nausea.

"It's fine. We're fine," I shouted over the nervous laughter, the occasional shriek, the dull roar of jet engines, and the incessant rattle of baggage trying to escape the overhead bins.

If they didn't spill out onto our heads, we were doing great. Way to test the latches, guys.

Sean kept crying, not that I could blame him. I'd held him during the flight so Moira could go to the bathroom, could take a nap. When she'd thanked me, I'd told her I was pregnant myself, and I hoped somebody would help me someday. It had been my first pregnancy announcement, and it had felt momentous at the time. I'd laughed a little making it, and I'd wanted to cry, too. Moira had looked at the three carats on my left hand and clearly wondered, *Why is somebody with that rock on her finger sitting in the middle section at the bumpy back of the plane?* And because she was a Kiwi, she hadn't asked, for which I'd been profoundly grateful. I'd done enough crying for a lifetime already. Although it was good I'd gotten it all in, if my lifetime was going to be over right now.

Just when I was thinking it, the airplane lurched hard to the right, then back left again, and I clapped a hand on my mouth and thought, *Oh, God. Oh, God.*

We couldn't actually crash, despite the pounding of my heart and the useless adrenaline flooding my body and making me shake. The pilots surely wanted to go home as much as we did, and they must know what they were doing. You didn't get those wings from a cereal box.

And I *couldn't* lose my baby. Hemi's baby. That wasn't happening. I just didn't want to throw up myself, because I'd already found out that they didn't put airsick bags in seatback pockets anymore. You had to go all the way to the toilet for that. Ask me how I knew.

The plane lurched again, then dropped hard, leaving my stomach well behind, and I stopped thinking about death. It was all about the nausea now. All. About. The. Nausea. Sean had gone into full-blown Scream Mode, a woman was moaning steadily across the aisle, and I clutched the seatback in front of me, laid my forehead against it, and tried not to think about the scrambled eggs, potatoes, yogurt, and, worst of all, sausage I'd wolfed down with the ravenous hunger known only to those in the first trimester.

Please, no. Not on the jeans. Not the sausage.

When the plane hit, it was still tilted to the left. Then it slammed down on the right. Hard. And we bounced. One wheel, then two. We were bouncing some more, and then we were coming down.

Somebody was screaming. I thought, *Karen. Hemi. My baby.* Which was when the lurching stopped, and we were rolling. We were down, we were safe, and the entire plane erupted in cheers and applause, in the exultant relief of three hundred passengers who'd been miraculously delivered, like the Maori adventurers of old, safely onto New Zealand soil.

I put my head back, closed my eyes, swallowed hard, and tried not to cry.

I hadn't died, and I only had one person's vomit on my clothes. Bonus.

not desperate

♡

Hope

Koro wasn't there.

Hemi's grandfather, that is. Wiremu Te Mana, the eighty-three-year-old patriarch of the family, who'd promised me the day before—if that had been the day before, because I'd lost track—that he'd be there to meet me at the Auckland Airport without fail. He hadn't arrived, and I was getting worried.

I stood on an impossibly hard floor and felt as slammed by the voices bouncing off the unforgiving surfaces as if they were actually punching into my weary body. The sound seemed to arrive and recede in waves, and I clutched the handle of my black suitcase just for something to hang onto, looked around, and tried to avoid the word "desperately."

The arrivals hall wasn't a big place. It's not like he could have missed me. Auckland may have boasted the biggest airport in New Zealand, but it wasn't exactly La Guardia. But then, you'd have to add the sheep to the people just to get New Zealand's entire population up to New York City levels, so that wasn't too surprising.

I was trying to think about that, because thinking about anything else was terrifying, and thinking at all was almost beyond me. My brain was doing a slow whirl, and my head felt like a balloon hovering somewhere above my body. I'd fumbled my passport into the scanner, answered the questions from the Customs officer as best I could—Why was I here? Because I hadn't had anyplace else to go?—claimed my bag from the carousel, ducked hastily into the restroom, and changed my jeans with trembling hands, barely restraining myself from stuffing them into the garbage. The only thing that had stopped me was the knowledge that I was broke again. Or broke still. Broke people didn't throw away perfectly good jeans just because they had toddler vomit on them and the smell was making their sensitive pregnant selves sick.

I'd hurried through the quick change, then a rapid brushing of my teeth before I'd dashed cold water onto a face that felt as if it had the grime of nations embedded in it, and realized only then that there was no way to dry it. I'd settled for wiping it on my shirt, in the end. The shirt wasn't a whole lot better than the jeans anyway.

The whole thing was a long, long way from first class, let alone Hemi's Gulfstream G650, but that was just too bad. Coming here had been my choice, Koro would be waiting for me, I would get a job, and it would all get better. I didn't have to solve all my problems right now. I just had to get through today so I could start over tomorrow.

Except Koro *wasn't* waiting.

Finally, I went over to the Vodafone kiosk and waited as

patiently as I could behind a young couple whose gigantic backpacks leaned against the counter beside them like fatigued travelers. Even though it took a good fifteen minutes, there was still no reassuringly broad-shouldered grandfather figure to be seen when the clerk had replaced my SIM card and I had restored my contacts and was dialing Koro's number.

Four rings. Voicemail.

"Uh," I said at the beep, "Hi. It's Hope. I'm here. I guess you're stuck in traffic." It was barely six-thirty in the morning, but I did know that Auckland sported one thing New York City shared. Traffic. "I'm just, uh, letting you know I'm waiting for you in the arrivals hall."

In the half hour that followed, I sat on an uncomfortable chair and called twice more, and he still didn't answer. The sinking feeling in my stomach wasn't just nausea now, and my fluttering heartbeat wasn't just for myself. Something had happened.

What now? I wanted to sit on the floor and cry like a little girl, but I hadn't been a little girl for a long, long time, so that wasn't an option.

What would Hemi do in my shoes? I'd left him, and I might have destroyed my future with him for good, but he was still the person whose judgment and initiative I admired most—well, except in the matter of interpersonal relationships. I longed to have him with me right now, because he'd *know* what to do, and then he'd make it happen.

Well, then, figure that out and do it.

Who did I know?

I knew Hemi and Koro and nobody else here, not to have their number. And I wasn't calling Hemi. What, I'd left him to establish my independence, and twenty-four hours later, I was calling him and asking him what to do, begging him to work his magic and rescue me? No.

All right—what could have happened?

Koro had changed his mind and wasn't coming for me. He'd talked to Hemi, and the two of them were trying to force me to go back.

No. Not possible. Hemi would never, ever have left me here alone, and neither would his grandfather. It was that Te Mana thing. My baby was going to have a father with protectiveness embedded in his very DNA. I got a flash of Hemi's big arms cradling somebody tiny and helpless, and knew exactly how gently and carefully he'd hold our baby. How fiercely he'd guard us both.

Stop that.

Right. Back to thinking rationally. Koro wouldn't have left me here on purpose, so… an accident on the road holding him up? An emergency at home? No, he'd have called me, surely. All right, a simple dead battery in his phone. Mine was on its last red sliver of battery life itself. Or the likeliest thing of all: he'd mixed up the day. I couldn't remember what day it was myself, now that I'd crossed the International Date Line and gained nearly twenty-four hours. Koro had looked at the confirmation I'd hastily emailed him and assumed it was for tomorrow. And today he was… well, sleeping, probably, with his phone off.

Go, or stay?

Go. Katikati was only a three-hour drive, and there was no point waiting here any longer. I'd leave Koro another message along the way telling him what I was doing and when I'd get there before my phone died entirely. I wasn't in Outer Mongolia, I was in New Zealand. There was an information booth in the corner, and if I knew anything at all about Kiwis,

I knew the person behind that counter would be helpful.

Right, then. I was going to Katikati, where at least I knew my way around and nothing was confusing, and there would be a shower and a bed somewhere. Where I could get ready to face tomorrow.

♡♡♡

It was actually more like six hours later by the time I'd trudged the couple of uphill miles from the Katikati i-Site, the information center where the bus had discharged me, to the little house on the hill. I'd wolfed down a chicken pie at a brief rest stop that felt like hours ago, but I was hungry again, and so far beyond "tired" that I seemed to be floating in some alternate space, with my consciousness fully outside the shell that was my body. And, yes, it was still raining, the wind was still blowing straight from Antarctica, and despite an anorak with the hood pulled up, I was soaked and shivering. For the last half mile, the part where I was dragging my suitcase behind me up a final steep hill that felt more like a mountain, with my backpack feeling like it held bricks instead of a laptop, I honestly wondered if I was going to make it.

I did, of course. You could always do more than you thought you could, and your limit was always another step farther ahead. I'd learned that long ago. And when I reached the driveway, Koro's car was there. A much-used small Toyota SUV, parked beside his boat.

I hadn't realized how much I'd feared he'd been in an accident until my knees threatened to buckle. He was fine, and he was home—at least there was light coming from inside.

I hauled the suitcase up four wooden steps to the broad

front porch, blessedly under cover and out of the rain, and knocked on the door.

Ten seconds, twenty, and I knocked again, louder this time. I was sweating despite the cold, and not just from the physical effort and the anxiety over my welcome. The minute I'd seen the house, my insistent bladder, high on hormones and the suggestive rain, had flashed "TOILET" in giant red letters and declared a state of emergency. I was shifting from foot to foot, wiggling like a five-year-old.

When there was still no answer, I tried the door. It was unlocked. Thank goodness for New Zealand. I pulled my suitcase hastily inside, slammed the door behind me, and didn't stop to deal with my streaming jacket and soaked boots, just headed straight for the bathroom.

Is there any relief in the world more blissful than finally peeing when you're all the way past desperate? It was very nearly orgasmic. At least, I was shuddering. Then I was washing my hands and face and drying them on an actual towel, and that wasn't bad, either.

Finally, I stripped off my dripping jacket and unzipped my boots. I'd have to wipe down the water I'd tracked in before Koro came home, because wearing shoes in a Maori home just wasn't done, let alone walking through the house in muddy boots. But after that, I'd get rid of my wet clothes, take a shower that used way too much hot water, see if Koro had any herbal tea, plug in my phone so I could text Karen, and then lie down and sleep for a day.

Koro wouldn't mind, surely. *Have a rest and a think,* he'd told me. *Come to me, my darling.* He wouldn't mind.

I picked up my jacket and shoes and left the bathroom, finally flipping on the light in the hallway that I hadn't bothered with on my mad dash.

Something made me look to the left, toward Koro's bedroom. I stood there for a moment as if I'd grown roots, my mind trying to take in what I was seeing. And then I heard, as if from far away, the *clunk* that was my boots hitting the floor, and I'd covered the five or six steps to the half-open bedroom door.

And the arm that was barely visible through it. The arm on the floor. That wasn't moving.

how to love

♡

Hemi

I'd come home from the airport on Tuesday night just because I hadn't been able to think of anything else to do. I'd wanted to go after Hope, and I'd known I couldn't.

When I got there, Karen came out from the living room so fast she nearly cannoned into me.

"Did you get her?" she demanded.

"No." I took off my shoes and followed her into the living room, and had to blink. Papers and magazines were scattered across the coffee table, Karen's sandals and a long-sleeved shirt lay strewn on the carpet, the TV was blaring, and it looked like an entire family had eaten a Chinese banquet and then fled the premises.

"What have you been doing?" I asked her. I picked up a remote, turned off the TV, and pressed the button to slide the hardwood panel over the screen for good measure.

"Who's been here?"

Her gaze slid away from mine. "Nobody." And when I kept looking at her, she said, "Well, just Noah, for a little while."

"What?" I'd been gone… barely two hours. Well, three. It was nearly eleven. "Noah the Buddhist? Unattached Noah? *Male* Noah?"

"I was *upset.* Hope was gone, and *you* were gone, and I didn't know what to do! I didn't know if you were going to go to New Zealand or coming home with Hope or *what.* And Mandy couldn't come over, because it was late, and I knew you'd freak out if I took the subway over there, because you're so overprotective and everything, so Noah came over to hang out." All that last part came out in a rush, her voice rising as she spoke. "And I thought you were bringing her *back.* You let her go? Why?"

"One minute." The Maori in me had risen, and it had to go somewhere. Seemed it was going here. "There is no boy in this house when nobody's home, and you're not to go to any boy's house alone, either. Period. And clean this up, please. You leave it for Hope. You leave it for me. You leave it for Inez. It's nobody's job to tidy up after you, and nobody else is going to do it. *You* are."

Her hands were on her slim hips now. She was wearing only a ribbed yellow tank top and short brown shorts, and I looked at her and knew exactly what Noah had seen.

I hadn't met him. I needed to. Pity I hated him already.

She began to stack plates, her movements rough and abrupt, and said, "*OK. Geez.* I should have gone with Hope. She at least *wants* me. At least she doesn't *yell* at me. And why can't I have a friend who's a guy? Why can't I be a normal person?"

When she turned around, I took a better look and said, "That would be why." Her hair was still only a couple inches long, kept short after her head had been shaved for her surgery, and there was no hiding the considerable love bite on her neck. Which would be why the cushions on the couch were disarranged as well. If I'd had a back door, I'd have guessed that Noah had made his escape out of it while I'd been on the way in.

Hope would have blushed and put her hand to her neck. Karen squared off to me again, dirty plates and all, and said, "So I've got a hickey. So what? People *kiss.* You are such a hypocrite! Why is it all right for you and not for me?" She was waving the dishes around forcefully enough that a knife and fork slid off and headed toward my bare feet, forcing me to take a jump back to avoid them.

I kept my voice level with a major effort. "Because I'm not sixteen? Barely?"

"No. Because you're *male.* I'll bet you'd had *sex* by the time you were sixteen. Probably when you were *twelve.* And I'll bet the girl wasn't eighteen, either. Or the *girls. That* was fine, but it's not fine if I do it? What about the girls you did it with? Why am I better than them? That's being a hypocrite, and it's slut shaming. Women are sexual beings, and we should be just as free to express our sexuality as men are."

I couldn't deal with this. The mess. The noise. The… the hormones. I was stuck, and I was so frustrated, I wanted to growl. Instead, I took a deep breath, let it out, and said, "Hope will talk to you about it." A weasel response, and I knew it, so I went back to firmer ground and said, "But no. Absolutely not. Noah is not here when Inez or I aren't, and you aren't at Noah's when nobody else is home, and you're to tell Inez or me where you're going when you leave, and who you're going with, and we'll be… we'll be checking."

How? How were you meant to check? I had no clue. When I'd been sixteen, I'd been living with a dad who'd been heaps more interested in what was in the bottle than what I was doing or who I was doing it with. And, yes, I'd been having sex every chance I got, or anything close to it I could manage. Mostly on the beach—the Kiwi teenager's second bedroom—or snatched moments in the back of a cinema or a party, or, best case of all, in a car. Never enough time, and always the risk of discovery, the thrill of the forbidden to lend spice to the encounter.

Why? Because most of those girls had had a dad. A dad who'd probably felt exactly the same way about his little girl and about blokes like me as I was feeling now, because he'd *known* what they were thinking and what they wanted to do, just like I did. And if Karen *were* doing the things those girls had done with me in the back seats of cars or behind a dune…

How had Hope coped with all this? I needed to talk to Inez. I needed to talk to Charles, too. How was I meant to approach *that* conversation?

I was still trying to sort it out when Karen marched past me, all but flung the dishes into the kitchen, then came back and began to throw things about in a fashion that, if it was "tidying," wasn't the kind I knew.

"You didn't bring her," she said, her back to me. "I thought she'd be coming home. I thought she'd be *back*. And now I'm in *purdah*."

"I reckon she needed to be alone for a while. And you're not in purdah. You can see all the boys you want. Just not alone."

"I thought you were going to try to get her back. I thought

that was the whole *point.*" She was tossing cushions about in a random fashion as if that made it better, and I resisted the urge to step in and fold the rumpled throw tossed across the arm of the couch, to pick up papers and stow remotes. Karen bent down, grabbed the knife and fork she'd dropped onto the rug and said, "She wanted to stay. I know she did. She came to see you, and you weren't even here. How come you guys keep wrecking it? Why can't you just *love* each other? You said you were going to *fix* it. What did you say? You were supposed to tell her you loved her. That's what she wanted to hear. You should have told her you'd take her for a walk, or to the art museum or a show or something. All those flirting things you used to do. You know, old-timey dating. She loved that."

"Yeh," I said, abandoning any shreds of pride that remained. Even Karen knew what I'd done wrong. "Got that, didn't I. I'll be doing it from now on, no worries." I should tell her that Hope was pregnant. But how could I, if Hope hadn't? I needed to talk to Hope first. I needed to *see* Hope.

My entire life was upside down. My meticulously ordered apartment was chaos. I kept finding myself shutting Karen's bedroom door when I walked by, because otherwise, the clothes on the floor seemed like they would actually roll out into the hallway and stage a coup. The woman who should be my wife, the mother of my child, was flying away from me at nine hundred kilometers an hour. Meanwhile, the woman who *was* my wife was trying to take away most of what I owned, I had whole buildings full of nervous employees and some very anxious bankers, and just when I needed a clear head to deal with all of it, I was more rattled than I could remember being for years. For fifteen years, in fact. Since I'd been married to Anika.

But this time, it wasn't having the woman that was causing the trouble. It was *not* having her.

"I'm going to fix it," I told Karen. "I'm going to fix everything."

"I should have gone," she said, grabbing her shirt and shoes from the floor and standing up, hugging them to her. "I should go."

"No." I put out a hand and ran it over her neat cap of shining dark hair, then pulled her in and gave her a quick cuddle, as exasperated as I was, because it was what Hope would have done. Hope rose above. "You shouldn't. You should keep me company, and tidy up after yourself, and learn to cook and drive and swim, and visit your girlfriend, and enjoy your first summer of being healthy. And wait for your sister to come home, so you can show her all of that and impress her."

Karen's brown eyes were shining now, and her voice wobbled a little as she said, "I miss her, you know? I slept with her my whole life, did she tell you that? At first it was so cool to have my own bed, and my own room, and my own *bathroom,* even, but… do you think she's coming back?'

"I know she is." I wasn't sure if I was convincing Karen or myself. "She won't leave us for long. She won't be able to. She loves us, and your sister knows how to love."

♡♡♡

I had a number of conversations the next morning. First with Inez.

"I want Karen to tell you where she's going when she leaves the house," I told her from my spot at the kitchen counter. "I want Charles to take her, and I'd like you to ring up and… check. With the mum, or whoever. She had a boy over here last night, and could be his parents are working and he's at home alone himself, and I think that'd be bad news. But be subtle," I thought to add. "Not like you're checking on her, eh. Just that you're *checking*, because Hope isn't here."

She gave a sniff, pulled the milk out of the fridge, and got busy at the cappuccino machine. "You think I'm stupid? I have three daughters. *Three*. I know how to check on girls. Sixteen is a bad age. They think they know everything, and they know nothing." She poured heated, milky foam over coffee with the attention of a barista, then slid the cup and saucer onto the counter in front of me and took away the empty cup sitting there. "Decaf."

"Decaf isn't going to do the job," I said.

"You are too tense. Decaf is better."

For a man who liked to be in control, I had a fair few women giving me their opinions. So I did what any wise man would do. I moved on. "And I should tell you that Hope's gone to New Zealand for a bit to see my grandfather."

I was taking a casual sip of coffee when Inez said, "She's pregnant, and she's run away." Which may have made me choke.

"She said she just found out," I said when I could speak again. "She said that last night. How could you possibly know?" And then I regretted it. I didn't share information. I didn't betray uncertainty.

Another sniff. She had a pad and pencil out, was making some sort of list. "What, you think it's because I'm a witch? Because I have magical powers from the Mayan people? No. I know because she stopped drinking her coffee and thought it tasted strange. Because she would only eat yogurt and toast for breakfast, and if I began cooking meat, she left the kitchen. Because I have three children."

"Pity I was the last to know," I muttered. "Could have told me, couldn't you."

"It was not my business," she said primly, and this time, *I* was the one who snorted.

"Karen doesn't know," I said. "Best let Hope share it."

"Again," she said, "I am not stupid. And you need to be at work, and I have many things to do here. Go."

"Charles is meant to be giving Karen driving lessons," I said, getting off the stool and choosing to pretend I hadn't just been ordered out of my own kitchen. "I'd be happier if he started doing that straight away. Keep her out of trouble, eh. I'll have a word with him today about that. And see that she cleans up after herself."

She was still writing, and she didn't look up. "Why do you think I allow her room to be that way? A way that hurts my head just to look at? Because it's no good for her for others to do things for her. She has a strong mind. A strong will. She will push. You need to push back."

"No worries. I got that."

"And now go," she ordered.

I looked at her and said, "Maybe I won't. Reckon I need to push back."

"Not with me. Me, you need. Go."

Well, she was right about that.

My conversation with Charles was considerably shorter. When I got into the car five minutes later, I said, "I want you to drive Karen more. Wherever she wants to go. And teach her to drive. Take her to get the… permit, or whatever it is, and then practice with her every day." I'd have Josh check into it and ring Karen with the details. For the eye surgery as well. Get that scheduled, and until then? I'd keep her busy.

"OK," Charles said.

"You won't be driving Hope for a bit longer," I said.

Nothing at all for a long minute, then he asked, "She OK?"

"Yeh. But she won't be back for a bit, so when you take Karen… the Y's all good, and so is her friend's. Mandy's. Otherwise, check with Inez before you drop her off."

His eyes flicked to mine in the rearview mirror. "Guys?"

"Yeh. Could be."

He nodded, and that was that. Problem sorted. Pity nothing else today would be that easy.

the wages of pride

♡

Hemi

For the rest of the day, I put my head down and worked. I put out fires, I reviewed the revised marketing plans for the Paris show and the launch of the Colors of the Earth line. I focused. I dealt. And I tried not to think about Hope.

I'd told Josh first thing what to do about Karen—the driver's license, the eye surgery—and then I'd set Karen aside. It was done, and I didn't do worry. Except that I did. From three o'clock on, when her plane would have landed, I waited for a message from Koro, or, better yet, one from Hope. And heard nothing.

She'll be waiting until she gets to Katikati, I told myself. *You'll hear then.*

Surely I would. Because last night, on the way home from the airport, I'd arranged for flowers to be delivered to Koro's house. Lavender roses, to be exact. I'd done what I hadn't managed since she'd moved in with me. I'd told Hope she mattered.

Had I felt self-conscious typing the message into the box, knowing that some florist in Tauranga would be printing my words onto a card? Had I felt raw, and exposed, and much too clearly revealed? Yeh. I had. But I always did what was necessary, and I had a feeling this was necessary.

She might need me to let her go. She also needed to know that I still loved her, that I wanted her, and that I wanted our baby, too. And I needed to tell her.

The rest of it, I'd wait to tell her on the phone. I needed to hear her voice, to hear her response, and I needed her to hear mine when I told her how I felt.

I'd asked the florist to make the delivery that afternoon and had paid extra to make sure it happened. I wanted those roses on Koro's table when Hope walked in the door. I wanted my note to be the first thing she saw. I knew she'd have to text me when she got them, because I knew my Hope.

Except she didn't. Five o'clock came and went, and then six o'clock did. I finally gave in and texted Koro, *You and Hope get home all right?* and got no reply. Probably still teaching me a lesson, because he had to know I'd be concerned.

Or half out of my mind.

Then it was seven-thirty, and I texted Karen and packed up to go home. It was Women's Wednesday, the sacrosanct evening when Hope and Karen would watch a movie while they ate dinner on the couch, with popcorn for dessert. Another thing I'd stopped sharing in once I'd achieved my objective and they'd moved in with me. This would be Karen's first Wednesday without her sister, though, and I needed to go home and do that with her. It would make

Hope feel better, and it would make Karen feel better, too. It might even make me feel better, come to that.

Karen was surprised, but she watched with me willingly enough. The idea of the driving lessons had helped clear up her earlier narkiness, I guessed. I even let her pick the film, which was why the credits were rolling on *Little Miss Sunshine* when my phone rang.

I had the phone out of my pocket so fast that the second ring had barely started when I'd noticed the New Zealand number and was saying, "Hello?" I was already headed out to the terrace, too. I wanted to be relaxed for this, or at least to sound that way. Because it was my cousin Tane's number, and there was only one reason he'd be ringing me. He had to be with Hope.

"Hemi." It was Hope's voice, not Tane's, and the single word sounded tense and stressed. But at least she'd rung me.

"Sweetheart. How are you? With the cuzzies already, eh. Karen and I were just watching this film and wishing you were here. Would've made you laugh." There, that was good. Letting her know I wouldn't be berating her, even before we got into it. Letting *her* relax.

"Hemi. I… I… It's Koro."

It was still heat-wave warm outside, and the gooseflesh had risen on my arms all the same. "Tell me."

"I just… he's alive. But I should have called you. Why didn't I call you?" Her voice was high, nearly out of control.

"Hope." I put all my command into it. "Stop. Take a breath. A deep one. Let it out, then take two more. Don't talk. Breathe."

I heard the sharp inhalation, then silence, and finally, in a slightly calmer tone, "OK."

"Right. Now tell me. What happened?"

"He didn't come to get me. I thought he must have forgotten, or got the date wrong, or changed his mind. I couldn't reach him, and I couldn't think what to do, so I just came anyway. And all these hours . . ."

The pitch of her voice was rising again. I said, "You don't have to tell me that now. You don't have to think about that now. Just tell me what happened."

"He said he fell. He was saying something when we were waiting for the ambulance. Muttering something. He was coming to get me, and somehow, he fell. He broke his arm, too, I think, or his shoulder, because it was all… wrong. Twisted wrong." Her voice wobbled on the words. "And he hit his head on the corner of the dresser. So hard. He bled so much, and the paramedic said he was in shock. It's cold here, and it was a long time. He's been taken to the hospital, and Tane—he's taking me there now. We're going, and he's called some other people. Your family. He saw the ambulance and came over. But Hemi." There were tears, now. "He'd been lying there for eight *hours*. I'm so… I'm so sorry."

"No," I said. "You didn't know. And you *did* find him, and got him help, too."

"If I'd called you, you could have had somebody check on him. He wouldn't have been there all this time."

"And if I'd called somebody else when I couldn't reach him," I said, "he wouldn't have been lying on the floor for eight hours. I didn't call, because it would've hurt my pride to do it. And you didn't call me because it would've hurt yours. How did you get there? To Katikati?"

"On the bus." Her voice was thready, so exhausted and distressed, and I felt a surge of worry to go along with the fear for Koro.

"Have you slept?"

"Not… not much."

Tane's voice, now, practically vibrating the phone out of my hand. "Cuz. You'd better get your arse out here. Koro's not too flash, and Hope isn't much better. Why the hell did you let her come like this, without taking better care of her? And why didn't you or Koro tell us she was coming? One of us could've gone to collect her, instead of her getting here dripping wet and dead tired, and Koro lying there with his head split open."

"I'm coming now," I said. "I'm on my way."

the sharp end

♡

Hope

I was more tired than I could remember ever being, at least since the worst times with Karen, but I couldn't sleep.

I was in Hemi's bed, in Hemi's teenage bedroom. But there was no Hemi to put his arms around me and tell me it would be all right, or that I hadn't done everything as wrong as I knew I had. Or maybe it was that there was no Karen for me to be strong for. For the first time in my life, I not only had nobody to comfort me—which was the normal state of affairs—but, so much worse, I had nobody to comfort. Because I'd left.

And every time I tried to shut out all the confusion, to close my eyes and find the sleep I craved more than any drug, I saw Koro.

Sprawled face-down across the bedroom floor, his pants half-on, his bathrobe askew around him, his body so still, it froze me, too. I'd struggled to turn him onto his side, thinking in some dim corner of my mind, *Recovery position,* while I'd thought about heart attacks and strokes. I'd seen the blood that had covered his face and flowed onto the floor, that was still seeping out from a gash in his scalp. I'd felt the iciness of his skin, and it had turned mine just as cold.

I'd felt frantically at his outflung wrist for a pulse, but hadn't been able to detect it beneath my numb, shaking fingers. But he was bleeding, and dead people didn't bleed.

It was only when I'd pulled out my phone that I remembered that it was dead. I spotted the old-fashioned corded landline by the bed, lunged for it, dialed 911… and got nothing. I hung up and dialed twice more before I figured it out. There must be a different emergency number in New Zealand, and I didn't know it.

My breath sounded loud and harsh in the room, competing with the wind and rain lashing the little house. When I heard myself whimper like a child, though, I pulled myself together. *There's nobody else here. Deal. Cope. You can't call for help? Then* get *help.*

I thrust my feet back into my boots and ran. Back out in the rain, in the wind, down the hill to a neighbor, too far away out here in the country. Up a long driveway, where I pounded on a door, waited, and heard nothing. Another dash to another house, and it was the same. I kept running, stuck in a nightmare, the kind where you try and try and you can't get there, can't get closer. Until, at the third house, I found somebody at home, and I was gasping out an explanation, and a woman was calling for the ambulance. Then I was running back up the hill again, my boots squelching with water, my hair streaming with rain. Back into the little house, and back to Koro.

I knelt by his side, held his hand, and waited for a siren. I covered him with a blanket, because that was all I could think of. Now, I was just trying to hang on and wait for somebody to get here, somebody who'd know what to do.

I wanted it not to be true. I wanted to go backward, to start over, but there's no rewind button for life.

When he opened his eyes, I nearly dropped his hand.

He looked straight at me, but his eyes didn't focus, and his voice, when it came, was cracked and dry. "Fell… down. Got to get up. Get… Hope. Hope's coming."

"I'm here, Koro." The tears I'd suppressed until now were trying to choke me. "It's Hope. I'm here. You fell, but you're going to be all right. You're going to be fine. Help is coming right now."

Finally, I heard the wail of the ambulance, and then Tane was in the doorway, big and solid as Hemi. I hadn't remembered until that moment that he and June lived *up* the hill. I'd run the wrong way. I scrambled to my feet, and as we watched the paramedics settled Koro gently onto a gurney, I asked, "Could you take me to the hospital with you? Please?"

Tane looked at me as if I were insane. "Course you're coming. But you'll need to change first."

It took me long seconds to realize what he was talking about. That everything I wore was soaked, all the way down to my underwear and boots, and I was shivering.

I changed once again, nearly passing out at the smell when I opened my suitcase, hardly believing that being airsick had mattered a few hours before. I called Hemi on the way to the hospital, which was one of the hardest things I'd ever done. And then we ended up someplace that was all too familiar, even though I'd never been in this particular waiting room before.

After that… after that, the hours wore by, sitting without news while family came and went and, mostly, stayed. Men and women, old and young, babies and children, many of whom I'm never met, until there were nearly a dozen people filling the chairs. Being introduced as "Hemi's Hope," and not knowing if it was true. Or maybe it was just that my brain still seemed to be outside my body, that I was running way past empty now, barely able to process.

One person, I did remember from before. Matiu, Tane's younger brother. As tall as Hemi, but slimmer and finer-featured, with eyes that gleamed with intelligence and humor. He sat beside me during the hours that followed, his long legs stuck out in front of him, and did something on a laptop. He had that in common with Hemi too, I guessed.

Me? I just sat, stared ahead of me, and thought, *Koro, please don't die.* Also, *Poor Hemi,* and *I'm sorry. I'm so sorry.* Not exactly the world's most productive thoughts.

When the doctor finally came out to see the family, it was Matiu, not one of the elder Te Manas, who went to talk to him while the rest of us waited, the anxiety level cranked up another notch as we looked at Matiu's back, the doctor's serious face.

When Matiu came back, he announced, "He's had surgery in his shoulder, but he's come through it OK, the stubborn old bugger," and there was a scattering of relieved laughter, and then some eyes briefly closed, lips moving in silent prayer. "Got a pin in his upper arm," Matiu went on, "but that's not too bad. Had an MRI on his brain, and that's the one they'll be watching, checking for swelling. Badly concussed, but he's a tough nut, eh. To last through the shock like that? Yeh, I'd say so. And that he doesn't have a bleed now—that's good. Not out of the woods yet, but lucky it wasn't a stroke after all, just an accident. And that Hope found him before he was worse." Making me feel better, probably, than I deserved.

Thank God, I thought, and not in that casual way you say it. In the real way. From down deep. What would it have done to Hemi to lose his grandfather? Koro was Hemi's father figure, his rock and his conscience and his stability. I knew it.

"Can we see him?" Tane asked.

"Soon as he's in recovery. One person. Reckon that should be you, Auntie," he told a sixtyish woman. Flora, I thought. "And then, when he's in a room, you can take it in turns to sit with him, whoever can stay. No kids. Just quiet, eh. Touch his hand. Have a word. Let him know you're there."

The talk swirled around me. I was getting that fading-in-and-out thing again, and Matiu came back to sit beside me and studied my face before saying, "He has his whole whanau with him. I'd say your bit's done. Why don't you go home for the night? I'll give you a lift."

"Oh." I was extraneous, I realized. Not family. Maybe I shouldn't have come in the first place. "Sure. I'll just… I'll go."

He smiled at me, something sweet in it that reminded me of Hemi at his most open, and I realized yet again why Karen had been so taken with him during our previous visit. "Nah," he said. "It's not that you're not welcome, just that you're knackered. Come on. I'll drop you. I have to go to work anyway."

"Where do you work?" I asked him when I was in his car, heading north toward the much smaller settlement of Katikati. I was trying to focus, to make conversation instead of sitting like a lump. "It's a night shift?"

"Tauranga Hospital."

"Oh. Wait. Isn't that where we just were?"

A flash of white teeth through the dark for that. "Nah. That was Grace, the private hospital. That's your boy Hemi. I knew he'd have said 'only the best for Koro,' and Grace is all about the orthopedics. I told Tane to bring him straight there. Me, though… nah. I'm on the sharp end where the excitement happens. ER."

"Oh. You're a . . ."

"Doctor. What, you thought Hemi was the only one of us with anything to show for himself? We don't quite measure up, maybe, but we don't do so badly."

"I never… I didn't . . ." I stumbled over the words.

"Never mind." He pulled up to the house. "Twelve hours tonight, for my sins. No rest for the wicked, eh."

When I went into the house again and flipped on the lights, feeling as if I'd left it days, not hours earlier, I saw what I'd missed then. A vase of lavender roses on the dining-room table, and in the midst of them, a tiny white envelope held on a stick.

Hope, it said, and when I opened it, it said more.

E te tau, toku aroha. Please rest now. If you need me, call me. I love you. Hemi.

My darling, it meant. *My love.*

I knew he must have arranged to send them before he'd known about his grandfather. The flowers had to have arrived the day before, in fact. And all the same, it felt as if he could see me. As if he'd been listening to me after all. I held the note, looked at my flowers, and cried at last. From relief. From fatigue. From confusion and longing and aching need. From everything.

Now I was in bed, and none of it would leave. I should

have eaten, but I'd only managed some crackers and cheese, and a shower had seemed about the limit of my capabilities. The thoughts came and went as if I were caught in a whirlwind, and I couldn't escape them. The sheets felt cold, and I couldn't warm up, even though I was wearing pajamas. Finally, I got out of bed, pulled on socks and a sweater from the suitcase I'd finally managed to unpack, crawled back under the covers and pulled them tight around me, and curled into a ball for warmth.

I tried not to think it. I thought it anyway. *Hemi, please come. Please come now. I need you.*

inconvenient emotions

♡

Hemi

It was after four on a New Zealand Friday afternoon by the time the jet touched down in Tauranga, and nearly five by the time I was walking into the small ward of the private hospital with Karen at my side.

I hadn't intended to take her. Or, rather, taking her hadn't entered into my thoughts at first. I'd changed my mind for a few reasons. First, she'd demanded to come. Second, I hadn't wanted to leave her alone, not with Noah the Unattached Buddhist hanging about. Third, I thought Hope would want to see her, and that Hope would realize how much she'd missed her sister, how much she needed to be with her again. To *live* with her again.

I was determined to use any ammunition I had, you see.

I wanted to see Hope more than I could remember ever wanting anything. But I *needed* to see Koro.

When I walked into the room, he was lying in bed, his eyes closed, his arm in a sling, the white bandage around his head contrasting with his gray-tinged skin, and he had tubes running from an IV bottle into his arm. Koro, who'd always stood tall and strong despite his age, lying there shrunken and wrong, like a mighty kauri fallen in the forest.

I knew that a man in his eighties couldn't live forever, and I needed him to all the same. Nothing else was thinkable, but seeing him like that forced me to think it.

And then there was Hope. Sitting beside him with a newspaper in her hands, her sweet voice saying, "Police urge members of the public to be vigilant . . ." When she saw us, she stopped reading. The paper fell from her hand and onto the bed, and Koro opened his eyes.

You read sometimes about the worst kind of dilemma. A shipwrecked man, maybe, treading water, with two people he loves struggling beside him and only one he can save. It was the type of question philosophers loved to pose, the type that had always seemed pointless to me. But now? That was how I felt. There was my Hope, pregnant with my baby, and all I wanted to do was take her in my arms and hold her tight and never let her go. But beside her was Koro, and he was alive.

I tried for words, but none had come by the time I was across the little room to Koro and taking his uninjured hand gently in mine.

He said, "Hemi. My son," but it didn't sound a bit like Koro. No strength to his voice, and his eyes weren't focusing right, either.

Neither were mine, for that matter. The tears were threatening to spill, and I still didn't trust my voice. Instead, I leaned down, pressed my forehead and nose gently to his in a hongi, breathed his breath, and thought, *Thank you, God.*

Thank you for my Koro.

Across from me, Karen was hugging Hope, who'd sprung to her feet. I stood upright, still holding Koro's hand, hard and calloused from a lifetime of work. He said, his words slow and slurred, "I took a tumble in the dark. Silly old bugger."

"Nah," I said. "Bit clumsy, maybe, that's all."

"Never mind," he said. "I'd have told you not to come, but I reckon you were glad enough of the excuse."

"Too right I was. And no worries. I was always going to come."

"Should've fallen ages ago, then," he said, and I had to squeeze his hand again and swallow past the lump in my throat.

I looked across the bed at Hope and saw the compassion and understanding in her eyes, and the lump may have grown even bigger. She wasn't going to be starting up with me again. Just now, she cared about Koro, she cared about Karen, and she cared about me. I could see it in her as if I could see her heart, because I could. Hope was an open book. I just hadn't bothered to read it.

"Eh, sweetheart," I managed, then couldn't think of what else to say, where to go with it.

The moment stretched out until Karen heaved a sigh and said, "Could you guys just hug or something?"

"Yeh," I said. "Yeh. We could."

Hope came to me this time. Straight around the end of the bed and into my arms, sliding into place like my missing piece. I held her tight, lifted her off her feet, and said, "I love you."

It wasn't the most eloquent declaration ever, but it seemed to do the business, because she wrapped her arms around me even more tightly as I set her down, then tucked her head under my chin and laid her cheek against my chest, seeming to need to inhale me the same way I was inhaling her familiar flower scent, the softness and the strength of her. Everything I'd missed. Everything I needed most.

"Good," Koro said. "Take the two of them and go. Tane and June are coming after work. Any minute."

"Came to see you, didn't I," I said, though I hadn't let go of Hope. "I'll wait until they arrive, at least."

"Nah, you won't. I'm tired, and I want to sleep. I saw you. Go away."

Karen laughed out loud. "Koro's as bossy as you, Hemi. That's awesome."

I hesitated a moment longer, but Koro closed his eyes and said, "Ignoring you. Bring Karen tomorrow."

I smiled, took his hand once more, and said, "We'll be back first thing in the morning. See you then."

After that, Karen, Hope, and I were walking out the main doors into a chilly winter evening, and I was trying to figure out what to say next.

Karen, of course, beat me to it. "Let me guess. I'm going to get dropped off to get something to eat while you and Hope talk. I'm psychic like that."

"No," I said. "We'll go home and have something to eat. It'll be good to be together." I meant it, too. It *was* good. "And then I'll take Hope for a bit of a walk, maybe, and a chat."

I hadn't seen her for nearly two weeks, and I'd been shocked when I'd held her, especially once I'd lifted her. She was wearing her familiar jeans, but they weren't nearly as snug as they should have been. Her collarbones, too, were much too prominent under her long-sleeved white tee, although her breasts were clearly larger. All things that might have been there to notice two weeks earlier, if I'd paid more attention.

"I'm not sure what there is at Koro's," Hope said, confirming my suspicions. "Not for all three of us to eat."

"We'll stop by and pick something up, then," I said, reaching the car and holding the door open for her. "Do a bit of cooking. What do you fancy?"

She laughed, just a breath of sound. "That sounds so normal. Sorry. I'm having a hard time wrapping my head around all this. Figuring out how to be."

"Right now," I said, "you don't have to be anything. We'll make it up as we go, eh."

All she was able to think of to eat, once we were back in Katikati and walking the endless aisles of Countdown, was, "Potatoes. But Koro probably has potatoes. And yogurt."

"Tummy?" I asked.

"Yeah. And I just . . ."

She trailed off, and I said, "Chicken, then." I picked up a packet of prepared boneless chicken breasts marinated with a bit of herb. She needed protein. I didn't have to be a doctor to know that. "I'll cook you a potato, no worries. Some kumara as well. Vitamins."

"You don't have to baby me," she said. "I'm fine. Just a little tired. It's been a long few days."

"If I don't have to baby you," I said, "I can't think why else I'd have been put on earth."

The minute the words were out of my mouth, I wished them back, but Karen said, "Why would you have to baby Hope?"

I looked at Hope, but all she said was, "You didn't tell her? I would have, but I thought you should know first."

"Tell me what?" Karen asked. "I wish somebody would

tell me *something*. Hello? I'm sixteen, not ten?"

"I'm pregnant," Hope said, and I saw her take a deep breath as if the word had scared her.

Karen was saying, "Get *out*. So *that's* why you've been so weird," but I barely heard her. I took Hope's hand instead.

She stopped, right there in the chill of the meat aisle, looking all her questions at me, and the tenderness was squeezing my heart so hard, it nearly hurt. I said, "I've never told you how I'd feel about that. I should have done. I'm over the moon. I'm . . ."

I was the one who had to stop then. *Harden up, boy,* I told myself, but I couldn't. I was choking up instead, and somehow, the tears had risen again, were waiting just behind my eyes.

Koro in hospital, and Hope growing our baby. The worst thing, and the best. All I could do was reach for her, and all she could do was come to me. I was still holding the plastic basket in one hand, but the other arm was around her, and I was kissing her hair, holding her to me, and thinking… I couldn't have said what. Thinking nothing. Feeling everything.

Karen said from behind me, "Whenever you're done, could I hug my sister? Because I'm going to be an aunt. How great is that?'

I let go of Hope and stepped away, and Hope hugged Karen, and Karen said, "I'd ask how come being pregnant meant you *left,* because that seems totally stupid to me. Not to mention why you didn't tell me. I *would,* except it would end up with me having to go away again so you guys could have a Big Important Angsty Talk. I'm probably too old to go on the horsey ride in front of the store, and there's nothing else to do here except read magazines about celebrities I never heard of. Plus, I'm hungry."

Hope laughed, though I could tell her own tears weren't far away, and said, "I've missed you too, sweetie. Let's go home and cook dinner."

♡♡♡

We didn't go for a walk after all that night, and we didn't have a chat, either. We cooked a quick dinner and ate it, and Karen told Hope about her upcoming driving lessons, and Hope smiled and asked questions, and I considered mentioning Noah the Buddhist but decided it could wait until tomorrow, along with everything else. And I thought about how good it felt to eat dinner with them, and how little I'd done it back in New York.

Hope and I did the washing up, because Koro'd never taken to the idea of a dishwasher, and when we were done, Hope said, "I'm sorry, guys, but I think I'm going to have to take a shower and go to bed. Jet lag, I guess."

"Too bad you didn't come in Hemi's jet," Karen said. "Those seats fold down into beds, did you know that? It's like being a rich person. Oh, wait. It *is* being a rich person."

"Mm," Hope said. She looked at me, hesitated, then said, "I don't know if there are sheets on Karen's bed. And I wonder… I hope . . ."

"Karen can take care of her own sheets," I said, and my heart had started to hammer. "She's sixteen, not ten, eh, Karen."

"Yeah," Karen said. "And I guess I'm going to go watch TV and read a book. Not that there's anything to watch. New Zealand seriously needs to get some better channels."

"You could just read instead," Hope said.

"Too boring," Karen said. "Multitasking is my life."

When she was gone, I looked at Hope and said, "You wonder what?"

Easy, boy, I told myself. *Don't rush her. Don't push her.* Even though self-control had never come harder.

"I know I left," she said slowly. She'd been looking at the tea towel in her hands, folding and refolding it, but now, she looked straight at me. "I was right to leave. I know that, too. But I still want to sleep with you. It would feel so much better, even though I should be too tired to care. I'm too tired for sex, and I know you probably want it, and that you're so angry at me for leaving. But from now on, I'm going to try much harder to tell you what I feel and what I need, and it seems . . ." She stopped and laughed a little, trying to make it lighter, to make herself less vulnerable, and hung the towel carefully over its rack. "It seems what I need most is to fall asleep with you holding me. So I'm asking for it."

I had one chance here. I was going to get it right. "From now on," I said, "I'm going to try much harder to listen. Go take your shower, baby. I'll come hold you."

While she was in the bathroom, I unpacked my things into the bedroom that had been the site of my most lurid teenage fantasies, not to mention some sex with Hope that had exceeded anything I could have imagined. Tonight, I was going to get none of that, and I didn't care.

She came into the bedroom again wearing a pair of pink pajamas and looking about sixteen herself, and I didn't kiss her, hard as it was not to do it. I was pretty sure we weren't there yet. Instead, I said, "I need a shower myself. Now, you see, if I'd been a billionaire, I'd have one on my jet. With gold taps, eh." Which made her laugh and lose some of the tension, and I smiled at her and said, "Five minutes."

I normally didn't wear anything to bed. Tonight, I did. I took the world's fastest shower, then pulled on a pair of black sleep pants. I could hear the TV in the lounge when I came out of the bathroom, and I hesitated, then headed in there and told Karen, "Don't stay up too late. We'll be off to see Koro first thing in the morning."

She looked up from her program and her book, both of which she was somehow taking in, and said, "Thanks for bringing me. I kind of needed to come, you know?"

For once, she didn't sound stroppy. I bent and kissed her forehead. "I kind of needed you to come myself. It's better for us all to be together."

"Do you think you can make it up with Hope?" she asked.

"I'll die trying." Once again, the words were out before I could recall them. "Starting now. Good night, sweetheart. Sleep well."

When I got back to the bedroom, the dim light on my side of the bed was the only one on, and Hope was curled up under the covers. I thought she was asleep already, but she turned when I came in and said, "I should have kissed Karen goodnight. I should have told her how glad I was to see her."

"Never mind." I came over to sit on the bed beside her and brushed the hair back from her cheek. "Tomorrow's soon enough. Besides, I did it. Told her I was glad she came, and kissed her goodnight as well."

"Oh." She sighed under my hand. "Good."

"Bit hard," I guessed, "to juggle everybody. To pay enough attention to everyone you love. Koro. Karen. Me. Even the baby, eh. Could be you lose yourself a bit in all of that."

"Now," she said, "if you get that, why do you have to be

so unreasonable?"

I laughed out loud. "Dunno. Hardwired, I reckon. We could talk about that tomorrow, maybe."

I went around to my side, then, climbed in, switched the light off, and settled the duvet over myself. The bed was too small for two, especially when one of them was my size, but that suited me. I moved closer to Hope, and she moved back into me, and when I wrapped my arm around her from behind, she sighed again.

"That's the best," she said. "It's so much warmer when you're here."

"For me, too," I told her in the darkness. Her slim body was soft against mine, but her flesh was cool, and I kept my arm gentle around her. *A shield,* I told myself. *Not a prison.* "Could be that even a strong woman needs somebody to keep her warm."

I think she slept well that night. I know I did.

still paying

♡

Hemi

Saturday morning, and we were all at the hospital again. I'd risen while Hope had slept and gone for a long run to clear my head and regain my optimism and fill my lungs with the clean air and endless space of my homeland. Hope and I still hadn't talked, and I still hadn't even kissed her, but things were easing between us already. Once we had a chance to work it out, they'd be that much easier. That much better.

You couldn't love somebody this much and not have it work out. It wasn't possible. Not even for me.

Koro was a bit brighter this morning. Auntie Flora was with him, and he was watching the morning news and talking back to the set. Looking more like himself.

"Right," he said when we appeared, clicking the program off with a snort of disgust. "You can go on, Flora, now I've got these three. Too big a crowd."

"I'm happy to stay," she said. "Morning, Hemi."

"Too early for the deathbed scene," he said. "All I have is a sore shoulder and a bit of an ache in my head. No help for that but time, and time's what I've got heaps of. You don't. You need to go to work."

She got up, kissed his cheek, and said, "See you tonight, then," then gave me my own kiss and cuddle. I was back with the whanau, and that was good.

When she'd gone, Koro said, "She chats too much. And I need to get out of here. Nurses in and out every five minutes, so I can't get a wink of sleep. Old men need their own beds. The doctor says tomorrow. Why not today? I'm ready, I can tell you that."

I said, "You'll need someone with you when you go home, you know, with your arm in a sling and you dizzy and all. The doctor told me about that, so there's no use denying it. We can't have you falling again."

He glared at me, and I said, "Besides, who's going to plant your garden? September's only a few weeks away, and the doctor's telling me six weeks for the arm, and probably that long for the head, too."

"Tane and the kids will do it," he said. "You know they will. You won't get me like that."

"Will they come weed it the way you want it?" I asked. "Water it?"

He closed his eyes again. "You talk too much as well. You never used to do that."

Hope was laughing and bending down to give Koro her own kiss, and he opened his eyes and said, "You're all right. You can stay."

It was all going better, you see. Until my dad walked into the room.

I hadn't seen him for nearly four years. I didn't want to see him now. He smiled at me, showing off a newly missing tooth at the side of his mouth, and his bleary eyes filled with tears. His once-powerful frame looked shriveled to sinew, and he appeared nearly as old as Koro, though he was barely sixty.

"My son," he said. "Hemi."

"Dad." I didn't move, and somehow, Hope was beside me, sliding her hand into mine. I held it like a lifeline. I didn't want to need it, but I did.

Koro said, "Good you've come, Daniel."

"How you goin', Dad?" He came forward, then, and bent to give Koro a hug. I wondered how strong the vodka would be on him. He drank it not because he liked it best, but because he thought nobody could smell it, and nobody would be able to tell. He was wrong. We could all tell. Every employer he'd ever had had been able to tell, too, which was why he'd never held a job longer than a year. He'd start out full of good intentions, and then he'd fail. Always.

"I'm better every day," Koro said. "Don't know why I'm still in here, but it's good to see you."

"I'd have been here sooner," my dad said, "but I couldn't get time off work."

"Too many people in this room," Koro said. "Too hard to focus. Karen can stay. The rest of you go and have a chat."

"I just got here," my father said.

"Yeh, and I'll see you again," Koro said. "But not just now. Go talk to your son. Go meet Hope."

It wasn't a suggestion. I said, "We'll have a coffee, then," and walked out of the room, still holding Hope's hand, while my dad trailed after. I could tell that Hope was looking up into my face, but I didn't look at her. Instead, I found the cafeteria, ordered a coffee for me, one with extra sugar for my dad, and a cup of herbal tea for Hope, and we went and sat down in front of a window with a view of a courtyard filled with fern trees and low-growing vegetation. Shades of green, meant to be soothing, but it was going to take more than that.

I was nearly vibrating with tension, so I took three long, slow breaths in and out, the way I'd learned to do long ago. I didn't have Hope's hand anymore, but she was sitting so close, her side was nearly touching mine. Her left hand was on the table beside me, and my ring was still on her finger, shining out a promise I was going to keep. No matter what, because I kept my promises. That was the difference between me and my father. One of them.

Get through it, I told myself, and said to my dad, "This is Hope Sinclair. My fiancée. This is my dad. Daniel Te Mana."

"Heard you were having some trouble with that," my dad said. "Not divorced from Anika after all."

"That's true." I kept my voice measured. I was controlled. I was calm. "But I will be soon enough. It's only a matter of weeks."

"After your money as well, I hear," he continued. "Pity."

"Never mind," I said. "She won't get it."

"What a first-class bitch she was, eh. Still is, I reckon. Marry a woman like your mum, they say. Ha. You did that, all right, and you're still paying the price, just like I did. Hope you've done better this time."

Another breath in and out, and Hope had hold of my hand now. "I have," I said. "And I'm not here to talk about my mum. Or Anika."

The coffees came, and we sipped them for a minute while I kept my control, wrapping it tight and close around me.

Finally, Hope said, "I've wanted to meet Hemi's parents. You must be very proud of him. He's pretty special, isn't he?" As if she hadn't heard any of the rest of it, or as if it didn't matter.

"He's done well," my dad said. "I'd have come to meet you sooner if I'd known about you. As it was, I'm the last to know. Had to hear it through Flora instead, just like I heard about Dad. I'd have turned up sooner this time, too, like I said, but I finally found a new job a couple months ago, after everybody else told me no, no matter how much experience I had. At least he took me on, though he's a hard man, gives me the dirtiest work. Panelbeaters. Not too good, but all I could get, just because of a couple of mistakes."

"Car repair," I told Hope. "Body shop."

"Yeh," my dad said. "Better than the mattress factory, though. So you see, it all worked out well in the end. All for the best. I'm on the road up now."

"Are you sober?" I asked, and his head snapped back, the anger flashing in his eyes for just a moment. The anger he'd shown so often when I'd been a kid, and not since. Not since I'd had money.

"Yeh," he said. "Have been since I got out of the program. Six months now. I've started again."

I'd believed that too many times already, and been disappointed every time, until I'd stopped believing. It hurt too much to have the belief shattered, and I couldn't afford to hurt that way. Not ever again.

My dad told Hope, "Hemi paid for the program. Four months inside, getting sober. He doesn't think I've been such a good dad to him, maybe, doesn't understand how life can knock you down, but he paid anyway. At least there's that."

"That's good," she said.

"He's a good man," my dad said, and I tried not to let myself hear that, tried to remember why he'd be saying it.

"Where are you living?" I asked.

"Got a room in Onehunga. Car's still running as well, but it's not too flash."

"No," I said.

"Haven't even asked, have I."

I stood up fast, and after a second, Hope scrambled up to join me. "You don't have to," I said. "I can hear it coming down the pike. I'm glad you're sober, if it's true, but the answer's still no. I've paid enough. I'm done paying."

I would never be done paying.

♡♡♡

Hope

I walked out with Hemi, and he didn't say anything, and I didn't ask. I held his hand as he headed back toward his grandfather's room, and finally, he said, "Sorry."

"No," I said. "Don't be sorry. Hey, *my* dad never even came back again. I'll bet he'd be there in a heartbeat if I had hundreds of millions of dollars, though."

"You *will* have hundreds of millions of dollars. And if he turns up, I'll be there to help you deal with him. Thanks for that. Who knows what you must've thought."

He said the last part fast, like he didn't mean it, and I knew that was because he'd meant it too much. I squeezed his hand and tried to send all my belief through it. "Thanks for letting me hear it. I have the feeling you're ashamed, but you have *nothing* to be ashamed of. You're even more amazing than I knew, do you realize that? You give so much, even when nobody could expect it of you, even if nobody will ever find out. You think you're hard, but you're so… so decent underneath, Hemi. And so you set limits. So you cut him off when he tried to go somewhere you couldn't stand to go. That was the right thing to do, and it made you look even stronger to me."

He stopped where he was, in the middle of an echoing corridor, and looked at me. His face would have seemed as inscrutable as ever to somebody else, but I saw his eyes, and he couldn't hide from me. "I hated you hearing that," he said, "and I would have said I didn't want you to, but could be I was wrong."

"Hey," I teased gently, "I got the 'w' word and everything. And if I helped, I'm glad."

"Wait till you meet my mother," he said, and started walking again. "She *won't* be sober. I'll have to invite them both to the wedding, and I'll have to chuck at least one of them out."

"And if you do," I said, "I'll just be that much more impressed."

no cinderella

♡

Hemi

Back in Koro's room, Karen was reading aloud, and Koro had his eyes closed.

"Don't stop," he said when she trailed off at sight of us. "I want to hear what happens."

"Harry Potter," Karen informed us, and I laughed despite my still-turbulent emotions.

My dad. And Hope. And Koro. It was all too much.

"Don't laugh," Karen said. "Have you ever read it?"

"No," I said. "And I wouldn't have said it'd be Koro's cuppa, either."

"Just because you haven't tried something," she said loftily, "that doesn't mean it's no good. Open your *mind,* Hemi."

Koro smiled, but his eyes were shrewd as he studied me. He might be dizzy, and his head might still be aching, but he saw too much all the same. "Leave your dad behind, did you?"

"Finishing his coffee," I said. "He'll be back."

"Leave Karen with me for a bit, then," Koro said. "Let her keep distracting me. You take Hope someplace more cheerful for a wee while. Say all the things you're scared to say, and let her say all the things you're scared to hear. Only one way out, and that's through."

I could have pointed out that I knew that, since I'd been pushing through all my life. But maybe not with Hope. Maybe I'd just thought I had. I'd done *something* wrong, and it seemed that everybody could see it but me. I'd better find out what it was if I was going to fix it.

"I'll be back," I promised. "I'll switch off with Karen."

Koro waved a hand that still had IV tubes running into it. "Or whoever else is coming. You know they'll be here soon enough. I have enough company, and I'll have more. You'll keep. Go."

♡♡♡

When Hope and I were in the car, I started to turn the key, then stopped myself. "I was going to say, 'We'll go to the beach.' But maybe I should say, 'How about the beach?'"

"The beach is good," she said. "The beach is perfect. Good job asking, though."

I nodded, put the car in gear, and went there. All the way through Tauranga to Mt. Maunganui and the kilometers-long stretch of sand where I'd given Hope her ring and we'd danced on the shore. If I was going to do this, I was going to do it with every happy memory I could invoke attached to it. If I were really meant to be honest, I'd need all the help I could get.

We were walking, then, on the firm sand at the water's edge in a fresh breeze that felt glorious after being cooped up in the jet for so long, the winter sun warmer than it had any right to be in August and only a few white clouds scudding across the blue sky. I was holding Hope's hand, and having her this close to me on a New Zealand beach was a pretty good place to be.

After a couple quiet minutes, during which I let the peace settle over me and seep into my bones, she said, "It's beautiful today. You should have seen how hard it was raining when I came."

"Mm," I said. "When you were caught out in it."

"Yes," she said. "Which I survived, even though I was cold and wet and tired and scared. I can always do more than I think I can. I remembered that afterwards."

The only way out is through. I plunged in. "You left because I didn't tell you about Anika, and because I asked people not to hire you. And because I didn't pay enough attention to you. And because you were pregnant, and you were afraid I'd… what? Not want the baby?"

She was silent a moment, and then she said, "I think those are just the symptoms, don't you?"

I started to say something, then stopped. I listened to the waves and felt their motion inside me, the coming in and going away again, the certainty and the effortlessness of it. I felt the wind on my cheek and said, "Tell me."

She looked up at me, all her questions in her eyes, and I said, "I'm listening. I want to know."

"Then," she said, after taking a breath that I could tell was for courage, "it's this. I left because I was so confused, but now, I think I left because I was losing myself. As soon as I said I'd marry you, especially as soon as Karen and I moved in with you, it seemed like you had to control everything. Or maybe it was as soon as you got back to work, back to the way you normally run things. You wanted to say not just where I worked, but who I saw, where I went, even what I knew and what I heard. I knew it must be because you were afraid, but I couldn't see how to fight that or how to reassure you enough. You're so strong, and even if I could have held my own—I grew up with fighting. I hate it, and I'm no good at it. I don't want to live that way. I want to have peace, but if the only way to have that is for me to do everything you say, that's not peace at all. That's powerlessness, and it's ownership. I can't be powerless, and I can't let myself be owned. Love can't mean giving up myself, like I'm not allowed to be a separate person. That's a choice I can't make. I'm no Cinderella. I can't be. I know what happens to her."

She stopped as if she were out of breath, as well she might be. I said, "And I'm no prince, I reckon," and earned a startled laugh from her. "Did I really do all that?"

Now she was the one hesitating, then going on. And she'd been wrong. She had courage and strength to burn. "Don't you think you did? And whether you see it or not—maybe you could think about where that might come from."

I forced myself to confront it. You didn't solve a problem by running away. You solved it by seeing it, learning the ins and outs of it, and then attacking it. I thought about the swim lessons, the news about my marriage, the article in the *Journal*, and the job interviews I'd known would come to nothing. About all the ways I'd let Hope down.

"Could be I did what I always do," I finally said. "I focused, and I got the job done. And when things got hard, I got myself under control, and then I controlled everything else I could. This time, maybe that included you. Could be I don't know how to do this. How to be in a . . ."

"A relationship," she said. "Just like I don't. The only one I've been in—my only long-term relationship—is with Karen. I had lousy models at home, I don't know how to do it as equals, as real partners, and neither do you. But we have to learn." She turned to face me. The wind was blowing her hair across her face, and she put up a hand to shove it back and said, "I want to tell you something, and I want you to try to hear it. The only way you'll lose me is if you shut me out and push me away. I don't want to go. It killed me to leave. But I couldn't get your attention. I couldn't get through, or I didn't try hard enough, and I was out of ideas. I felt myself being swallowed up in you, and then the baby thing came along and made it worse, and I panicked."

"Because I didn't do this," I guessed. "I didn't take you on a walk, I didn't take you to Paris, and I didn't send you flowers. I thought I was done. I thought the courting was over, and I could go back to… normal. Back to work."

"That's not what matters," she said. "It isn't about sending flowers, even though I love getting them. I *knew* you loved me. I still know it. But I needed more… you. I felt like a doll. I felt myself *acting* like a doll. I want you to hold me, but I want to hold you, too. I want to feel like part of your life, and I need to know you need me."

I laughed, and she stiffened. "Sorry," I said. "I don't need you much, no. Only as much as I need air, maybe. Only as much as I need to breathe."

Her eyes were so intent, her heart so open, and she was twisting my own heart, finding my most vulnerable spots. It was terrifying. "Really?" she asked. "Because I didn't feel that way."

"Maybe it scared me to show it." There. I'd done it. It was out there. "I don't do weakness, and I don't do fear. I can't afford to."

She'd stopped walking. She had her hands on my forearms as if she needed to touch me, needed to hold me. Maybe for strength, or maybe to give it to me. Maybe so.

"Last night," she said. "When you were willing just to lie with me and hold me and keep me warm. That night in San Francisco, a long time ago, when we'd almost broken up, and you did the same thing. You did it then for the same reason you did it last night. You did it because you loved me, even though you didn't know it then. When I'm in your arms, I feel safe. I feel your love surrounding me. But can't you see, Hemi… I don't need to feel safe every minute. I don't need to be in the circle of your protection all the time. I know it's there, and that's enough. I need to be in the world as *me,* and to know you're proud of me for doing that, just like I'm so proud of you. After that, I need you to come back to when I need to rest, and I want to be that for you, too. I want to be your resting place. I want to be your safe spot, where you can open your heart and know you're loved for exactly who you are. How can needing somebody like that be weak, if we're giving it to each other? How can that not be strength?"

I could hardly breathe. I could hardly speak. "You are that," I finally said. "You're my prize." She started back, and I said urgently, "Wait. You're my… I don't know. What you said. My shelter, maybe. I'm out in the storm, and then I come back to you. Like a sailor. Or a Maori."

"That's beautiful," she said. "And I love to hear it. But if you have to be under control all the time, if you're controlling *me,* how can I see you? How can I help you? Especially if the only time you show yourself to me is in bed?"

I didn't answer, and she hurried on. "I hear myself saying all this, and I cringe. I feel like all I'm doing is complaining, when you've given me so much, and that's part of the problem. I don't want to nag, and I don't want to fight. And I love having sex with you. I want to have it almost every night, and I love that you want me so much. But I want to know you better than that, and I want you to know me. I want you to love me not just for my weakness, not just because you can take care of me, but for my strength, too. I want you to see that I'm not so different from you. I need to get somewhere, the same way you've always burned to. I want you to love the fighter in me, just like I love the fighter in you."

"If I didn't," I said, "I wouldn't love you much right now. You say you don't know how to fight. You're making a pretty good fist of it all the same."

"I don't think this is fighting," she said. "This is discussing. This is sharing. This is risking it all, saying it's too important to give up. This is what I need. You listening to me, and you *talking* to me."

I laughed. "You don't ask much, do you?"

She smiled, then. "Only to change. They say people don't change, but I think they can. I think I can learn to put my hand on you and tell you I need your time, I need your attention. And I think you can learn to give it to me. I think I can learn to tell you no, and that you can learn to win in a new way. I think we can both try, if it matters enough."

"Oh, sweetheart," I said, my heart right there in my throat, "it matters enough."

"Then," she said, "maybe we should talk about where to go from here."

rubbish at negotiation

♡

Hope

I'd been expecting storms. I'd been expecting to be shut down. I'd been thinking we were at "do or die," and part of me, the part that had never dared to believe my life could really work out this way, had whispered that it would be "die." I couldn't live under a man's control, not even a man I loved as much as Hemi.

The thought that he could be flexible? Yes, you could say that was a new concept. But to help him become less rigid, I was going to have to become much stronger. I'd said we'd both have to change, and I'd meant it.

I was still turning it over in my mind when he said, "Let's sit a bit, eh." He led me over to our tree, the one where he'd given me my ring, and I looked at him suspiciously and said, "You planned this."

That barely-there smile touched his mouth. "I plan most

of what I do. Want to take back all those lovely things you said about me?"

"No. If I love you, I love all of you. Even when you frustrate me and make me crazy."

He sat on a huge, twisting branch that ran perpendicular to the sand, pulling me gently down with him. Behind us was an urban area filled with stores and business and hospitals, with people and all their problems, but we were alone in a green and gray grotto, the gentle swish and roar of the waves our rhythmic background music, kilometers of empty beach spreading in each direction. Sheltered, and alone together, wrapped in the embrace of the sea.

"I reckon," he said, "that means I love all of you, too. Even when you won't go along with my perfectly reasonable plans."

This time, I laughed, and he smiled for real, put his arm around me and pulled me closer, and said, "Did I mention I was over the moon about this baby of ours?"

"Mm." He was right there, so I had to bury my face in his neck just to inhale his delicious scent, all spice and warm man. A touch of aftershave, and a whole lot of Hemi. I would've known his smell anywhere. I would've known it blindfolded.

That was when he did the thing that melted all my resistance. He put his hand gently over my lower belly and said, "You were the best thing that ever happened to me. Except now there's this, too. Now there are both of you. When I start to think of it, sometimes I have to stop, because I can't . . ."

"You're overwhelmed," I said. "Like me."

"I am." Surely his eyes were glistening a little, and his hand was so big, so warm and solid on my belly. As if he really could hold both of us under his protection, could keep us both safe there, and what a seductive idea that was, even after everything I'd just said.

"We conceived it here, you know," I told him. "Probably at Koro's. Could even have been the night you asked me to marry you."

"Bloody hell." He ran his hand slowly down my back and up again, leaving tingles in its wake in that way only he could. "I spanked a pregnant woman. I spanked *my* pregnant woman, and I spanked hard enough to hurt, or at least right up to the edge of the line, and more than once. Doesn't make me too happy to remember that."

"That isn't the part that has the baby in it," I had to tease. "And in case you couldn't tell—I loved it."

"Not doing it anymore," he said. "Not while you're pregnant, I'm not."

"What if I'm really, really naughty?" I had a hand in his hair and was kissing his neck now, just because it was so brown and strong, and I hadn't touched him in two weeks, and what was worse, he hadn't touched *me*. Plus, there were those pregnancy hormones. For once, they weren't making me sick. They were just making me… hormonal.

"Then I'll have to find some other way to get you under control," he said. "But I'm going to be careful, and I'm going to check in more. I'll say everything you want to hear, but you're not getting anything rough. I don't want to hurt you, sweetheart."

"Would that keeping-me-under-control thing be why you aren't kissing me right now?" I asked. "Did I ever tell you how annoying that was to *me?* That first day, when you touched me on my *arms,* and then my shoulders, until I thought I was going to embarrass myself right there on my couch, and then you refused to kiss me? All that buildup, and not a bit of payoff for about two weeks? Then the first time you *did* kiss me, up against that wall in Paris… it felt like you were going to steal the soul right out of my body. And after that, how long did you torture me?"

"Things are always so much better if you have to wait for them." He was caressing me now, not that much differently than he had that first time, his hand tracing lightly over the neckline of my scoop-necked T-shirt. He knew exactly how to make me tingle, and was he ever willing to take his time to do it. "And they're even better if somebody else is making you do the waiting. At least so I hear. From my point of view, I'd say they're better if *I'm* making you do the waiting. Nothing I love more than watching you squirm underneath me." His mouth was at my ear now. "Except maybe hearing you beg," he whispered, and just the touch of his lips on that sensitive spot made me shudder. "Now, that?" he said, sitting up again, way too much self-satisfaction in his eyes. "I'm willing to do that, pregnant or no, because there's something about knowing you're pregnant that's making me want it even more, reprehensible fella that I am. There are some ways I do want to own you, no matter how much I'm meant to be letting you fly free otherwise, and I'm afraid that's not going to change. But we're talking about this baby of ours, not about your sweet little body and everything I'm going to be doing to it… tonight. It was really that long ago? You're that far gone?"

"Nine weeks." I tore my mind away with a major effort from the places he'd sent it. The man could talk dirty like nobody I'd ever imagined.

Tonight. I knew I was shuddering again, and knew he saw it, and that he knew exactly why. "It looks like a little person now, I guess," I said, returning to the point under discussion. "A very tiny person."

"And it's made you sick. You've lost weight. Too thin here." He ran a slow couple of fingers from my collarbones down to the edge of my neckline as if he didn't know how sensitive that spot was. Liar.

"Also normal," I said. "Though I guess I need to make a doctor's appointment, now that I'm here. So what do you think?" I moved on, because we didn't need to go back into Hemi Te Mana Protectiveness Mode at this moment, where he'd, what? Arrange for daily checkups? Hire a nutritionist and a chef? "Do you want a boy or a girl?"

"Doesn't matter, surely. Whatever it is, the deed's done. And I'll be rapt about either one, no worries."

"Huh," I said in surprise. "I thought men always wanted a son. But that was what I told Guy. Karen's dad. *He* only wanted a boy, and he was positive he could get one. He insisted that my mom buy only boy clothes. You never saw a girl baby with so many outfits featuring dogs and fire trucks and dinosaurs. Why are dogs a boy decoration? I *told* him the baby was already made, and he said, 'Anything can happen.' Dumbest thing I'd ever heard. I already knew about chromosomes, and I was nine. But then, he was an idiot."

Hemi was smiling again. "The brains must've come from your mum, then, because you got them too, I've noticed. But I'd love a daughter, and I'd love a son. In fact, since we're meant to be communicating here, and this one has been a curious hole in our negotiations, I'll tell you that I'd love two or three. Four, if you're willing. I want all the babies you'll give me, and I've been thinking about that since well before I asked you to marry me."

I was going to be a mother. I was going to make Hemi a

father, too, and he was going to be such a good one. "Was that supposed to be another thing I didn't need to know?" I asked him, staying sassy with an effort. "Didn't work out so well, did it?"

"No, because you surprised me. I didn't even have to bring it up."

"Antibiotics," I explained. "Apparently they interfere. And apparently we're both fertile."

"Well, that's good news, anyway. Since I'm betting you'll make me some pretty good babies, and I want to keep you doing it. So. Do we get to go home, so I can watch the process and keep you as spoiled and satisfied as I want you? Whilst remaining fully independent, of course," he added, not entirely convincingly.

"Ah. Well, no." Here we were. The tricky part. "I don't think that would be a good idea. This is all so new. I'm just figuring it out, and it's too easy, when everything we have is yours, and it's all on your schedule and your rules, for me to feel like I have to fit into that. I want to do it differently, but I think I need… practice first. And time to figure out my future."

"Practice." He wasn't inscrutable now. His face was hard. "What kind of practice?"

"Well, here's Koro. Probably going home tomorrow, and he needs somebody to stay with him, right, while he's still fragile? What if that somebody was me?"

"I can hire somebody. And you know the whanau will be coming round as well."

"He'll hate you hiring somebody. And of course they can all come around. But he'll need somebody to sleep there, don't you think? And I'll bet he'd like it to be me. Keeping his eye on you and me, giving me advice on how to deal with your highhandedness? It'd make him feel useful, and he'd *be* useful, because I could use all the advice I can get."

"You think you're helping your case," he said. "You're not. You *and* Koro? How'm I meant to stand up against that?"

I turned toward him a little more and put my hand on his cheek. I loved him so much it hurt, but that wasn't enough. "Hemi," I said, keeping it soft. Keeping it loving, because that was what it was. "I want to work this out. I want it more than anything. But I also need to see if we can do it without sex, or without so much sex, because it's so easy to take all our… frustrations there, to do all our communicating that way, and not talk enough. Especially since that's all I want to do right now. I'm dying for you, and I'm guessing you're dying for me, too. But I need to know that you *will* talk to me, and that I *can* hold my own. I need to get clear, and I need to get strong, and that's so hard to do with you right there."

He didn't say anything at all, and I waited, then waited some more. Finally, he said, "I want to say, 'Absolutely not.' I know that'd be wrong, but I can't think what else to say."

"Because you only know how to be in charge. That's why."

He was all the way past "hard" now. He was scowling, but somehow, it didn't intimidate me as much as it might have. "I'm hating this."

I had to laugh a little at that, and to give him a kiss, too. He hadn't kissed me yet, and I needed to brush my lips over his, to feel that electric *zing* as every nerve ending lit up from my mouth to my toes. I needed to feel his hand coming out to hold me at my waist, because he couldn't help it any more than I could help touching him.

It was only a moment, but it was a good one. I pulled back

and said, "Well, how about if I had Karen, too? I miss her like crazy, and that way, you could have your orderly life back for a while, and we could both think about how we'd… how we'd work better together. We could talk. We could work it out without the sex there to make us think we'd solved something we hadn't. Koro's in the cast until around the last week of September, they say. We could use that as a rough time frame, don't you think?"

"Karen's school has to start up before then. When?"

"Early September, right after Labor Day. So I send her back, if you're willing to take her. It would still get us through that first month with Koro, which is when he'll need the most help. And then I could be there to make sure he was all right at night."

"Karen has this fella," he said, surprising me. "Noah the Unattached Buddhist. Had him at the house the night you left, in fact, while I was going after you. Gave her the biggest love bite on her neck you ever saw."

"Oh," I said. "Wow. All right. That's not too surprising, I guess, even though she didn't tell me. Huh. She's catching up fast." Too fast for me.

"I wasn't sure what to say about that," he said. "Told her he couldn't come over when she was alone, but about the 'why not' of it . . ."

"Hemi Te Mana at a loss," I teased. "Not being able to make a decision."

He was half-scowling, half-smiling. "It wasn't funny. Bloody uncomfortable, tell you the truth. She asked why she shouldn't have sex, since I'd probably done it when I was younger than her, and with girls her age. Couldn't come up with a proper answer for that one."

"So how old *were* you?" I glanced at him sideways from

under my lashes.

"Not telling," he said promptly. "And I never wanted to hurt anybody, but now? I wonder. I probably did. Not 'hurt' hurt," he went on hastily. "Not if… anyway. Just that I was never serious about anybody. I didn't do force, and I didn't do coercion. Then or now."

"Except for telling women who worked for you that you wanted to fuck them," I pointed out.

"Ah. That was an experiment." His smile was a bit sheepish. "We'll call it a fail, eh."

"You read me wrong."

"I saw the response to me. Didn't see the rest of the woman. My loss."

"Mm. But Karen. I'll have to think about that. How to talk about it. Birth control. Responsible choices. But I think it'd help if you tell her what… what boys can be like, maybe. I think you'd have more impact. Though you know you're going to get the rolling eyes."

"I can do that, rolling eyes and all. Nobody better for the job, sadly. But we're off the subject."

"No," I said. "I don't think we are. I want to stay for a while, and I'd like Karen to stay with me. That way, I can see if I can get a short-term job, too. I'd love to work for somebody who *liked* me, and to feel like I was being… at least satisfactory. My pride's kind of bruised, you know? Battered, you could say." I tried to joke, even though it was no joke at all. I'd spent five years working for bosses who'd belittled me and told me I was nothing. If that was them, I needed to change the pattern. If it was me, I needed to know why, so I could fix it.

Hemi said, "Not many short-term marketing jobs in Katikati."

"Nope. But there are some jobs I could do, I'll bet. And I need to find one."

I'd found a piece of bark and was busy shredding it, because I was nervous again. Not Hemi, though. He just got more still. I knew he was processing, deciding, all those scarily fast neurons zipping around his brain and drawing conclusions. Finally, he said, "I still want to say 'absolutely not.' You have no idea how much."

"Oh," I said, "I think I have some idea."

"But it won't work."

"No. It won't. I think this is our best way forward. I think it'll help both of us to… renegotiate from a more level position."

"Right, then. Rules?"

He was going for it. I couldn't believe it. He really *did* care enough. Half of me wanted to throw myself into his arms and tell him that was enough, and to please take me home right now. The other half reined Miss Undisciplined in and said, "If you wanted to come visit, that would be awesome. I know you're so busy, and everything's so hard right now. That's what keeps getting in my way. I keep thinking, 'Hope, he's so busy and under so much stress. You can't ask any more of him.' And then I feel… last on your list. So I'm going to tell you. I'd love you to visit. I'd love to hear from you in between. I'd love you to talk to me."

"Texts," he said. "Emails. Phone calls. All the things I stopped doing once you were in my bed every night."

"You think you're jumping through hoops. I can see how you could think that."

He smiled suddenly, and I was so surprised that I dropped my piece of bark. "Sweetheart. If we ever buy you a car? Let me do the negotiation, eh. Because you're rubbish."

"Oh, I don't know," I said. "Seems like I'm getting what I asked for."

"Yeh." He tucked a strand of hair behind my ear and smiled down at me, his eyes so warm, and I was melting once again. "But the car salesman isn't going to be hopelessly in love with you."

same old story, same old song

♡

Hope

Did he kiss me then? Of course he didn't. He had a plan, I could tell, and it was going to be worth waiting for.

Have you ever wanted to be swept off your feet? I had. I *did.* I was a sucker for it, in fact, and Hemi could sweep like nobody's business.

We walked back along the beach, and he asked, "All right?" I guess I'd gone too quiet.

"Sure."

"You're worrying. Don't worry. We're going to be all good, you'll see."

"I'm not worrying. I'm just… I'm . . ."

He looked down at me, his expression impossible to read. "Hope," he said softly, "what are you?"

"I'm a dirty girl," I said with a sigh. "I should be having elevated thoughts about love and life and motherhood and my higher purpose and all that, and I'm not. Maybe you should be the one thinking twice."

There was a light in his eyes now that I could read just fine. "You need to be straightened out?"

That gave me such a hard rush, I nearly shuddered again. "Maybe."

He sighed. "And here I was, planning to be nothing but tender and adoring with my sweet little pregnant bride."

"You were not," I said, trying not to laugh. "You are a dirty liar."

He laughed out loud himself. "Well, mostly I was." He let go of my hand and gave me a light slap on the bottom that made me jump.

"Hey," I said. "I thought we weren't doing that anymore."

"Just a tap." He was still smiling. "If a man can't give his woman a little tap on the bum when she needs it, what's the point in living?"

"There is so much wrong with that statement." I tried to frown at him, but it wasn't working.

"Well, you can tell me tonight," he said. "Maybe. Or could be all you'll be able to say is 'Please.' We'll see which it is."

Which was all wonderful. And then we went back to the hospital.

When we walked into Koro's room, Karen was still there, and so were June and Tane. And Daniel, sitting at his father's bedside.

It was odd, really. He looked like Koro, and he looked like Hemi. Tall and broad-shouldered, with strong features and bronzed skin. And yet he looked nothing like them. He had none of their power, none of their force of personality. None of their strength.

Even as I was thinking it, I felt Hemi tensing up beside

me. Koro, though, merely said, "There you are. Good. Take Karen home, and the rest of you lot can go on as well. I need to rest for a bit, especially as I'm meant to be going home tomorrow."

"About that," Hemi said. "What do you think about Hope staying with you?" Which tells you all about Hemi and how hard he was trying. He hadn't wanted me to stay, but he'd listened to me, he'd agreed, and now, he was jumping straight in to help me do it.

"Thought she *was* staying," Koro said. "Thought that was the whole idea. Were you thinking I'd tell her to go on home with you? Not until she's ready."

Everybody was looking pretty interested. I said, "I'd like to stay with you, and I'd like to help out. Thank you."

"Oh," June said, giving me a curious glance. "Well, that makes life easier. I was just on the phone with the others this morning, trying to work out a schedule."

"Nobody has to work out a schedule," Koro said. "I won't be helpless."

"You'll need some help in the bath and all," June said. "At least at first. In and out, with the dizzy spells, the arm. D'you want Hope doing that? Better be me, I'm thinking."

Koro scowled at her. "Not showing you my bare backside, thank you very much."

She laughed, not one bit fazed. "I've got two sons. There's nothing you can show me that's going to be a surprise, or that I haven't seen too much of."

Koro was still frowning, and Tane said, the amusement clear to see on his face, "I'll come help with the bath, eh. Or Matiu will, if I can't. No worries. As I'm guessing Hemi's going to be taking that jet of his home, off to do important things."

"No choice," Hemi said.

"Always got a choice, haven't you," Daniel said. "Whanau comes first, mate."

Hemi seemed to get bigger before my eyes, and I could tell that only his willpower was holding him back. Time to step in. I said, "Nobody knows that better than Hemi, wouldn't you say?" and gave Daniel my best innocent look. "He's in a pretty critical place with the business, yet he came all this way. Because of Koro, and to be with me. We're expecting a baby, you see."

I said it to take the spotlight off Hemi. Besides, surely Hemi's father would want to know he would be a grandfather.

For a moment, it seemed to be working, as June let out an exclamation and gave me a quick hug, while a smile spread across Tane's face before he was pumping Hemi's hand and slapping him on the back. Koro just looked thoroughly satisfied.

Daniel didn't do any of that. He looked me up and down, long and slow, and then he looked at Hemi. "Expecting a baby, and she's staying here? Not going home to be with you?"

"Not for a bit," Hemi said, his face and voice equally expressionless. "Koro needs the help just now, and Hope's right. It *is* a critical time for me."

"If you're going to be a dad," Daniel said, "maybe you should start acting like a family man for once. Take Koro back to New York with you, get him looked after properly, and this time, see your woman goes with you as well, where she belongs."

I truly thought for a moment that Hemi was going to jump across the space between them and throttle his father.

He didn't, of course. He just gathered his energy into himself and stood motionless.

"He didn't suggest that," Koro said, "because he knew I'd say, 'Like bloody hell I'm going.' I've been to New York. Catch me spending my time in the Big Smoke where I can't hear the birds and can't catch a fish, everybody talking on their phones night and day and never bothering to look up at the people around them, and nobody who'll answer a civil "Morning" from a stranger. I'll stay here with my whanau, thank you very much, and if Hemi wants to see me, he can visit. I reckon you couldn't keep him away."

I thought Hemi was going to say something about me, but he didn't. He just stood there, betraying none of the vibrating tension I knew he was feeling, and stared at his father. It was a pretty scary look.

"Sounds like you've all decided already," Daniel said. "As usual. I'd best be off. I promised a mate my company for the All Blacks match tonight. He's just come out of the program, and only a month sober. Keep him from going to the pub, back with the old crowd. Temptation's a hard thing, eh. Old patterns."

He shook hands with Tane, then turned to Hemi and said, "Walk me to my car, mate."

Hemi said, "Aren't you going to say goodbye to Hope and her sister?"

"Course," Daniel said. I held out my hand, but he grabbed me instead, pulled me in, and held me too tight, smothering me with the smell of cigarettes. My stomach instantly rebelled, and I stiffened in the grip of his clutching hands.

I hated being grabbed by big men, especially when they wouldn't let me get away. And if you think that's what Hemi did, you don't understand my boundaries and the way Hemi watched for and respected them. Or the way his father didn't. All I can say is, my body knew the difference.

When Daniel finally let me go, I stood back and focused on breathing, but he wasn't done. "Think about being a good wife to Hemi," he said, his eyes shining with the tears that I could already see came too easily to him. "Such a thing as loyalty and supporting your man through the hard times. You could think about that."

The room was nothing but silence until Hemi said, "I'll walk you out, Dad." His voice was hard and cold as steel, and he didn't even glance my way, just stalked out beside his father.

"Whoa," Karen said into the silence that followed their exit. "I guess I'm glad I didn't get any words of wisdom. Or a hug."

"All right?" Tane asked me.

"Sure."

Koro said, "Sit down," and I didn't argue. I sank into the chair Daniel had vacated and thought, *Wow.*

Tane said to June, "If I ever do that to one of our sons? Shoot me quick."

It was so unexpected, I laughed, and so did everybody else except Koro.

"Yeh," Tane told me with a grin. "Never mind. He'll be far away. The Pacific Ocean's a wide and wonderful thing."

I thought, *Thank goodness.* And then I thought, *Oh, Hemi.* And I hadn't even met his mother yet.

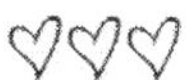

Hemi

I didn't want to hang about and chat with my dad, but he paused at the open door to his car, looked at me with resignation that made my blood boil, and said, "You don't have to marry her just because she's pregnant."

I was controlled. That was who I was. At least it was the man I had made myself into. "I do have to marry her," I said. "I'm going to marry her. You'll be invited to the wedding, because Koro will want you there. And if you get drunk, I'll be the one chucking you out. Drive safely."

"I told you," he said. "I'm sober. If I'm not safe, it won't be my fault. It'll be these tires, because they're buggered."

I held his gaze. "Tell me you don't have a bet on that All Blacks match. More than one, probably, because somebody's in form, and the jokers at the TAB haven't figured it out. You've got inside info on who's likely to score the first try, and you can't lose, because this is your big chance, and you deserve it. How much? A hundred? How many tires would that buy?"

A flash of anger in the dark eyes. "Your sister says you're a cold bastard. Why d'you reckon she'd say that?"

I breathed in and out. "Because I don't listen to excuses. Because I expect the same effort out of anybody else that I'm willing to put in."

"You don't understand human weakness. You don't understand life."

"No. I understand it, and I don't let it beat me. I push back."

I left him standing there. Did it feel good? No. But then, it never did.

Back into the hospital, then. Back to Koro, and a roomful

of people I could be grateful for with my whole heart. Back to Hope.

But first, I had to deal with something else. I walked through the door to Koro's room, pulled out my wallet, and said, "What did he borrow?"

June looked at Tane, and my cousin sighed and said, "Fifty."

I handed the bills over without a word, and he pocketed them and said, "Sorry, mate. Hard to say no. He's my uncle."

I nodded, and then my gaze fell on Koro.

"Not your business," he said.

"Almost a hundred," Karen said softly from my side. "Everything Koro had in his wallet."

"He'll spend it on cigarettes and the TAB," I told Koro. "Next time you see him, he'll be driving on those same tires, have that same story."

He shrugged. "Have to believe, don't I. No choice. He's my son."

I didn't know what to say to that. I never had.

whatever you fancy

♡

Hope

We were in Hemi's car again, headed north toward Katikati, when Karen said from the back seat, "No offense, Hemi, but your dad's kind of a jerk."

I'd had my hand on his thigh, wanting to help but not knowing how else to do it, and I felt his muscle stiffen for a split second. And then he laughed, and it relaxed under my hand. "Yeh," he said. "He is. At least he wasn't drunk. Used to turn up at my rugby games pissed, have a go at the coaches and generally make a nuisance of himself, until he got himself banned for good for charging at the ref. That was a hell of a day. One of many memorable moments."

"Whoa," Karen said. "That'd be majorly embarrassing. Didn't you just, like, want to sink through the ground?"

"Maybe at first," he said. "When I was younger. After that, I pretended he wasn't there and focused on what I was doing instead. What I could control. He couldn't embarrass me if I didn't show it. Good for me, probably, that I learned that lesson early."

He didn't say any more than that, but he didn't have to. I'd wondered what could possibly have forged that iron self-control, that nearly desperate need to be in command of not just himself, but every situation he was in. I had a feeling I had my answer. If I was terrified I'd end up like my mother, Hemi was even more terrified of ending up like his dad. Feelings were weakness, and showing vulnerability was offering yourself up for humiliation and pain.

For now, I kept my hand on his leg and didn't talk. He didn't need me jumping all over that. He'd told me, had given me that gift, and I was going to respect it.

"So can we all just agree on that and go have lunch?" Karen asked. "Because I'm starved, and Hope probably needs to feed the munchkin."

"Sadly," I said, "it's true."

"Then I reckon I know what my job is," Hemi said, sounding a whole lot more relaxed.

The second I got into the café, a small, cozy place a block from the Katikati beach, my stomach made an important announcement. I told Hemi, "I need something really fast. A… I don't know. A muffin. Something. Right now."

"All right," he said, looking a bit startled. "Uh… what else would you like?"

"I don't know," I said. "I don't *care*. Food."

He must have seen how agitated I was, because he told the woman behind the counter, "Can we get a savory muffin straight away, please? Pregnant partner. Emergency, eh."

She smiled, put a muffin on a plate, and handed it over, and I took it to a table and tried not to fall on it like a

Labrador who'd just heard the rattle of kibble in the dish. But by the time Hemi and Karen arrived at the table carrying glasses and a carafe of water, the muffin was history.

"Thanks," I said. "I'm all better now. I can even wait for my lunch. I'm ready to talk to Karen."

"Uh-oh," she said. "Why me? You guys could just deal with your own stuff, you know. Don't bring me into it. I'm fine. I'm just here because I wanted to see you and Koro. *I* didn't have any burning need for more drama. I'm the teenager here. I'm the brain tumor survivor, too. How come I'm the only normal person in this room?"

"Well, see," I said, "that's the perfect segue. I need you to stay here with me and help with Koro for a few weeks and be your nice normal self."

She studied me for a few seconds. "Let me guess. Hemi told you that I'm actually, you know, having a normal teenage life, seeing a—gasp—*boy,* so now I must be whisked away to New Zealand before I, what? Start having group sex? Get pregnant? Oh, wait. *I'm* not the one who did that. Or maybe it's because I left my shoes on the floor. I ate in the living room and forgot to pick up, and Mr. Clean can't handle it. Time for military school. Geez. I'm a *person,* you know, not a robot."

"Well, no," I said. "Actually, that's not it. There are boys everywhere, so how would that change anything? And if you're here, you'll be leaving your shoes on *Koro's* floor, and I know it. But I need your help, and so does Koro. I need to stay here for a while, and if you stayed, too, I could get a job. You could cook, because how will Koro manage with one hand? And you're a better cook than I am already. Plus, I miss you. I *really* miss you." Darn it, there were those tears again, right there behind my eyes.

"You know what would be even simpler?" she said. "Let's see. You could come *home?*"

"Please, sweetie," I said. "It's just a few weeks. Please stay with me. I need your help." And then I held my breath. I didn't think I'd ever said that before, and it felt so scary to say it now, to hear her refuse again, to think that she might not love me as much as I loved her. Hemi must have realized that, too, because he had hold of my hand under the table.

Karen sighed. "All right. But I was going to take driving lessons, and keep on with my swim lessons. *And* get surgery on my eyes."

Hemi said, "I'll have Josh reschedule the surgery. I'll come back here for you, what? End of August? We'll fix it for then, so you'll be good to go when school starts. And I'm guessing you can find a way to get driving lessons and swim lessons here. Everything's easier in New Zealand. You'll see."

"Which would be why you moved away," Karen said.

"Except making money," he said. "That's easier in New York."

♡♡♡

Hemi

As we ate lunch, I was racking my brain. I'd be here one more night, and then I'd be leaving Hope fifteen thousand kilometers away for who knew how many weeks, surrounded by other blokes who'd see in her exactly what I saw and who'd want exactly what I did. And, yes, Eugene would have said that wasn't trusting enough, but I couldn't help thinking it. Besides, I *was* leaving her, wasn't I? I was doing what she asked, and I was even trying to be understanding about it.

That was going to have to be enough, because it was all I could manage.

I needed to give her something special today, though, to remind her why she wanted to wait for me. I knew what would have worked for *me* along those lines, but I was pretty sure I was meant to do something else, too.

I may have been a slow learner up to now, but I'd sussed out that giving her the best sex I had to offer, even with a cuddle and a bit of loving chat afterwards, didn't meet all her intimacy needs. Seemed odd to me, because there wasn't much more I could have asked beyond that myself, but maybe I was grasping that we weren't wired entirely the same after all. That women actually *were* different, and pregnant women might be even more so. And if my achingly sweet, exasperatingly stubborn, undeniably fierce little fiancée needed more from me? I was going to give it to her. You did what you had to do to get the job done, and my job just now was to get her back, and keep her there.

I said, aiming for casual, "It's a gorgeous day, and there's that swimming pool and all. Seems to me that after we finish here, we could check it out, get you signed up for those lessons, maybe. I've never seen your progress with that, either of you. What do you reckon? Or we could do a . . ." I cast my mind about a bit more. "A visit to the bird gardens, maybe. A walk to the top of the Mount. A visit to the art gallery. Whatever you fancy."

Hope asked, "Don't you have work to do?"

"Yeh, I do. But I could spend a couple hours with you first, and I'd like to. And here's that negotiation practice again, sweetheart. Don't let me off the hook that easily."

"I want to swim," Karen said. "But I didn't bring my suit."

"I did," Hope said. "And swimming sounds really good, at

least as much as I can manage. Thank you, Hemi."

There you were. Points. I'd got it right. "I don't have mine, either," I said. "No worries. A wee shopping trip, and we're golden."

We did that, and they both seemed quite happy about it. Hope didn't even make any murmurs when I paid for Karen's new things, which was progress indeed. We headed for the pool after a stop to pick up Hope's togs, and I was changed and in the water fast.

The first brief shock of cold, then the calm the rhythmic breathing and motion always brought, plus the pure pleasure of swimming under the open sky, were the perfect antidote to the lingering tension from my dad's visit and everything else the past couple days had offered up. I'd already powered through ten fast laps when I touched the side of the pool and looked up to see Hope and Karen emerging from the ladies' changing room.

It was a good thing I was in the water when they dropped their towels and walked toward me. Karen jumped straight in and began to swim in a perfectly creditable crawl, but Hope sat on the concrete edge, then slid carefully into the lane next to mine. She was so short that only her upper eighteen inches or so were visible, but those inches were choice.

"Sweetheart," I said, "how could I have missed that?"

It was the same white bikini she'd worn at the Polynesian Spa, but if it had looked good then? It looked even better now. First, despite her slimness, which had almost become frailty now, I'd seen the tiniest, sweetest little swell of belly below her navel, and had been nearly overwhelmed by a sudden, fierce longing to put my hand there. I needed to feel that, to trace every beautiful contour, and then to kiss it, because it was mine. And after that, I needed to show her exactly how much I loved seeing it.

Tonight, I reminded myself. Because the other place where she'd changed, I absolutely had to keep my hands off just now.

I'd always loved her sweet little breasts, all her delicate curves. She was tiny, but so perfectly made. But now… she wasn't so tiny anymore.

"I finally got a figure," she said, reading my mind with perfect ease. "Too bad I'll only keep it for a month or so. I should have bought a new suit myself, I guess. I didn't realize how much I'd be, well, spilling over."

It was true. That bikini top wasn't really big enough to do the job she was asking it to.

"Are you all good to swim?" I asked. "Need me to come over there and give you a bit of help?"

She laughed, and it sounded so happy, it twisted at my heart. "I have the oddest feeling about exactly how helpful you'd be. Besides, I learned how, remember? You just watch, boy."

"Like I could do anything else," I said, and she laughed again.

She wasn't as far along with the swimming as Karen, but she wasn't going too badly. And then, because I really couldn't stand there and perve at my own fiancée all afternoon, I shoved my goggles back on and did another twenty laps or so. And if I looked over occasionally to watch Hope swimming, chatting to Karen, or, best of all, doing some floating, looking exactly the way I was going to be seeing her tonight, on her back and blissful? Well, I could hardly help myself.

After our swim, Hope signed herself and Karen up for more lessons, and she didn't even object when I paid for them. And when I stopped at the bank and opened an account for the two of them, all she did was sigh and say, "Hemi… how does this help my reestablishment plan, exactly?"

"You don't have to use it for anything, ah, frivolous," I said, and then went on with what I thought was some pretty faultless logic. "But you and Karen will be caring for Koro, won't you? If you weren't here, I'd be paying somebody else, or a team of somebodies, more likely, and that wouldn't come cheap. Plus groceries and whatever else he needs. Besides, who knows what he's giving my dad. Could help me with that, couldn't you, so he's not caught short. And if you had an emergency, you wouldn't have to worry."

Hope took the cards, tucked one into her wallet, and handed the other to Karen. "You keep sneaking in under my defenses. I know why you're so successful. You are the most single-minded man I've ever known." But she was smiling when she said it.

We headed back up the hill to Koro's, then, and Karen said along the way, "Tane and June invited me to have dinner with them tonight, and to sleep over. So I could get to know my cousins better, they said, which was nice of them, even though their kids won't actually be my cousins at all."

I made a mental note to thank Tane next time I saw him. "Course they will," I said. "You'll find the definition of 'cousin' is pretty fluid to a Maori. You could say we have heaps. Your whanau's more than your mum and dad. Or, in your case, your sister."

"Huh," she said. "That'll be novel. Anyway, I said yes, because I *thought* this would be my last night in New Zealand until you guys finally got married. Ha. Little did I know I was going to be a resident. But they have a ping-pong table, so that's cool. Besides, otherwise I'd be hanging around here, trying to read my book while you guys show me a whole bunch more of that 'Do as I say, not as I do,' making out right in front of me and staring deep into each others' eyes. So awkward. Leading by example, right? Showing me how not to give in to my hormonal urges?"

"We're engaged," Hope said, and I could see her smile trying to escape. "It's allowed."

Karen snorted, as well she might. "I hate to tell you this, but you started doing that a long time ago."

"Your sister's also nine years older than you," I said. "And I'm in love with her, not just some fella looking to hook up."

Another snort. "I was *there,* Hemi. Maybe try again."

"All right," I said. "She said no."

"Oh, so guys only respect you if you say no? They act like they want sex and they'll leave if they don't get it, but if they *do* get it, they leave because you're a slut? Who thinks like that anymore? That just makes guys sound like jerks."

I shook my head, feeling like a bull being pestered by an annoying fly. "If you don't become a lawyer, the world will be missing out on a perfect match. But you're right. Guys *are* jerks, at least some of them are, especially the young ones. I know I was, but your sister made me work for it until the relationship was on her terms and wasn't all about what I wanted. She's still doing it. She tells me what she needs from me, and then she holds my feet to the fire until I give it to her. And you know I love her, or I wouldn't be telling you all this," I added, pulling into Koro's drive once again. "Bloody uncomfortable, isn't it."

"Open communication is key between adolescents and their authority figures," she said. "Even though your sexual politics were forged in fire at about the same time as the One

Ring, and you aren't really my authority figure."

I started to say, "Of course I am," but held myself back at the last minute. Fortunately, Hope did it for me, just as she'd done with my dad. "Of course he is," she said. "He's your secondary authority figure. And his sexual politics are pretty much on target, from everything I've ever seen. Sad but true. If you want a good guy, you have to be picky. He has to *know* you're picky. Then, whatever you choose to do or not do, and however long it lasts, you're left with your self-respect and pride intact, because it was a hundred percent your choice."

I wasn't sure I liked the sound of "secondary," but it didn't seem that I got a vote. "You could ask Tane," I suggested. "He's got sons, and a daughter as well. Bet he'll say the same, and he's not nearly as much of a caveman as I am, or so I hear."

"Yeah, right," Karen said, opening the car door. "That's a conversation I'll be having."

She went into the house, and Hope looked at me, and I looked back at her. "Well," she finally said, "at least they have a ping-pong table. Would you like to rethink your decision to be involved with either of us?"

I couldn't help smiling. I reached over, put a gentle hand behind her head and another on her shoulder, pulled her into me, felt her body yielding to me, and finally kissed her the way I'd wanted to ever since I'd seen her again. Slow and deep and the way I needed it, taking her mouth hard enough that she'd feel it, making it mine. Until she was making some noises, those little whimpers that drove me wild. Until she was clutching at my shoulder, hanging on, and I had my hand in her hair, tugging her head gently back in the way I loved most, and everything about her response was telling me that she wanted me to lay her down then and there.

And when I took that gorgeously full lower lip between my teeth and gave it a nip? She gasped, her whole body jerked, and I finally did the other thing I'd been longing to do. I slid my hand into the low neckline of that snug tee, straight inside her bra, palmed her breast, and bit her lip again. And felt her squirm. Hard.

I let go of her, sat back, and said, "No. On consideration, I think I'm going to have to insist on keeping you."

She was lying back against the seat, her color up, an audible hitch in her breath, and all she could say was, "Hemi."

She wanted to hear it all, so I gave her what she needed. But then, giving Hope what she needed was the greatest pleasure of my life.

"Yeh," I told her. "I have that work to do. And then I'd like to make an appointment to remind you who you'll be waiting for, and what he expects from you. You may hold my feet to the fire, but I can hold yours, too. I can do more than that. I can hold your ankles, and I can hold your knees, and tonight, I'm going to do it. We'll have another chat about your independence when I've taken all your clothes off, you're on your back in my bed, I've got my hands on your pretty thighs, and I'm holding them apart while you squirm to get loose. When I've got my mouth on you, and I'm reminding you what my tongue is for and exactly how much you need it. We can have another chat about it when my hands are on the backs of your legs, when I've got them shoved up so you're spread wide open for me, and all you want is more. When you find out just how long I'm willing to play with you, and just how far you're willing to go."

feet to the fire

♡

Hope

Maybe you can see why distance was necessary to maintain my self-control during my regrouping period.

What did he do after that? Did he kiss me again? No, he did not. He got out of the car, then came around and opened my door like the gentleman he most definitely wasn't.

I looked at him with narrowed eyes and said, "What I told Karen is true. It's still a hundred percent my choice."

"Now, sweetheart," he said, only the barest movement at the corner of his mouth betraying his real feelings, "when did I ever say it wasn't? It's my job to make you want it. It's your job to decide whether you do."

"Yeah, well," I muttered, "you're too good at your job." And this time, his smile might have escaped.

He was setting me up for later, that was all. Too bad he was the master at that. Or lucky for me that he was. One or the other, because it sure had worked. I was a quivering, tingling bundle of arousal right now, and he still looked as cool as ever.

Except that I knew he wasn't, because if he knew my dirty secrets? I knew his, too.

I didn't know what we were doing tonight. Going out, or staying in. The only thing I knew for sure was that Hemi knew which it was going to be, and what was going to happen.

Well, I might have a plan, too. I hung up my suit and towel, then took off all my clothes and took my time rubbing wildflower-scented body butter into my skin. I applied just enough makeup to look like I wasn't wearing any and fixed my hair in a tousled bedhead look before changing into soft black cotton leggings and a long, stretchy white shirt with a low crossover neckline, a gathered front, and a hem barely long enough for decency. A tiny gold heart on a chain around my neck, and Hemi's ring on my finger. All soft and clinging and innocently, sweetly seductive, like I didn't know what I was doing.

I almost hadn't packed this shirt. I was glad now that I had. Hemi was going to try his best to knock my socks off tonight, but he was going to be facing some competition. If he knew how to push my buttons? I knew how to push his, too.

I'd never been much good at sports, but there was a game or two I was good at playing all the same. I'd been a late bloomer, but I had what Hemi needed. Of that, I was sure.

He was at the dining room table, working on his laptop with his usual focus, when I came in with my own computer. I set up at right angles to him, then wriggled around some, pulled my hem down, which also had the effect of exposing my newly acquired cleavage, and shoved a foot under myself so I was curled into the chair, angled a tiny bit toward him.

Did he look up? Yes, he did. And then he kept looking.

I didn't pay any attention. I found my document, propped an elbow on the table, shoved my hand into my hair, messing it up some more, bit my lower lip, and sighed. And he watched that, too.

He went back to work, eventually, without a comment, and I smiled a little inside and kept my own focus on applying for the working holiday visa I'd need to get a job here, then did some more research on everything I'd need to know and everything I'd need to do. Hemi sat still, his face intent, his fingers flying, and if he looked at me from time to time? Maybe I did my best to distract him.

Tomorrow, he'd be leaving, back to his fourteen-hour days, back to running his empire and managing his crises without distraction. Tonight, though, he was mine.

It was almost six when Tane's oldest, sixteen-year-old Nikau, showed up at the door. Karen, who'd come into the living room at the sound of the doorbell, said, "I could just have walked up the hill, you know. I mean, it's nice of you to come get me and all, but unless I'm going to be attacked by a wild pig or something, I think I was pretty safe."

"Karen . . ." I began.

Nikau, already almost as tall as his father, looked startled, then grinned. "Yeh, nah, maybe you're not all that, eh. I came to deliver some fish to Uncle Hemi as well." He handed Hemi a squashy parcel in a plastic carrier bag and said, "Dad said you'd be expecting it, Uncle. We caught it this morning."

"Cheers," he said.

Karen said, "Whoops. I guess I blew it, huh?" And I thought, *You think?*

"Nah," Nikau said. "Just don't say something like that to Dad, and you're all good."

"Oh," she said. "Is that some kind of New Zealand thing about respect for your elders?"

"Some kind of Maori thing," Hemi said as Nikau looked startled again. "Could be you'll learn something."

She *laughed*. Oh, man. I really had to teach her some better manners. Then she picked up her backpack and said, "I'll see you guys tomorrow morning, then. Or tonight, if they kick me out for being rude."

"At least you get that," I said. "For heaven's sake, Karen."

"Won't be happening," Hemi said. "Hospitality's another Maori thing. See you in the morning."

Once he closed the door on them, he hefted the plastic packet, looked at me for a long moment, and headed into the kitchen.

Oh, I thought. *Refrigerator.* In another second, I heard it shutting, and Hemi came back out to join me.

He wasn't wearing jeans tonight. I'd already noticed that. He'd changed after the pool, too, while I'd been in the bathroom. Now, he had on black trousers in a fine wool, together with one of his white dress shirts with the sleeves rolled up to show the lowest few inches of his swirling tattoo, not to mention the forearms I never got tired of looking at, with their thick bands of muscle under the bronzed skin.

When I'd emerged from the locker room with Karen that afternoon and had slid into the pool next to him, I'd wanted to stare. It was easy to forget, after a couple weeks, exactly how spectacular that body was. The slabs of pectorals, the bulk of shoulders and arms, and, best of all, that wonderful V-shape as shoulders tapered into broad chest and then on down to his trim waist.

It wasn't all visible right then, of course. You couldn't, for example, see the thin, dark line of hair running from his navel into the top of his swim trunks or the strength of his thighs. But you could imagine them. And the sight of those muscles, that skin, that blue-black tattoo, and the close-cropped dark head, all of it glistening with water? It was pretty special. In fact, there was a group of older ladies doing some kind of water aerobics in the next lane who I could swear weren't exercising nearly as much as they ought to have been.

I'd ignored him then, too. I'd been sassy, and he'd loved it. I'd left him wanting more. He might act like he had all the power, but we both knew it wasn't true.

Now, with Karen gone, I sat back down in front of my computer, but he slid it out from under my hands, closed it, and said, "Oh, no."

"Excuse me?" I tossed my head and frowned at him. "Do you get to say that?'

"Yeh. I do." He closed his own, then, and set them both on a low table near the front door. "How hungry are you? Need me to fix you a snack?"

"Um . . ." I did a little more nibbling on my bottom lip, because he liked to watch it. "Not too bad. I'm good for another hour. Are we going out?"

"Now, Hope," he said, coming toward me, picking me bodily up out of my chair and setting me on my feet. "You know I'm making you snapper tonight. But not yet. Seems I've got some feet to hold to the fire first."

I expected him to take me into the bedroom, but he didn't. He flipped a switch at the wall so the only illumination came from a table lamp, pulled blinds closed all around the room, then picked up his phone and pushed buttons until the room was filled with music. Low and dark, soft and sweet, but with an urgent, sensual edge. A male voice, singing about desire and longing and getting what you needed most from a woman.

"That's better," Hemi said. "You've been teasing me all afternoon. Time for me to tease you."

♡♡♡

Hemi

When Hope had disappeared into the bedroom after our outing with a saucy glance back at me, I'd had all I could do not to follow her in there.

Karen had still been with us, though, so I couldn't. The two hours that passed until she left were some of the longest I'd ever spent. Especially with all Hope's little sighs, the wriggles and readjustments, her index finger tracing her lower lip as she stared at her screen in a fascination I'd known she was pretending.

Now, Karen was gone, the music and the lights were both low, and Hope was on the couch, her hair tumbled around her shoulders, one edge of that stretchy shirt slipping over to one side, showing a thin pink ribbon of bra strap. All she had to do was lie back and look at me with those eyes, her pretty mouth a little parted, and I was halfway gone.

"Hope," I said, and this time, it was *my* finger tracing her lips, forcing her mouth to open more for me, "do you want me to take off your clothes?"

Her eyes widened even more, and I could swear she was breathing harder already. "Yes."

I smiled and felt the dark satisfaction of it all the way down my body. "But they're so pretty, and you wore them just for me. So I think I'm going to have to explore a little first. Besides—I need to kiss you, and you need to be kissed."

I had weeks to make up for, so I took my time. I started out by sucking that passionate, plump lower lip into my mouth as I stroked my thumb down the side of her neck, trailed the backs of my fingers over her bare shoulder, and shoved her shirt a little farther to one side. I traced the pretty pink strap of her bra down, then followed the low V-neck around and down, touching the delicate skin between her breasts with a thumbnail, letting it rasp down into my favorite valley as I took her gasp into my mouth. I did all of that, until I needed more, until I was laying her back against the cushions and getting my arm around her, my hand holding the back of her neck firmly enough that she'd know she was mine.

I was going to be careful, but I was going to be possessive. She might not like that in all aspects of our life together, but she liked it here, and she needed it. And so did I.

I was right, because just like that, she was shuddering and saying, "Hemi."

I smiled inside, but I didn't answer her. Instead, I held the back of her neck a little harder, then trailed my lips across her cheek to her ear and felt her start to tremble. I took my time nibbling on the lobe, then moved to her throat. When I began to kiss her there, she was already moaning, and we'd barely started. And when I did it better, when I took a gentle bite at the spot where her neck met her shoulder and then kissed and bit my slow way back up, she started to squirm.

I couldn't feel the silky skin of her legs under my hands, though, and I needed to. I needed to wind her up, to make it good for her, to make it last, and to do that? I needed her legs. I sat up, got both hands under her stretchy white top, and pulled the leggings down, taking her socks with them.

"Oh, yeh," I said when my hands were running up her calves, pushing her knees gently apart. "That's better." My hands drifted over her thighs, and she sucked in a breath and held it.

"How badly do you need an orgasm, sweetheart?" I asked her. My thumbs were moving higher, then higher still. They were nearly there, and she was whimpering.

"So . . ." she managed to say. "So badly. Hemi. Please."

"Open your eyes," I told her. Her head was back, her eyes closed, her mouth open. I watched her lids fluttering open, and I smiled.

"Normally," I said, "I'd tease you more first. Normally, I'd make you wait. I'd make you beg. But I think, tonight... you've missed me too much."

When I shoved her top up to her waist and exposed the pink thong with the black lace overlay, the one I'd bought her in Paris, I thought I was the one who'd missed her too much. I got my hands under the straps and pulled the tiny scrap of material down her legs, and she said, "Ah . . ." and started to close her eyes again.

"No," I said. "Watch me." And she did. She watched while I pulled her hips to the edge of the couch, and while I sank to my knees in front of her. And she watched while I did what I'd promised. I had a hand on each knee, and I was positioning her for me, and then I was opening her with one hand while I explored her with the other. Not one bit quickly. She might be embarrassed, but I didn't care. She was mine, and I needed to see her, and touch her, and taste her, and feel her. Absolutely everywhere.

She'd changed here, too. She was pinker, softer, fuller. More delicious, more swollen, and if I'd thought Hope was responsive before? Now, I could hardly hold her down. I'd barely begun to kiss her, to suck her into my mouth, and she was already writhing, calling out. I could feel her back arching, and her hands were in my hair, hanging on desperately. And when I slipped a careful finger inside her, then another one, and found the spot? I thought she was going to explode.

It felt like seconds. I knew it wasn't nearly long enough before she was bucking, moaning, and calling my name. She was coming into my mouth, then climbing again, over and over. And all I could do was keep going. All I could give her was more.

♡♡♡

Hope

He'd promised me he wouldn't be rough, and he wasn't. He wasn't one bit rough, and he didn't make me work for it. He just gave it to me again and again like he didn't know what "done" was, like all he wanted was to take my pleasure into his mouth, and then to give me more. He showed me exactly why he was the only man who could ever satisfy me. And when I was limp and shaking, wrung out and used up, he stood, picked me up, carried me into the bedroom, laid me down on the bed, turned on the light beside it, and stood over me like the conquering warrior he was.

"I'm going to fuck you so carefully tonight," he told me, and I shuddered again. I was so satisfied, but I wasn't one bit done. I was still so aroused, in fact, that my entire body felt like one aching need. "I'm going to get you where I want you, and then I'm going to make you come over and over for me.

You need it, and I need to do it to you."

He was drawing my shirt over my head, unfastening the clasp of my bra. I was sprawled across his bed, my legs parted, all of me exposed for him, wearing only that tiny golden heart and his ring. And he still had all his clothes on.

"I should . . ." I said. I rose on my elbows, and he pushed me back down with a gentle hand on my shoulder.

"No," he said. "There's no 'should' tonight. You don't have to do anything. I'm going to do it all."

His hand was on my lower belly, tracing gently over the little bit of swelling there, and he said, "This is nice. This is so pretty."

"That's your baby," I said, and smiled at him.

He kissed me there, and the tenderness in it tried to bring tears to my eyes even through my excitement. Then he stroked over my belly, up my side, until he finally reached my breast. I jumped, and he asked, "Are they sore?"

"Yes. Tender. Feels good," I managed as his hand traced carefully over the swell of my breast and grazed a peak that had been hard for what felt like hours. "Just… tender."

"Mm." He got onto a knee on the bed, and then he was over me, kissing his way from my neck to my breast, exploring me with so much gentleness, reading my sighs, taking it slow, taking it easy.

I said, "I need to feel you. I need to see you." My hands went to the buttons of his shirt, and I began to unfasten them, to stroke my way over his broad chest, and felt his instant reaction.

How could a man have as much self-control as Hemi? How could he do all this without needing anything for himself? So I told him so. "You're the most amazing lover," I said. "You make me feel so good. But right now, I need to feel you inside me. I need to feel you taking your own pleasure. I want you to do everything that feels good to you. Everything you want. I want you to tell me what that is, and to show me what you need. I'll do whatever you say, because obeying you excites me. Please, Hemi—let me please you now."

I shoved his shirt off his shoulders, and he finished taking it off, then stood and got rid of the rest of his clothes. After that, he stood there, and I drank him in. My Maori god, all muscle and sinew, controlled strength and powerful intent. And all of it was for me.

After that, he did just what he'd said he would, and he did what I'd asked. He took his pleasure, and he did everything he wanted. He told me what to do, and I did it. And whether I was on my knees, taking him deep in my mouth, obeying every gasped command, or lying on my back with his hands on the backs of my thighs, feeling him stroking deep, or on my elbows and knees, his hand at the back of my neck holding me down, my forehead on my hands, my entire body jerking hard at every thrust… wherever I was, and through everything he did to me—he was heartbreaking careful, he was breathtakingly thorough, and he let me know that I was absolutely and completely his.

And just for now, just for tonight… I let myself be that and nothing more. Sometimes, your will truly isn't your own, because giving it up is such exquisite pleasure.

Independence matters, and autonomy is a wonderful thing. But sometimes… sometimes, surrender feels so good.

wairua

♡

Hope

I was nearly dozing, wrapped in Hemi's arms, when he asked, "Hungry?"

"Mm." I rolled over and pushed myself up. "Yes. How did you know?"

There was no smugness, no calculation in his smile. All I saw was contentment when he said, "Hang on, then, and I'll fix your dinner."

I tried to fall asleep again, but as exhausted as I was, I really *was* too hungry. Hemi was back in less than five minutes, though, with a plate and a mug that he set on my bedside table.

"Oh," I said, and tried not to be disappointed. Three crackers, topped with bits of cheese, and a cup of herbal tea.

He laughed. "No worries, baby. That's your snack, so this doesn't become another emergency." He went to the closet, pulled out a soft flannel shirt in a green and black plaid, picked up my thong from the floor, and handed them to me. "So you stay warm. Dressed for dinner, eh."

When he came back again fifteen minutes later, carrying a tray this time, he stopped in the doorway and said, "I could sell a few pairs of undies with that picture."

"What? Me in your shirt, with my hair a mess?"

"Yeh. You in your pretty thong and a man's shirt five sizes too big for you, your hair all mussed and your gorgeous mouth looking like it's been well kissed, sitting cross-legged on rumpled white sheets. That'd sell some undies."

"Well," I said, "you might do the same." He was wearing only one thing, but it was a good one: a pair of black boxer briefs that didn't do much to disguise the substantial Te Mana assets. "All that tattoo, and all those muscles? But this is a private viewing. One customer only."

He handed me my plate, and we ate like that, sitting up against the headboard. Delicate white fish in a whisper-thin golden coating that Hemi told me was beer batter, chunks of potato and kumara roasted to perfect crunchy goodness, and a salad of baby greens that he'd tossed in olive oil, lemon juice, pepper, and a little bit of mustard. All the savory flavors I craved most now, and who'd known Hemi could do that, or that he'd be willing to?

Afterwards, I had just about enough strength to brush my teeth before I was crawling back into bed. I'm not sure when Hemi got in beside me, but at some point, I woke and he was there. I fell asleep again with his arm around me and his hand on my belly. Holding me, and holding onto the life inside me. Letting me know he was going to keep holding on. Letting me believe it.

I fell asleep feeling safe.

♡♡♡

I woke the next morning to find that it was already seven, and I'd nearly slept the clock around. And I also woke to find a couple digestive biscuits on a plate by my bed. I ate them before I got up, and that made it easier. How had Hemi known?

I found him working, of course, but he shut his laptop when I came in and smiled at me. "Morning, beautiful girl."

"Morning." I leaned down to give him a kiss, and he pulled me gently into his lap, bent me back over his arm, and gave me a better one.

"Thanks for my biscuits," I said when he finally let me up again.

"Mm." More smile, then. "I talked to Tane this morning. He said they'll keep Karen over there till it's time to collect Koro. He also told me about the biscuits. Teaching me to be a good husband, eh." The hand stroking over my hair told me he meant what he said.

"What about Koro?"

"Rang him as well. He said he'll be released at eleven, and he wants us to come then. He said no sooner, because he'd have a roomful, and all the company was making him tired. Grumpy old bugger. Sure you're ready to take that on? You can still come home, and I'd rather you did."

I kissed his cheek, then ran a hand down it, loving the morning-smoothness of it as much as I'd loved the faint roughness against my skin the night before. "I haven't changed my mind. I love you more than I can say, but I need to do this. *We* need it. And of course I'm ready. He's only out of sorts because he hurts, and he's not at home, and he feels powerless. I've done a little bit of nursing, you know."

He sighed. "Right, then. And I do know. First your mum, then Karen. Too much nursing."

"No. The right amount. It's always better when you can do something to help, and it's best of all when the person will be getting well."

We cooked breakfast and ate it together, and then we took a walk down through the kiwifruit orchards toward the sea, stopped into the same café to pick up a coffee for Hemi, and walked back up the hill again. The late-winter breeze was chilly, but the sun was warm, and surely there was no sky as blue as New Zealand's, no clouds whiter, no air as clean or invigorating. Or maybe that was just Hemi, and sex, and love, and… Hemi.

"You're all good," I said when we were back in the house and I saw him reach for the phone in his back pocket, then stop himself. "If you have something to do, go ahead and do it."

His smile was rueful. "I'm trying to focus on you, but I do need to take a wee look at this."

"That's fine. I have a few things to do myself." My resume, mainly. I wasn't sure I'd be applying for the kind of job that required it, but if I did, I'd be ready.

It was actually strangely compatible, sitting there. Hemi had given me his attention and his time, and now, we could both be busy. Parallel play, like two toddlers. He'd put on a pair of headphones and was wearing his fiercest look of concentration, clicking at his laptop, staring at it, then clicking again. I sneaked peeks at him, but I couldn't guess what had him so… upset? Focused? Something.

I finally hit "Save," sat back, and took a breath, and Hemi took the headphones off and said, "Would you want to give me your opinion?"

"Uh… sure. About what?"

"The launch of the Colors of the Earth line. You had some good ideas at the meeting. Thought you might have an opinion now, and I'd like to hear it."

I was so surprised, I about fell over. I almost asked him if he really meant it, if he truly wanted to know what I thought or if this was some sort of ploy in the Get Hope Back campaign, but I thought better of it. Hemi didn't say things he didn't mean. "Sure," I said instead. "I'd love to." I bit back the words "for what my opinion's worth." I had a feeling that didn't meet Te Mana Negotiation Standards.

Hemi unplugged the headphones, shoved the laptop closer to me, and clicked again to start a video. A driving rock beat, that fashion show staple, filled the room as a series of slides flashed before me. Design drawings of dresses on models, and finished garments. A simulated show, in other words.

I listened and watched until the end, then said, "Huh. Can I see it again?" and did.

"These are the ads," he said when the show had finished and I still hadn't said anything, because I was still thinking. He clicked another few times, and I read the copy and did the rest of the clicking through myself.

A lot of it, I recognized from my proofreading duties, but I was seeing it matched with the photographs for the first time. The lush greens and exotic vegetation of the New Zealand bush, the empty sweep of spectacular golden, crescent-shaped beaches and azure water so clear and pure, it stabbed you to the heart. Beautiful women of all colors and shapes and sizes, wearing headdresses made of flowers and leaves. Long hair and big eyes and, most of all—clothing in vibrant shades and lush, gorgeous fabrics. Dresses and tops and trousers that any woman's hands would itch to stroke, that she'd yearn to drape herself in because if she wore them, she'd be beautiful.

"The images… they're breathtaking," I said slowly.

"But?" Hemi's eyes were intent on mine.

"Well, two things. I saw this copy before. I thought it was too florid then. Now, I really think so. You've got all these long sentences, all this over-the-top copy, when the images really speak for themselves. I feel like you need more… contrast. Like… choppy and sweet. Tender and tough. You know? The clothes are really *so* gorgeous. I can't believe you did this. At least," I hurried to add, "I *can* believe it, but I think they're your best work ever. That's all I'm saying."

He made an impatient gesture. "Never mind my ego. Go on."

"Well, don't you think it might be more effective if it were more . . ." My hands moved, wanting to try, wanting to write, and Hemi slid a pad of paper and a pen over. "Like this," I said, and wrote,

Too much is never enough.

Beautiful is a state of mind.

Taste the color. Hear the movement. Feel the life.

"I mean, those are just ideas," I hurried to say when Hemi said nothing. "Off the top of my head. But sort of staccato, you know, but in an italic font, maybe. So the contrast again. And I feel like the show… like it needs more of that, too. More contrast. More edge. Like… you're doing that now, with the hard music, but it feels wrong, doesn't it? Isn't that why you were frowning, why you asked me? See, I think you could go bold with that, like you are with the models. Bold, but not in a hard way. In a *different* way. In *your* way. The way a feminine woman can be bold, can be strong, and still be soft.

Gentle but strong, like you last night. Gentle, but so sure."

I was carried away now, and I couldn't have stopped if I'd wanted to. I was going for it. I was putting it out there. "One of the first things I noticed about you was that you never, ever raised your voice. The more emotional you get, especially the more *angry* you get, the more quiet and still you become, and what happens? Everybody turns to look. Everybody stops talking and holds their breath. I'll tell you, that is seriously scary. Serious power. It's like a whisper is more powerful than a shout. And that's these clothes, too. They don't have to be bold and edgy to be powerful. They just have to be more beautiful, like they're not afraid to be feminine. Like they can whisper."

"They can whisper," Hemi said slowly. "She can whisper."

"Yes. *Yes.* So… Maori music. I've listened to some of it, doing my research on you, you know." I tried to joke, because I still wasn't sure what he thought, but I needed to express myself, to *tell* him, and the words kept tumbling out. "And some of it… like the bone flute, especially… it's so haunting. It grabs you. It compels you. You *have* to pay attention. When you hear that loud rock music, you almost want to curl up, to go inside, to hide. The bone flute, it brings you out. It's like what you'd play to make the animals quiet, to calm them and open their hearts."

He didn't say anything, but he didn't stop me, either, so I went on. "And another thing. The clothes. That's where you could do the edge. I think, maybe… like, boots. In the show, she could have on funky leather boots, you know, with cutouts, maybe? Sexy, tough, rocker-girl. Nature isn't always beautiful. It's tough, and it's tender. That's where you see the softness best, when it's against the hardness."

He sat still as stone, and I said, "Those are just ideas. Just my ideas for tweaks. I mean, I'm not saying there's anything wrong. Everything's so beautiful, and with the diverse models? It's going to be a hit. It's going to be wonderful. But just… tweaks," I finished lamely, then trailed off. "Wow," I finally said, then tried to laugh. "Bet you're sorry you asked. Never mind. Henry said the worst thing in a marketing assistant was somebody with no experience, but with delusions of grandeur. The kind who wanted to plan strategy and write copy without any idea what she was doing, and what did I just do? Exactly that. But maybe that can give you some of your own ideas."

I waited, and then I waited some more. The seconds ticked by, and I found that I was holding my breath. Finally, Hemi did what I'd never have expected. He smiled like the sun coming out, and then he laughed out loud and picked me up out of my chair and off my feet. He swung me in a circle, right there in his Koro's tiny living room, and I was twirling, spinning, and laughing, too.

When he set me down at last, he kissed me, but not with the calculation he'd shown the night before. This came from his heart, and I put my hands on his cheeks and kissed him back, his joy coming straight through from his body to mine, as if we were one flesh, one spirit.

Finally, he stood back, but he still had his arms around my lower back, was still holding me so close. "Sweetheart," he said, "I knew there had to be more than one reason I loved you so much. Because you are brilliant."

"I… I am?" My heart was pounding, and the happiness in him was a golden thing, a shining thing. I wanted to stay in this moment forever, watching him feel that. Knowing he was showing it only to me, and that I'd helped him find it.

Soulmates. That's what it felt like. His soul touching mine.

Something sacred. Something powerful, but not in a solemn way. In a bright way, a beautiful way.

He said, "There's a Maori word. Wairua. Spirit. The immortal principle, the shining essence. It's not a separate thing, or even a religious thing. It's the foundation, the most sacred part of who we are, the part that lives on after our body is gone. It can bubble to the surface, or it can glow beneath, shining out in our eyes, in our voice, in our deeds. And sweetheart—your wairua, it's… it's a light that shines so strong in you. And it's beautiful."

I was crying now. I couldn't help it. Tears of joy, not sorrow. Tears of gratitude that wouldn't stay inside me, that had to come out, that had to be shown, to be seen. I was holding Hemi, I was crying, and there was so much love there. So much love, my body couldn't contain it. It had to come out in my tears.

"I love you," I told him. "Because you listen. Because you hear. Because you're so much more than what you show the world, but you show it to me, and I'm so grateful to see it."

He looked at me, his face for once perfectly open, perfectly joyful. The face he must have shown as a boy, before the hard realities of his life had closed him off and shut him down.

And if life has perfect moments, the ones you'll remember forever? The sweet, precious pearls of joy you can hold in your heart, the treasures that will still be yours when you're too old for anything but memories? Surely this was one. Surely this was mine.

coming and going

♡

Hemi

All too soon, Karen was home again. No time to take Hope back to bed, no matter how much I needed to do it. No time to show her all the things that, no matter what she thought, I knew I could tell her so much better with my willing body than with any clumsy, halting words I could dredge up. No time to make her own body hum and shudder and convulse until all she could do was sigh with satisfaction and fall asleep draped across my chest, or to make sure she'd remember exactly what she was missing when I was gone.

Instead, it was time to drive back to the hospital and bring Koro home. Time for me to go home myself, where I'd have the space I needed to handle all the problems closing in on me, unhampered by distractions and untidiness of any sort.

If that didn't sound as good as it once had, I needed to adjust my attitude fast. I did what I had to do, and just now, this was it. Otherwise, I could lose most of what I'd spent a lifetime building, and lose Hope along with it. Despite what she'd said, I knew that no woman wanted a loser. My dad was proof enough of that.

When we walked back into the hospital room late that Sunday morning, it was as crowded as I'd expected. Three vases of flowers crowded the meager table space, and a couple of bright helium balloons bounced against the ceiling. And then there were all the people. Tane and June and their kids, together with Auntie Flora. And for the first time since I'd been here, my cousin Matiu, leaning against the wall checking his phone.

"Good," Koro said at sight of me. "They say they're going to let me out at last, and I wasn't about to wait for you."

"We've heard the instructions from the doctor already," Matiu said, shoving the phone back into his pocket. "All good. Got a printout for Hope as well."

"Hi, Matiu," Karen said, bright and eager as a sparrow. "I thought maybe you weren't around anymore."

"Nah," he said with that patented smile that, Tane had told me, still had girls falling at his feet. "Been working, for my sins. I'll follow you home, Hemi, so I can fill Hope in and get Koro well settled. I can give him a bit of a check once we get there, make sure nothing's gone awry during the journey."

Koro said, "Think I can ride in a car for twenty minutes and go sit in my own house without needing a physical, thank you very much. Those nurses have been in here every time I turn around. Dunno what they're checking for. If my heart had stopped, they'd know it. I've got a bit of a sore head and arm, and nothing else in the world the matter with me."

"Hmm," Matiu said, the light in his eyes and the twitch at the corner of his mouth the only signs of the smile he was suppressing. "Call it being cautious with the whanau's treasure."

Koro snorted at that, and Matiu looked more amused than ever. Everything was a joke with him even now, and as always, it annoyed me. He said, "Tane and I will switch off coming out to help Koro with his bath and all, depending on my schedule, and that'll be good as well. I can keep my eye on the arm, and if Hope has any questions, I can answer them, and do anything else she and Koro need. Hope doesn't have a driving license, I hear."

"I don't," Hope said. "Which I realize makes more work for the others."

"No worries," Matiu said. "We can give you a hand with that as well, I'm thinking. Karen, too, as she's turned sixteen. Driving lessons, eh. Between Tane and June and me, we should be able to get that sorted." He flashed some more grin at the two of them. If women were drawn to me because I was closed off, with Matiu, it was the opposite. He was everything that promised a good time, even if he never promised a single thing more. Or delivered it.

Well, that wasn't quite fair. He was a doctor as well, and that hadn't been easy. In any case, Karen seemed to have no qualms, whatever I'd told her about men. She smiled back at Matiu and murmured, "Oh, goody," at Hope, and that wasn't the best.

Hope winced beside me, and I realized I was squeezing her hand too tightly and relaxed my own with an effort. We'd talked about driving lessons, after all. If she needed to be able to drive and swim to feel ready to marry me, then I reckoned she should learn to drive and swim. And if I'd rather be the one overseeing all that? I'd already seen how my attempts at full control had worked out. As for Karen, I had to admit that

Hope didn't seem any worse at managing her than I was. And Matiu was my cousin. He'd hardly set his considerable sights on my soon-to-be sister-in-law, all sixteen years old of her.

Better for Karen, surely, to have a bit of a crush, if it happened, than to deal with an actual hormone-crazed boy who'd be coming around when I wasn't there, taking her for a walk through the orchards, maneuvering to be alone with her in exactly the same way I'd done with every girl I could get my hands on in my own younger days. She'd have Koro around to give every bloke the look, after all. Koro's look was as effective as my own, concussion or no, and his mana was second to none.

Hope, seemingly unaware of any treacherous undercurrents, said, "Driving lessons would be amazing for both of us. Efficient, too, if we can get them together. I'm guessing it would be a whole lot easier to start learning here than in New York City."

"How long will you be staying?" Matiu asked.

"Three weeks for Karen," Hope said. "Six or so for me, maybe more. We'll see."

That earned some interested looks I could have done without, until Koro said, "I know Hemi knows how to drive, anyway, and it's high time he shook up a nurse and got me out of here. I want my own chair, my own bed, and my own garden. Want my own food, come to that. We'll stop at Countdown along the way. I can have a sandwich at my own table, and not a minute too soon."

♡♡♡

A couple hours later, and there was no putting it off.

I thought I'd hardened myself against temptation long ago.

I'd practiced discipline and self-control for so many years, they were second nature. Today, though—today, I wanted something else. I wanted to take Hope on another walk, to back her up against the smooth bark of an avocado tree in Koro's back garden or, better yet, to pull her down into my lap on a handy bench, because Hope in my lap was one of my favorite things. I wanted to take my time kissing her until her mouth was swollen and her eyes were closed, until my hands were all over her and her entire body was yielding to mine, until I'd lost my own inhibitions and could whisper everything I yearned to say about the way I needed her. No fear, and no restraint.

After that, I wanted to sit with Koro, watch the recap of the weekend's rugby, and drink a beer. I wanted to cook dinner with Hope and Karen and eat it at the little table in the best house in the world. I wanted to be the one who helped Koro with his bath and put him to bed, and then I wanted to take Hope to our own bed and take care of her in every way there was.

I wanted to be the man of my family. But to do that, I had to set my wishes aside and leave all of them. Life wasn't about doing what you wanted. It was about doing what you had to do.

Saying goodbye to Koro came first. In the end, the drive home and the wait in the Countdown carpark while the rest of us did a quick shop had tired him more than he'd been willing to admit, and there'd been a tinge of gray to his skin by the time Matiu and I had been helping him into the house. He hadn't objected too strenuously when we'd got him into his pj's and helped him climb into bed again before Matiu left.

"Hope and Karen are making you a sandwich," I said.

"And Matiu will be back tonight."

"I'm not deaf," he said with little enough heat that I recognized it for the pro forma protest it was. "I know he's coming back. Can hardly get rid of him, can I."

"Good." I put the TV remote next to his hand and rearranged a vase of flowers on the bedside table so he could reach the water glass more easily. "I can be back within the day if I'm needed. By you *or* Hope. Maybe you can remind her of that."

As soon as I'd said it, I knew it was weak, but Koro's tired, wise old eyes had already shifted to mine. "No worries, my son. She loves you, and she's not your mum. What's a month or two compared to a lifetime? Nothing. Laying the foundation, that's all."

"You've been talking to her." When could he have done that?

"I don't need to talk to her to know that. I know it's hard for you to follow somebody else's lead, but in this, the woman sets the pace. No way around it. She tells you when you've got there, but once you have, there'll be no budging her. She'll be solid as the ridge post in the marae, exactly like your Kuia was for me. A woman to build your life around."

I was having some trouble with my eyes. I took his hand, as weathered and gnarled as the pohutukawa where Hope and I had sat the day before, squeezed it gently, and leaned forward to hongi him again.

"Go," he said. "I'm all good, and you have things to do. You're better there."

"Three weeks," I told him. "Then I'm back to collect Karen, and to see the two of you."

"Three weeks," he said. "I'll be up and around, and your heart will be easier, because you'll see that you don't have to be with her to take care of your woman. I reckon you may do that better now than when you had her with you."

"I'll be doing that," I said, and then, because the words wouldn't stay inside, I added, "Take care of yourself. Please."

Please don't die, I managed not to say. *I can't lose you. Not that.*

"I'll be here," he said, seeming to understand me without the words. "Now go tell her everything you want her to know, including the hardest bits. It's all good, my son. You've done tougher things."

Hope walked outside with me for that. I was glad that at least it wasn't raining, so we could take our time. My pilot was going to be waiting a few extra minutes, but that was what I paid him for.

I tossed my luggage in the boot, then slammed it shut and leaned against the door, wrapping my arms around Hope and giving her a slow, thorough kiss as her own arms twined around my neck.

I could have kissed her forever, and she was the one who broke it off, then brushed her nose against mine in a playful gesture and smiled into my eyes. Her mouth may have trembled a bit around the edges, but her voice was firm when she said, "Take care of yourself, Hemi. And know that I'll take care of your grandfather. I'll do my very best, and so will you."

"I know you will," I said. "You always do. But it's not too late to change your mind. Surely you know how much I love you, and how much I'm willing to do to prove it. I can get Koro looked after. Come home with me."

Her eyes softened, and her hand was on my cheek when she said, "This is better. It's hard on both of us, but it's better. You think it's about you, that you can change, and maybe you're right. You're strong enough to do anything. But it *isn't* about you, not really. It's about me. It's about both of us holding strong together, not one person needing to carry the other, or the other person needing to be carried."

"It's not you, it's me?" I said. "Not something any bloke wants to hear."

"Practice, that's all. We'll both practice, and we'll get better. That's the point of practice."

I drove away, in the end, because I had no choice. And I watched her in the rearview mirror, a small, stalwart figure with her hand raised and a smile on her face, until I turned the corner and left her behind.

I didn't do helpless. Not ever. But I was damned if I could figure out how to do anything else.

comparisons

♡

Hope

Wednesdays can be weird.

On a wet one ten days later, I woke to news that was either good or bad, depending on your point of view.

I'd got out of bed at six-thirty, but Koro had beaten me. He was in the kitchen with a cup of tea and the newspaper, and not in his robe, either.

"Hey," I said, going over and giving him a kiss on the cheek, "look at you. Want some help with those buttons?" He was wearing a white T-shirt and jeans, with a flannel shirt hanging open over the shirt. Not quite neat enough for Koro, but major progress from staying in his robe until one of his nephews showed up to help him into his clothes. I knew it must have hurt getting his arm in and out of the sling, but I wasn't going to mention that. Koro, like Hemi, had pride to burn.

"I'd say no," he said with the lightening around the eyes that was the Te Mana version of a smile, "but I reckon I've used up all my grumpy bugger points already."

"Never." I fastened the shirt's buttons for him and loved that he let me do it. I didn't suggest that I could help tuck it in. I wasn't pushing my luck. "Only the tiniest dent in the allowable total, and I've practically forgotten it already. How's the head?"

He flapped his uninjured hand. "I'll live." Indeed, he was looking and sounding less foggy day by day, although he still tired much too easily. "Even managed to read a bit of the paper today. Sorry I did, of course."

I popped a couple pieces of bread into the toaster, then spooned a little chopped ginger into a mug and added a tea bag, hot water, and my spoonful of manuka honey. "Sometimes," I confessed, "I look at the news and want to pay to put the newspaper *back*. What was it today?"

He didn't tell me. Instead, he shoved the *Herald* across the table at me. I sat down, took a sip of tea, picked up the paper, and dropped it again. "Whoa."

Two faces stared back at me, and a shiver went straight down my spine. The first shot, Hemi at his darkest and most formidable, was nothing but a thrill. The one below that wasn't quite as good, though.

Hemi again. With his wife.

A younger, slimmer, happier man looked back at me, the look on his face one I'd only seen on rare occasions when the two of us had been alone. His arm was wrapped protectively around an absolutely glowing Anika, who stood laughing with one hand holding down the skirt of a full white dress, with the other slim, graceful arm over her head to pull back the sheet of dark hair that whipped around her head like a victorious battle flag. Her smile matched his. Two beautiful people in love.

Hemi and Anika Te Mana in happier times, the caption read, and I thought, *No kidding.*

I read the headline, then. *Cheating, lying, and the odd ménage a trois: Te Mana case takes a raunchy turn.*

"Oh, boy," I muttered, but at that moment, my toast popped up, which delayed things a little bit more.

You don't think fixing your toast outweighs learning about a critical development in your fiancé's life? All I can say is, you've clearly never been pregnant. Finally, though, I was sitting down again, falling on my toast with my usual starved-dog delicacy and reading between bites.

> *Sensational new information surfaced yesterday that could threaten Hamilton-based Anika Cavendish's claim to an estimated 125 million dollars, half the assets acquired by estranged husband Hemi Te Mana during the couple's seventeen-year marriage, scheduled to end in divorce court in mid-September. The payout, fashion industry sources speculate, could spell disaster for the tycoon's U.S.-based business empire.*
>
> *Cavendish's suit, which is not yet scheduled for trial, took an unexpected turn when a University friend of the couple alleged a sexual relationship between Cavendish and star witness Beauden McAllister.*
>
> *The length of time the couple lived together remains at the heart of the dispute. A couple is required to split their property evenly only if they share the same residence for three years or more. McAllister, Te Mana's former roommate, is reported to have sworn under oath that Cavendish moved into Te Mana's apartment while the two men were still sharing a room in a flat near Auckland University. Other witnesses are expected to testify*

that the couple did not start living together until they rented their own flat, starting two years and ten months before the couple separated, with Te Mana moving to the United States while Cavendish stayed behind in New Zealand.

Kiwi designer Violet Renfrow, friendly with both Te Mana and Cavendish in Uni days, has now alleged that McAllister was having a sexual relationship with Cavendish soon after Te Mana left New Zealand, which could cast doubt on the truth of McAllister's testimony. According to Renfrow, "I popped by the flat one morning to consult with Anika on a project we were doing together. It was just a couple weeks after Hemi left, but she came to the door in a shortie robe and nothing I could see under it. I could see Beauden McAllister, Hemi's old roommate, behind her pulling his shirt on. And after he left and I asked her about it? She laughed and said, 'If Hemi cares, he knows what to do about me. But come on, Vi. You know and I know that he's not coming back. Life's short, and Beaudie's hot. What, do you want to play, too? He'd be game.' That was the part that surprised me most. Not that she'd cheat—that didn't surprise me a bit—but that she'd be so open about it, to the point of asking me to join in. She didn't care whether I told Hemi. I think she wanted me to. She wanted to hurt him for leaving her, and she had her ways to pull a man in and get him to do what she wanted. So, no. Trust Beauden to tell the truth about her I would not."

Cavendish's neighbors, meanwhile, report even more startling activities at the tidy townhouse in Hamilton's stylish centre that Te Mana's wife has owned for the past five years. "There were noises coming from over there that you wouldn't want your children to hear, let's just say," said one former neighbor who asked to remain anonymous. "There's kinky, and then there's the kind of thing she got up to. We didn't want to pry into her business, and we try to think the best of our neighbors, but when you hear what we heard—well, there's not much else you can think, and it becomes your business.

"I hope I'm as tolerant as the next woman," the former neighbor continued, "but when we'd finally had enough, we slipped a note under the door asking for a little respect. She came over afterwards and told me off like I'll never forget. Had a look on her face that chilled my blood when she said, 'Your hubby must have drilled a hole through the wall, from the interest you're taking. Is it you that's jealous or him? Looking for lessons, is he? Next time, we'll take care to make it better.' Live and let live is one thing, but if she was married when she did all that, those weren't the vows I took. I know what I'd call her, and it isn't 'wife.'"

There was more. What Hemi's attorney had said, what Anika's had said in response, and how nobody's behavior mattered, because the law only cared whether Hemi and Anika had lived together for three years. And about the suppression order Anika's attorney had requested to avoid further trial by public opinion. A case of too little, too late, it seemed to me.

I was still working my way through all that, taking another sip of tea to calm myself and thinking what a bad enemy Hemi would make, when Koro shook his head and said, "Hard to read. I hate to see her bringing shame to herself and her whanau like that, however much it'll help Hemi."

I couldn't meet his eyes. Instead, I buried my face in my mug. What would Koro think if he knew the kinds of things Hemi and I did together?

No matter how filthy those things had been, I'd never *felt* dirty, except in the most delicious, intensely secret way. It had always felt like Hemi alone knew the woman beneath my innocent exterior, as if he and he alone was in charge of bringing her out, playing with her, and putting her away, secret once more.

I'd said I didn't want to be Hemi's doll, and I'd told the truth. I did enjoy being his plaything at times, though.

See? It even *sounds* dirty. How could you explain that to anybody, let alone a man in his eighties? Especially your incredibly inventive lover's beloved grandfather?

Koro had been watching me, to my disquiet. Now, he spoke again. "What two people get up to in the privacy of their bedroom—that's between the two of them. But when you go about shaming your husband to his friends or embarrassing an innocent neighbor who just wants a bit of peace, that's different. Secrets are all good. Every couple should have a few. What good are they, though, if they don't stay secret?"

I dared a glance at him, and he said, "That's why you have marriage, eh. So you have somebody to keep your secrets. She didn't keep his, but I'm guessing he'll do better this time."

"Yes," I said. "He will."

He did smile, then. "That's enough of that, I reckon. This will pass, and it'll be a memory to talk about together, another brick for the two of you to build on. They won't all be smooth, and they shouldn't be. You can't get a good grip on smooth. You need the rough times as well. That's where you both see what you're made of. That's what gives you faith."

♡♡♡

Imagine how much I wanted to talk to Hemi after all that. Too bad the time was all wrong. Instead, I started to get dressed, then stood in the middle of his bedroom in my underwear and texted him, because I couldn't stand not to.

Interesting article in the Herald today. You play hardball.

After a couple minutes, I got back, *That was the idea. Too rough for you?*

It wasn't what Koro had been talking about, but I went with it. I'd bet Anika had never teased, not the way I could. I might not be able to do "intense" as well as the Black Widow, but I did sweet and innocent and fun like nobody's business. I'd had twenty-five years of practice.

I like it rough, though, I texted back, in that secret space of ours and loving it. *And I like watching you win as much as I like letting you win.*

Bloody hell, I got back. *I'm in a meeting.*

It had worked, so I ran with it some more. *Oh? Am I distracting you? You'd better call me tonight, then, and tell me exactly how disappointed you are in me.*

No, I wasn't Anika. Tonight, I'd congratulate him on his salvo in the nasty war she'd pulled him into. He'd been born to win, and if she couldn't see it, she wasn't as smart as she thought she was. And what I'd said was true. I loved watching him win. I loved the powerful side of him, and I loved the vulnerable side, too. Tonight, I'd invite him to show me both. I'd talk to him, I'd listen to him, and when we'd done that? I'd let him win.

I'd said we needed to concentrate on something other than sex if we wanted our relationship to move forward. I'd been right. But oh, how I missed him.

another fabulous growth opportunity

♡

Hope

There was still all that real life to get through before tonight, though. All those fabulous growth opportunities I needed to experience in order to make myself into the woman I wanted to be, not to mention into a partner who could stand up to a man as powerful as Hemi. The only way to get stronger was to face the hard things and do them, and I knew it. That was why, a half hour later, I ran out of the house behind Matiu and hopped into the right side of his car, my heart picking up the pace right on cue.

Note One. You are in control.

The affirmation didn't work all that well, but it beat putting my arms over my head and whimpering, "I can't do this." Replacing negative thoughts with positive ones. Seeking progress, not perfection. All those good things. Except that I still had to drive.

"First time in the rain, eh," Matiu said, reading my nervousness and flashing me a reassuring grin. "First time for everything, I reckon. Let's go have an adventure. Lights. Windscreen wipers. You've got this."

He and Tane had been switching off, and not only with helping Koro dress in the mornings and bathe in the evenings. They'd also been giving Karen and me driving lessons, one of them taking us out every night since we'd taken the written test and received our learner licenses. It meant we'd started out our career of endangering the local population by driving in the dark, but as Matiu had said that first day, "Always easier to go from harder to easier than the other way round." We were less hazardous than we'd have been in New York City, anyway. There was that.

I switched on the lights and wipers, released the parking brake, put the car into reverse, and pressed cautiously on the accelerator, my breathing picking up as the car did. "Oh, man," I was muttering under my breath. "Oh, *man.*" I could barely *see.*

"Have to actually give it some gas," Matiu said, sounding like he was about to laugh.

"I'm not sure how… slippery it is," I tried to explain.

"It's rain, not ice. Come on, Hope." He put his hand over mine and gave it a squeeze. "Down the hill and away we go. Don't want to be late to work. Sonya would probably give you the sack."

"Oh, you're helpful," I muttered, but I did get the car turned around and headed down the hill again.

By the time I got to the nearly empty parking lot by the beach, pulled to a stop, and did all the steps in reverse, I was so tense, I was nearly shaking. "Whew," I managed to say. "OK. Driving in the rain is different." Especially when I'd braked at the bottom of the hill and the car had taken so much more time to stop than I'd realized, until I'd ended up jamming my foot on the brake and sending both Matiu and me hard into the seatbelts. That had been a moment.

Matiu shook his head. "Karen's sure she's ready to compete in the Grand Prix, and you drive like my granny. Are you sure you're sisters?"

"Half sisters." My heart would stop racing soon, surely. "Maybe that's why, but I doubt it."

"Sometime," he said, "you'll have to tell me that story. But just now, there's probably a farmer walking into the ER with a hatchet sticking out of his head, about to ask me to give it a quick yank, there's a boy, because he's got stock to move."

I laughed. "It's a little different from Brooklyn and gunshot wounds, I'm guessing."

"Could be. I had a good one yesterday. This crusty old joker comes in with a nail straight through his hand, shoves it at me, and says, 'Give it a good hard pull, mate. Tried to pull it out myself already, but couldn't get a good enough grip. Asked the missus to use the claw end of the hammer, but she wouldn't do it. Bloody soft. Drove me here instead, which is a bloody waste of both our time.' I'm trying to explain about tetanus and puncture wounds, and he gives a snort and says, 'A new danger every day, seems to me. Killer bacteria, mad cows, some new mosquito that'll turn you mad if the cows don't get you first. I've got along without knowing about any of that for sixty-three years, and I can get along without knowing about them now. But then, if you lot couldn't convince the general public that every sneeze was double pneumonia, you'd be out of a job. Just do it."

I was smiling, my tension forgotten. Matiu had that effect. "So what did you do?"

Laughter danced in his dark eyes. "Asked if he wanted a bullet to bite on while I pulled the nail out. He didn't think I was funny. Told me I was a cheeky bugger. He didn't need the bullet, though. I'd be willing to bet you he's out moving that stock today, snapping at the missus when she asks him if he's changed the bandage and put that ointment on like the doctor said. If he comes back in with an infection, I'm likely to give him that jab straight into the bum just to show him. Kiwi blokes and medicine aren't always an easy mix. More likely to pour some whisky on it and bind it up with duct tape. Women, now… they're much better."

I zipped my anorak and said, "On that note, I'm out of here. Nobody in there with a hatchet in his head, I hope, but I need to go anyway."

He was out of the car on the words, coming around to my side, ready to slide into the driver's seat. "See you this afternoon, then. Four o'clock."

"I can walk home. It's not supposed to rain all day."

"Nah. I need to see you going above thirty. I've got a short day myself, and I'm ready to help you live dangerously. We'll collect Karen and drive all the way to Tauranga. Tackle the roundabout, and then do a bit of a shop for the three of you on the way home. More practice in the Countdown carpark."

I would have argued—probably just because "tackling the roundabout" sounded like the least attractive activity ever—but this wasn't the time. Matiu was getting soaked, the water streaming over him, flattening his black hair to his scalp, and if I didn't get inside right now, I was going to be late. So instead, I said, "Thanks. See you then," and ran.

Inside the little café, my boss, the blonde, comfortably middle-aged Sonya, was sliding plates holding quiche, bacon and egg pie, and frittatas into the cabinet, and my stomach gave its usual lurch at the sight and smell of all that food.

Waitressing wasn't the perfect job for a woman with incessant morning sickness, but it was the one that had been available. Anyway, the midwife I'd finally visited two days before had told me, with typical Kiwi cheerfulness, that there was nothing to do but "bear with it, love, until it's over. Another few weeks and you're golden." Which I was clinging to with the desperation of a drowning man, especially at that moment. The smell of bacon and eggs hung in the air like a cloud and caused saliva to pool in my mouth, and not in a good way.

I pulled off my anorak and hung it up by the door, concentrating on deep breaths, and Sonya said, "There you are, darling."

"Sorry," I said automatically. "Am I late?"

She waved a hand. "No worries. You had Matiu out there getting wet, I notice. He's a handsome fella, isn't he. Seems unfair he'd be a doctor as well."

"He sure is." I started my own morning routine of emptying the dishwasher, checking the tables. "I'd say he's got charm to burn."

"Burning it on you, eh."

"Nope. That's just his normal mode."

"Right."

I didn't bother to correct her. Half of Katikati already knew too much about my business, and the other half was rapidly catching up. But I was wearing a gigantic rock on my finger that could tell its own story, Hemi was fully aware that his cousins were giving me driving lessons, and I was tired of living my life explaining and apologizing.

On the upside, I was learning to drive *and* to swim, and my boss didn't hate me. Which was novel.

alpha tendencies

♡

Hope

Much later that day, I woke with a start from a doze, groped around distractedly for long seconds, then finally located the phone on the duvet, stabbed at the screen, and said, "Hello?"

There at last was the voice I'd longed to hear, the one that was better than any other. It sounded as amused as his cousin's, but you know what they say: scarce commodities are the most valuable. Hemi's amusement and warmth were as scarce as they could be—and were shown almost solely to me.

"Only so early a fella can get up," he said, "at least I would have said so before I met you. Could be I'll have to try for four instead of five next time, though, because I've waited all day and night for this."

"Mm." It had been two days since we'd talked. It felt like forever. I blinked and shoved myself up on an elbow to check the old-fashioned alarm clock at the bedside. "It *is* after nine, you know. And all right, I know it's five a.m. there, but what can I say? I had a busy day. I drove on a roundabout. Well, not *on* it. I didn't mess up quite that badly. Around it. And maybe I'm worth your early start, you know?"

"Maybe you are." Just hearing that smooth, low voice could make everything start tingling, and it was happening now. "Nah, I'd say you definitely are. Nothing I like more than talking to you in bed, except being in your bed. I'm guessing you're still missing me, the way you've been teasing me. Texting me like that—now, that was naughty."

"Could be I am. Missing you *and* naughty. Maybe you could remind me that you're coming back." Flirting with somebody who'll give you not just the fun of it, but that almost-dangerous edge, too—is there anything better? Not for me.

"I'm coming back," he said. "No worries. But I've got something to tide you over as well. A parcel's arriving for you day after tomorrow. You may not want to open it in front of Koro. In fact, don't open it at all, not until I tell you. You can ring me this time, no matter how early it is for me, because I may have to do a bit of… explaining. I'm going to need you awake for that."

I did my best to keep things under control, even though I knew it was a lost cause. *Anika,* I thought, then kicked her to the curb. "A parcel, huh? Flowers aren't enough, even though you've already replaced them twice? They don't even have a chance to die before you've got another bunch there. Koro told me today that it smelled like 'a bloody bordello' in here. He says *he's* the patient, remember? Of course, then he said in a big hurry, "Don't tell Hemi that, though. Likely to fill my room with lilies, the way he's going, and I'm not dead yet."

Hemi's rich, low laugh spiraled its slow, smoky way down my body. "Good to know. Sounds like he's feeling better."

"He is." I wriggled further up and shoved the pillow more comfortably under my back. "I think that's mostly Karen. She makes him laugh, and you should hear her putting dinner on the table and pointing out that it's better than anything I've ever made. I've considered reminding her that I was always away from home working during those years when I cooked those inferior meals, but I hate to spoil her fun."

"Both Koro and I have a weakness for a cheeky girl, I reckon," he said. "So tell me about the roundabout. Having an adventure, eh."

"That's what Matiu said, and boy, did he laugh when I did it. I hate to confess this to you."

"Ah. That's always good. I'm waiting."

"Well, if I have to tell, I have to, I guess." I did my best to pout, although being an irresistibly sexy tease had never exactly been in my skill set. "I drove around twice before I figured it out, and then I had to drive around another time to do it. And I may have… squeaked a little." That surprised a laugh out of him. "Hey. There was traffic."

"I do love the way you squeak. What did Matiu do?"

"He *didn't* grab the wheel. I can tell you're waiting to hear me say that. He just got really stern, like you. Really calm. Must have been his doctor voice. He said . . ." I lowered my voice. "'Hope. Listen to me. Indicate for your turn, check your mirror, and do it.' It was very impressive. I was so shocked, I did it. The men in your family and their alpha tendencies."

A second, then he asked, "What about Karen?"

"Oh, she had no problem, of course. But we will just note here that *she's* the one Matiu's grabbed the wheel on. More than once. She thinks she's an expert, and she sits back there and criticizes my driving. It's extremely annoying. You wait, she'll do it to you, too. I'd pay money to see that. Or even better—to Charles. That'll be an experience to witness. 'Charles, the speed limit here is 25.' Yeah, that'll go over big."

"So has Matiu been giving you your lessons? Thought that was going to be Tane."

"It's both of them, but Matiu has more time, so he's been doing a little more of it."

"Mm. Are you having fun, baby?"

"You know," I said, "I am. Maybe that's terrible to say, because I do miss you, and I hate not being with you, with everything you're going through, but… it's good, too. The job's not horrible, and I can't tell you how new that is. I'm not tense all the time, waiting to be fired, or at least to be told I'm stupid. I'm not… desperate, and that's pretty great. And being with Koro, the lessons—all that's good." I hesitated a moment, then said, "I did something, too. A little impulsively. I hope you like it."

"What's that?"

My heart was beating faster. If Hemi didn't think it was any big deal… and he might not. I didn't know how a man would feel. Or more accurately, I didn't know how *Hemi* would feel. He seemed so different from me at times, it was as if he were not just another gender, but another species. "You may think it's stupid," I started to say, then stopped myself mid-sentence. "Scratch that. I was just telling myself today that I wasn't going to apologize or explain myself to everybody, and here I am doing it."

"You could practice your new resolve on me," he said, "since I love you. Safe territory."

The simplicity of it took my breath away. "I could," I

finally said. "I will. Here you go. I'm sending it. Hang on."

I took the phone from my ear, scrolled to the right app, and fifteen seconds later, heard the chime of a sent message. Then I waited.

It took at least a minute before Hemi said in a completely different tone of voice, "And you thought I might not like this." And I breathed again.

It was a picture. Of me, to be exact. Me in the bathroom mirror. Two shots, side and front, in my underwear and a bra which was going to need replacing very soon, along with all the others. One hand framing my lower abdomen, which was still nothing like huge, but bigger than it had been ten days ago when Hemi had last seen it.

"I thought," I said, feeling strangely shy, "that I could do it every week. As a sort of record. You could compare, and so could I. I thought it might help us feel… close. Because I was missing you so much today."

"I think you're right," he said. "I think I love it. The only problem is, I want to get on the plane right now. That little belly . . ."

"I know." Once again, the stupid tears were right there behind my eyes. "It's… I know it's so normal, the most natural thing in the world, but it's happening to *me,* to us, and it feels like the first time ever. That there could be a person growing, to be able to *see* it getting bigger. To know that in a few months, we'll be able to feel it moving inside me. Our little swimmer. And I know that my being here with that happening feels to you like I'm playing games, but it matters so much that we get it right. For both of us, and for the… for whoever this is. I want to do it *right.*"

"I know you do." There was no teasing in his voice now. "And so do I."

"One way or another," I said, "the thing with Anika is going to be over, and we can get married. I want us to be ready for that." I hesitated, then went on, "I was… surprised to see that in the paper this morning. I think Koro was disappointed. You might want to talk to him. Because that was you, wasn't it, who made it happen?"

A long beat, then he said, "It was. I told her she didn't know what she was getting into. I want her to know that if she keeps going, she'll be the one who hurts. I'm guessing she knows it now."

"And you don't feel bad about that?"

"I would have once. That's why she did it. She thinks I'm that bloke she knew. I'm not."

"Good," I said.

He laughed, and just like that, the grim, ruthless tycoon was gone, the Hemi who was mine alone taking his place. "You showing me your bloodthirsty side?"

"No," I said. "I'm showing you the side of me—the *all* of me—who believes in you."

Another pause, and his voice wasn't quite as smooth as usual when he said, "Then I reckon I'd better do my best to keep impressing you, and maybe it wouldn't hurt to tell you that you may have had a couple good ideas yourself."

He wanted to move on, so I said, "You mean—the show? The changes?"

"I do. The push to change the copy for those ads—that didn't go down a treat, and neither did the sourcing of the footwear, but we're nearly there. I'll ask Josh to set up a secure portal for the two of us so I can share a few things with you. I'll have him add a folder for those photos you sent me as well, and any others you take. Save them going through email, eh, so you feel safe sharing anything you like."

He said all that like it meant nothing, when it meant everything. My throat was tight when I said, "I'd love that. To have a safe way to send you pictures, sure. But more than that. To see what you've done for the show. I'd love it."

"Do you know," he said, "it's nearly eerie. When I first thought up the Colors of the Earth line, in that restaurant with you in San Francisco, I thought exactly what you said. Tender and tough, hard and soft. I had the vision, but then I lost that bit. How did you come up with that?"

"I don't know. It just popped into my mind. Maybe because I love shoes too much."

"Wouldn't have known it from the ones you were wearing at the start."

"Call it an unrequited love."

He began to talk more about the line, then, and I nearly held my breath to hear it. About his vision, and how the changes he'd set in motion had played out. About tense meetings with fear and doubt crackling in the air, and his own certainty as he'd laid down the law. He finished with, "I wouldn't normally say any of this to anyone. Bad idea to discuss internal divisions. You end up setting one side against another, stirring the pot without even meaning to. Better to listen to all sides, decide, make it clear, and move on. The team's only as a secure as its leader."

"Mm," I said. "You can talk it out with me, though, because I don't work for you. I have no agenda except yours, and you know it. It's almost like talking to yourself."

"Now," he said, "if I accept that, it means you were right to quit."

"Well, I *was* right to quit," I said serenely, and he laughed out loud.

"You're tired," he said, "and I need to get going.

Remember, though—day after tomorrow, you'll get that parcel, and you're not to open it. Tonight was for business. Next time, we'll focus on seeing how much I can make you miss me. I'd tell you more about that today, but I don't think I will. You know how much I enjoy making you wait for it."

Which was a completely unfair thing to tell a woman lying in bed alone with her heart so softened it was aching and her hormones at full alert, especially when she was already asking herself why in the world she wasn't with you.

But then, as Hemi had once told me, he didn't play fair.

closer all the time

♡

Hemi

I rang off, but I kept my laptop open to Hope's picture. She'd titled it *10-1/2 Weeks.*

She hadn't been trying to be sexy, and she was so sexy all the same. It was the secret smile on her face, the cant of her hip, the hand stroking over that tiny belly. She'd worn my favorite pink bra and thong for it, the ones that were trimmed with black lace. I'd taken them off her that last night, and I'd bought them for her at a time when I'd thought she was the woman I needed in my bed and nothing more. She'd let me do that, had worn them every time since, just because she loved to please me.

I got a sudden image of a whole checkerboard of photos, thirty more weeks of them. Of that belly getting bigger and bigger as our baby grew, and the idea that I'd be seeing those photos without seeing *her*—it was an absolutely physical pain, a dagger straight into my chest.

There was anger there, too, and I couldn't pretend there wasn't. Frustration as well. She'd told me what needed to change, I'd got it, and I was proving it. Why was she still so far away, and not even talking about coming home? She belonged with me, and we both knew it.

There was Koro, though. That was the complication. He was sounding better, his voice regaining some of its strength, but I couldn't forget the first sight of him helpless and dazed in hospital, or the gray tinge to his skin when Matiu and I had put him to bed on that final afternoon. Hope was looking after him, and that was better than anyone else doing it, even with the whanau popping by at all hours to do their own looking after. Outside of Koro himself, there was nobody I trusted more than Hope.

And then there was Karen, all the noise and the mess and the chaos of her. I'd thought longingly from time to time, after Hope and Karen had moved in, about coming home at night and being surrounded by the order and peace I'd always craved instead of dirty dishes and shoes and electronics and teenage hormones. Now, I had what I'd wished for, but somehow, peace had become emptiness, and restfulness had become echoing silence.

I was delaying getting out of bed right now, in fact, because it would be so quiet out there. Which was something I never did.

That was enough of that. I sent off a quick email to Josh about setting up that portal for Hope and me, shut the laptop, and threw back the duvet. Five-thirty. Time to get up and start my day.

The phone buzzed like a wasp, nearly bouncing on the bed, and my heart leaped as I picked it up. Hope again, telling me she'd changed her mind? Or just wanting to tell me one last thing, because ringing off was as hard for her as it was for me? And then I saw the name on the screen.

"Hemi." The single word had enough edge to it to slice the toughest skin, the way only my sister Ana could do. Well, her and my mum. "When were you going to tell me about Koro?"

"I didn't think about it." I didn't stay in bed. I moved into the bathroom and squeezed toothpaste onto the brush. Moving helped when I talked to my sister.

"You didn't *think* about it?" Her voice rose in a predictable pattern.

"No." I shoved the toothbrush into my mouth. I was willing to bet she'd be talking for a wee while.

"I had to hear it from Dad," she said. "He said he'd seen you at last, and then he said why. Did you think that I would've liked to be there? That he's my Koro as well, and that I miss him, and I'd care?"

I spat the toothpaste into the sink. The recitation hadn't taken her as long as I'd expected. "One sec," I mumbled, then rinsed my mouth. "No. I didn't think of it. I was busy getting over there myself. Maybe Dad should've called you. He knew soon enough. Maybe you should ring Koro when you don't want something from him. Could keep you in the loop. Anyway, he's all good. Had a fall, that's all. A scare for the rest of us, and a bit of downtime for him."

"That's casual," she said. "Or cold, more like, but that's no surprise. I'm your sister and his grandchild, and you can't bring yourself to think about me more than that? And what are you doing? Are you *eating* while you talk to me?"

I set the phone on the cold marble slab and pressed the button for the speaker, then lathered my face, took my razor from the drawer, and began to shave. "No. I'm getting up. It's five-thirty here. You could've thought."

"Why? You'd be up anyway. Mr. Ambition. Mr. Discipline. Like that's all there is. Forgetting your whanau, forgetting you're even Maori, ashamed of where you come from, trying to turn yourself into some rich pakeha bugger who doesn't think about anything but how he'll make his next dollar. How can you forget your only sister, your niece and nephews? Not to mention Dad and how you've treated him after all the work he's done this year, all the progress he's made. He said you acted like he wasn't even there. You cut him deep. Why do you still have to hurt him? Mum, too. She told me you haven't called for a month."

"Paid her rent, though, haven't I."

Ana started talking again at that, the words coming fast and sharp and hard, and I tipped my jaw up and focused on the tricky bits beneath.

I had a sudden flash of Hope, then, the memory so strong it was as if she were there. Leaning against the counter in a short white nightdress on a Saturday morning when she'd lingered in the bathroom to watch me shave, or maybe just to spend another quiet minute with me.

I'd finished up, then splashed water over my face and come up again, and she'd been right there holding a hand towel. Her touch had been so gentle while she'd dried me off, and then she'd pressed her lips to my throat exactly where I was shaving now and murmured, as I'd reached a hand around to pull her hard against me, "That much hot shouldn't be legal. All I have to do is look at you. You turn me helpless."

I felt the sting first, then saw the red line appear and swore aloud.

"What?" It was Ana's voice, sharper than ever.

"Nothing." She was talking again, so I kept shaving, watched the blood dripping into the sink, and felt a harder stab, of annoyance this time. That I'd let myself get distracted, had allowed myself to be affected by Ana's words, the memory of Hope, or both.

You're such a good man. That had been Hope, not Ana, obviously.

"Mum's asking about Koro as well," Ana said. "You know how much she loves him. You could've called us. Bloody selfish."

I knew nothing of the sort. Well, I knew I was selfish. That much was true. "Is that why you called, then?" I was stroking up from the other side of my throat now, watching the trail of crimson inch down wet brown skin and pool at my collarbone, the sting of the cut the least of my worries. "Or did you want something?"

"I want to see him," she said. "Of course I want to see him. I'll have to bring the baby, but I'll leave the boys at home. One ticket, that's all."

"Really. That I'd pay for, eh. Where were you thinking you'd stay?"

"With Koro, of course. Be some company for him, because I'm guessing you've left Tane and June to look after him. Or maybe you've paid for some outsider, like that's enough and you're finished."

"No," I said. "You won't stay with him. No room at his place. Hope's there, and she'll be there for weeks yet."

A pregnant silence followed, and I used it to rinse my face, then went into the toilet cubicle for a square of paper and ripped off a bit to mop up and staunch the flow. I was bleeding like a hemophiliac. I wanted to swear again, but I didn't. Instead, I breathed slowly out, then in.

There. That was better.

"*Hope's* there?" Ana asked. "Still? Dad said she was staying for a bit, but all this time, and more? I thought this was meant to be your love match at last."

"Are you almost done?" I asked. "Because I'm getting in the shower. There's no room for you at Koro's. Hope's sister is with her as well, helping look after him. And I'm not buying you a ticket anyway. He's better every day. I paid for all of you to fly over at Christmas, and I know you'll be asking me to do it again. That's going to have to be enough."

"The money's nothing to you."

Easy to dismiss the value of somebody else's money when you were asking him for it. This wasn't the first time I'd noticed that. "Maybe you haven't heard." I knew she would've. "Anika's threatening to take half of everything I've got. Reckon I'd better start economizing."

I heard her start to speak, then stop herself, and I knew why that was. That she'd begun to say that she hoped Anika would do it, and then had realized what it would mean. No more plane tickets and no more rescues, not if the money *wasn't* nothing to me anymore.

"I should've known it'd be useless to ask you," she said instead. "Anyone who's quite happy to leave his pregnant girlfriend halfway around the world for weeks on end, exactly like he left his wife? Yeh, Dad told me about that, too, and that she was staying behind and you were all good with it. And you wonder why Anika left you. Don't exactly know women, do you? We like a man to hold on. We like him to *care.*"

The man in the mirror was looking grim. Time to get my perspective back. Whose life would I rather have, hers or mine? Mine all the way. What I was hearing was envy, because I *did* have a good life. It was getting better every day, too. I had the photo to prove it.

"Careful," I said. "Next Christmas is coming closer all the time. Think about those tickets."

sweet anticipation

♡

Hope

What is it about Friday night? Having a date for that one particular night somehow feels so much better than not having one, even if it might turn out to be a dud, and no matter how much you try to tell yourself it's not important. And if you *know* it's going to be good, if he's told you he's going to make it special—well, that sweet anticipation can make your body hum all the way through a long, wet Thursday. And by the time Friday rolls around, that hum might just become a buzz, and then a downright throb. It might make your bike ride down the hill to work an entirely pleasurable experience, in fact, with every push of your feet on the pedals stimulating you a little more.

It might also make every look and every smile from a male customer feel like it's telling you, *Baby, you're so pretty. You're so sexy.* You might become hyper-aware, even as you're walking back to the kitchen, maybe twitching your hips a tiny bit more than strictly necessary, that under your jeans and the scoop-necked red tee that spells out *Katikati Beach Café*, you're wearing some underwear your lover would have to touch you through, things he'd need to take off you so slowly. It might make you feel like a purely female creature made of sighs and softness, the pheromones wafting off her silken skin and curling their way like smoke right down inside a man, making him watch her, making him crave her.

Well, it *might.* I was just guessing here, because it wasn't something I'd had much experience with in my first twenty-four years of life. The idea was probably fairly delusional, to tell the truth. I was a five-foot-two, ninety-five-pound, 32B woman with a baby bump, and nobody's idea of a sultry vixen. But that was how I felt—how Hemi made me feel—even from all that distance. Powerful in a purely feminine way, and so tantalizingly seductive that I was turning *myself* on.

I didn't have to ride my bicycle home, either, because Matiu turned up with Karen and his car, put my bike on the roof rack, and promptly killed my buzz by making me practice parallel parking, with Karen offering helpful comments from the backseat like, "Whoa. Way to hit the curb. Maybe don't yank so hard on the wheel, Hope. It's not *Grand Theft Auto.* No extra credit for collisions."

Matiu, fortunately, just smiled and said, "Pull out and try again. You're going well, no worries. All you need is practice."

I did practice, and I got better—gradually—and then it was Karen's turn.

She took it much too fast, of course. In fact, she ran straight up onto the curb, bumped back down again, tapped the bumper of the car behind her, lurched forward, hit the brakes just before she hit *that* car, and said, "There you go. I'm in. First time."

"Good on ya," Matiu said, "other than that the driving examiner's just dived for cover and given you a failing mark. Points for style, though. Except that you may want to get out and check that we aren't going to have to leave a note on that poor bugger's windscreen."

"Ha," she said. "That's what the bumper's *for.* And that was just my *first* time. You watch. This time, no curb."

Matiu said, "I do like a woman with attitude," and she laughed, then did it again without the bumper-car imitation.

"See, Hope," she had to say. *"That's* how."

"Nah," Matiu said. "Hope's just on a different path. If I had to guess which of you will get the better mark on her test, I'm backing Hope all the way."

"But if you have to guess who'll have more fun doing it," Karen said, "you're backing me."

"She's easier to teach, though," Matiu said. "Listens and everything. So rewarding, too. Hearing her suck in her breath like that, watching her get her courage up and finally do it."

"Gee, thanks," Karen said. "I'm making a note that men like helpless women. The Stone Age called, and it wants its attitude back."

"Could be," Matiu said. "Can't help it, and I wouldn't be the only one. Call me a keen student of biology, if you like." And I thought, *Whoa, there, buddy. That was a little too flirty.* Matiu sometimes had trouble turning it off, I'd noticed.

He must have picked up on my reaction, because he said, "Take us back to the house now, Karen. Show us how it's done."

Koro was in his usual spot in the recliner when we got

home. He switched off the TV and pushed himself up to stand, brushed off Matiu's helping hand with an irritable swat, and said, "Parcel came for you, Hope, as well as more flowers. How much space does Hemi imagine I have?"

I'd already seen both. I was turning pink just looking at the innocuous cardboard box. Not to mention the roses.

Not lavender this time. These had been sent to make a different statement. Deep, rich crimson, and no mere dozen of them.

A huge mass of enormous blooms sat in a crystal vase that had come from someplace much more special than a florist's shelf, the flowers seeming to glow in the lamplight, unfurling their lush petals and releasing their gloriously heady scent into the air of the little house. Reminding me irresistibly of that last night, when the music and the lights had both been turned down low. A night when Hemi taken off my clothes, made me weak, made me come, and made me his. As if I'd been anything else since the first day I'd met him, when he'd touched my cheek, licked his fingers, smiled into my eyes, and stolen me away. Body, heart, and soul.

"Whoa," Karen said. "Paging the Love Doctor. Love Doctor, stat."

I barely heard her. I was pulling the envelope off its spike and opening it, then taking out the card inside.

Five words.

Red for passion. Call me.

My mouth had gone dry, and I shoved the card back in his envelope as if somebody would see it. Well, that wasn't crazy, because all three of the others *were* watching me.

"I'll just… take these into the bedroom," I decided. I juggled the package and tried to pick up the huge vase, hugging it against me, but it rocked down to the table again as

I realized it was a two-handed job, and a heavy one at that.

Matiu said, "I'll get it." Before I could object, he lifted the vase and headed for the back of the house, leaving me to follow behind with the package, the card, my jacket, and my purse.

He didn't seem to have any problem finding the right room, but then, I guessed he'd been there before. He set the vase carefully on the dresser, didn't look at the bed, and said, confirming my suspicions, "It's been a while since I was in here. Never saw too much of Hemi growing up. Nearly ten years older than me, and he only lived here a couple years."

"Yes," I said, which was a pretty stupid answer. I set the package and card down beside my flowers, longed with everything in me to rip open the cardboard box and see what was inside, and heard Hemi say, *You're not to open it. Wait for me.*

"I'll go get Koro into the shower," Matiu said, and I nodded and said, "Thanks. And for the lesson, too. Stay for dinner if you like," and thought about time zones and a grandfather and sister who needed my attention, a lover who was asleep and absolutely required his rest, and thirty indecently opulent roses as rich as velvet, as red as blood. And wondered what was in my box.

surprise package

♡

Hope

Matiu had gone home. Koro, worn out by pain and the hard work of knitting old bones, had gone to bed. Karen was in the living room, watching TV with her earphones in.

And me? I was lying in Hemi's bed with music playing softly on my phone and a cardboard box beside me, pretending to read a book and wishing it would hurry up and be nine o'clock. Five a.m. in New York, as early as I dared to call him.

On the thought, my phone rang with the brush of drums and sweet lick of guitar that was my sexy, self-indulgent Hemi ringtone. I grabbed for it and said, "You're early."

That dark-chocolate voice. "Told you to call me."

"I wanted to let you sleep first."

"I don't need to sleep. I need you."

Just like that, there was that thrum again, licking into me

exactly as if Hemi's mouth were trailing across my cheek right now, his clever fingers tracing my neckline, making me start to burn. "I need you, too," I said, keeping my voice down, not because somebody would hear me but because it sounded better that way. More secret. More intimate.

"Did you open your parcel?"

"No. You said not to."

"Good."

"I got your flowers, though. I loved them. But they're so . . ." I hesitated.

"Yes?"

"So much. Such a… statement."

"Could be I needed to make a statement. Could be I needed you to hear my statement. Are you in bed?"

Another pulse. "Yes."

"Got your laptop?"

"Uh… my *laptop?*"

"Go get it. Bring it over and set it beside you."

Oh, boy. Why did I have a feeling that things were about to get dirty?

"Got it," I said, climbing back into bed again and fluffing up the pillows behind me.

"We're switching over. Onto the computer. I'm ringing off now, but I'll be back."

A few seconds later, and I was clicking the touchpad and seeing Hemi on my screen, sitting up in bed himself. His face, his bare shoulders and chest rich brown against the white sheets and duvet, the tattoo I loved to trace and kiss standing out in its vivid blue-black.

He was seeing me, too, because he said, "That's pretty, baby."

"Mm." I was wearing a pink nightgown he liked. "I've

been wearing pj's, but I wanted to feel sexy for you tonight, even though I didn't think you'd see me. I took a shower and used your favorite body butter, too, wishing the whole time that you were here to touch me and feel how soft I am. And now you *are* seeing me, and I'm seeing you, too. How good is that? Even though I'm not sure how much I want to show you. Not on camera."

"But you see," he said, his voice so thrillingly low, so nearly dangerous, "it's not about what you want to show me. It's about what I'm going to tell you to do."

I didn't even answer that. I couldn't. My breath was gone.

He didn't smile. "Ready to open your box?"

This one, I answered. "You know I am. I'm dying to."

"Right, then. Do it."

It had a tab on the side, and I pulled it, then shoved the flaps back. "Two things in here," I said.

"Open the one wrapped in tissue first."

I did it, then sighed. "Hemi… that's really pretty."

"You're gorgeous the way you are," he said, and even on the screen, his liquid brown eyes drew me in and threatened to drown me. "But I want to watch you take that pink nightdress off and put on the one I sent you."

I wanted this more than anything, but I couldn't help a shiver of nerves. "Nobody can see this, right? This call?"

"Nobody," he promised. "It's safe to show me. Come on, baby. Change your clothes for me. I need to see you naked."

I couldn't have resisted that if I'd tried, although to be fair, there was no way I was trying. I wriggled to my knees, then adjusted the laptop screen. "Can you see me?"

I could swear that his gaze was less focused than it had been a minute ago. Just seeing me in my nightgown had had that effect on him, and the power of my femininity surged through me again, as if the pheromones could reach him over all the distance between us, just as his were reaching me. I kept my gaze on him, pulled the short nightgown slowly up and over my head, and dropped it on the bed.

He swallowed. I saw it. "Now take off the thong."

I didn't smile, either. I just looked at him and did it. A thumb on either side of the waistband, a slow, sensuous wriggle down my hips, and then it had joined the nightgown, and I was naked. Smooth, perfumed, and burning for his touch.

He sighed. "Sweetheart. If I hadn't picked up that outfit for you and hadn't been thinking about seeing you in it ever since, I wouldn't make you put it on, because looking at you like that . . ."

"Mm." I smiled, slow and seductive, and reached for the filmy bit of cobweb that had been wrapped in the tissue paper.

Another thong, first, made of delicate lace, in an ivory that looked warm against my skin. And then the other part.

I guess you'd call it a chemise. A barely-there wisp of sleeveless ivory lace made up of an almost-but-not-quite-opaque bodice that fastened with a single ivory ribbon, then fell away on either transparent side to end in a floating drift of lace just beneath the hips, revealing much more than it concealed. I tied the ribbon into a bow between my breasts, then lay back against the pillows again.

"Is it pretty?" I asked, knowing I was preening and loving it.

"So pretty," he said. "Got your belly showing for me. That's why I chose it. I wanted to see you in that lace, and I wanted to see that little belly."

I stroked my hand over the bump that was a tiny bit more

visible now. "So what's the rest of my present?" I asked softly. "I noticed there's something else in there for me."

"Ah." He sighed. "Look and see."

I did. And felt the heat rise again. "Hemi… I'm not going to show you *that.*"

"Oh," he said, "I think you are. It's got a couple special features I expect you to enjoy. I'm going to enjoy them, too. You need to feel good, baby, and so do I. I'm going to make you do it all the way from here, and I can't wait."

The thing was pink, and it was… big. I held it up, flipped a switch, and it began to buzz.

Yep. It was a vibrator. Of the dual-mode rabbit variety, made to stimulate everything that Hemi wasn't here to take care of. Not exactly something I'd had room for in my suitcase or my thoughts when I'd left home, on a night when sex had been the last thing on my mind.

Time to get sassy. "You sure you want this? I'm pretty skilled on my own, and I know you'd like to watch that." I put the vibrator down, picked up the tube of lube Mr. Thoughtful had packed into the box, and waggled it at him. "I might even *let* you watch it. If you talk dirty enough to me that I have to get busy, that is. You'd love that, and we both know it."

"We do." He wasn't buying the sass. His face was absolutely serious when he said, "But here's what you're going to do. Get out the candles and light them, then turn out the light, lie back, and adjust your screen so I can see you. So I can record you. Then we're going to get started. You and me."

A lick of pure nervousness this time. Excitement, arousal, and uncertainty, a heady, scary mix. The curtains across the room stirred in the cool breeze and wafted the spicy scent of red roses to me. I was dressed in lace, and Hemi, I knew, was dressed in nothing. I was going to let him watch me, but was I willing to let him *film* me?

"Give it to me, Hope," he said, as if he could read my mind. "You've always trusted me. Trust me in this."

I did it. Of course I did. I pulled the heavy candles and matches out of the drawer, set one on each bedside table, and lit them, and knew Hemi was enjoying watching me do it. Then I turned out the lamp and lay back against the pillows, the flickering candlelight soft around me. And then I looked into my lover's eyes.

Hunger. That was what I saw. That was the power I had, even as I gave it up to him. I made him hungry, and then I satisfied him. I gave him what he needed most, and I was the only one in the world who could do it right.

"That's good." His voice was a little husky, and I loved hearing it. "Now turn your music on. The good stuff. Let's hear it."

Music, soft, smooth, and so sexy. Candlelight. Roses. Lace. And Hemi talking to me.

"Close your eyes," he told me. "Lie there and feel. I'm there with you, lying over you. Kissing your mouth the way you love it. Like it's mine."

A few sentences, and he already had me going. My fingers went up to my mouth as if it had a mind of its own, and Hemi said, "That's it. Feel that. Now I'm kissing my way over to your neck, and you're already arching your back, aren't you? Because you want it so much. You need it so badly."

I did. My fingers were going there, as greedy for the feel of my skin as if it really were his mouth that needed to kiss me, his hands that needed to stroke me. I left a trail of sparks in every place I touched, and when my hand drifted down my throat to the mesmerizing beat of the music, the dark pleasure of Hemi's voice, my back *was* arching. I needed that hand. I needed it now.

"I'm slowing down," Hemi said. "Working on your neck, your throat, and you're trying to pull me in, pull me down. Until I've had enough, and I grab your wrists and tie them together, pull them over your head and fasten them down tight. Because I need to take my time, and because I want you helpless."

"Hemi." It was a breath, and that was all.

"Yeh. That's nice, isn't it? Thinking about how that feels. Thinking about how much you love it. And now that I've got you where I want you, I'm untying that little bow. I'm letting that sweet little chemise fall off your body so I can see you, and touch you, and kiss you. Everywhere."

It was my hand untying the bow, but in my mind, it was his. I had one arm stretched over my head as if it truly were tied there, and the other was tracing around a sensitized, aching breasts. Giving me the gentle touch I needed now, and the teasing I craved.

"You want me to get there," Hemi said. "You're begging me to. And I'm going slower. Closer and closer, but not quite there."

My hand, now, stroking over the valley between my breasts, and even that was enough to make me squirm. Around and around, closer and closer, waiting for permission to touch. Permission to feel.

"You can't stand it," Hemi said. "You're telling me so. And finally, when you think another moment will be too long, my mouth is there, and you're making those noises, letting me know how much you love it, making me do it more."

Oh, that felt *good.* My eyes were closed, my head full of the scent of roses, with Hemi's voice pouring over me like syrup.

He let me enjoy it for a while, and then he told me, "I need to see you now. Take off that thong, sweetheart. Spread your legs for me."

My eyes opened, and there he was, looking at me. I said, "It's recording, though."

"Yeh," he said, "it is. Do it. Let me see. Let me watch."

My hands went to the wide band of lace, and I was pulling it down, pulling it off. "That's right," he said. "Now spread your legs. Let me look."

I whimpered, and heard myself do it. And Hemi's expression changed again, hardened. He stared at me, and slowly, I did it. I spread my legs and showed myself to him. Lace around me, hiding nothing. Open to his gaze, and to his will.

"Touch yourself," he said. "Because I'm touching you. Tying your ankles now, putting a pillow under your hips so you're all the way open for me. All the way helpless. Ready for anything I want to do to you."

I couldn't have done anything else, but there was no way I was resisting. My hand was caressing, stroking, settling in as Hemi continued to talk. Telling me everything he'd be doing to me, and it was as if he were there. His muscular body on top of mine, taking me over, driving me higher.

I was almost too far gone when he said, "Pick up the vibrator, put some of that lube on it, and turn it on."

This time, I didn't protest. I sucked in a breath and did it. And when he said, "Shove it in. Hard. Now," I did it. My whole body jerked, my torso rising from the bed as both silicone-softened arms assaulted me.

My hand fumbled for the switch, pressed it, but nothing

happened, and Hemi… *laughed.*

"Here's the special thing, sweetheart," he told me. "I control it, not you. Just like I'm there. Your job is to hold it inside you. My job is to do everything else. I'm going to drive you wild."

And he did. I had a hand over my mouth, was biting down, hanging on. And Hemi was doing everything. Harder, then softer, then, when I relaxed, harder again, until I was climbing, needing to soar. He took me ruthlessly back down again, frustrating me mercilessly, making me need to moan, to beg, even as I knew I couldn't, that I had to be quiet, and that I couldn't stand to be. Not another minute. Not… another… no.

That was when the arm inside me began to do something else. It wasn't just vibrating now. It was *spinning.* And I was gone. My hand hard over my mouth, everything in me stiffening, tightening, winding up so high, I was teetering. And Hemi pushed me higher. He pushed me over, and he pushed me down. And then he did it again.

He wore me out. He drove me crazy. He made me wild.

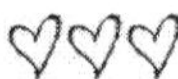

Hemi

Hope could barely stand it. And neither could I.

I worked the controls from my phone with every bit of finesse I had. By now, I knew how to read Hope's sighs, her smallest movements, her little noises. But from a distance, without the smell of her, the taste of her, the feel of her—I was missing so much. I was navigating in the dark. It was impossibly, achingly frustrating, and it was exactly what I needed.

Watching Hope be pleased. Watching her burn. Watching her come again and again, each time more intense than the last, losing every bit of her sweet reserve. Watching her surrender to me.

It was too hard. It was too much. It was nowhere close to enough.

When she was lying still at last, sprawled across the bed with her chest rising and falling with the force of her breath, I told her, "Sweetheart. You're so beautiful. I miss you so much."

She opened her eyes and smiled at me, slow, sweet, and languorous, and one hand came out to touch the computer screen as if she needed me as much as I needed her, except that wasn't possible. "I miss you, too," she said softly. "So much. And I love you. Thank you. I just wish I could do it to you. I wish I could make you feel that good."

"You have," I said. "You do. And you will, every time I watch this."

"Oh." Her eyes widened for a second, and then she said, "All right. It scares me a little to be out there like that, but I want to give you the same pleasure you've given me."

"I'm going to put this in our folder. So you can see it, too, and so you'll know it's safe. Our secret, just like everything else we've done."

Her throat moved convulsively as she swallowed. "Josh can't see it, can he?"

"No," I promised. "Not possible. Password protected, remember?" Locked behind every safeguard I could think of. To protect my business secrets, and now, to protect something even more precious. To protect Hope.

"You need to go to sleep now," I told her. "I'm not

forgetting how hard you're working, growing that baby."

"Mm," she said, her eyes so soft. "I love growing your baby."

"Love you, sweetheart," I told her.

In another minute, we'd disconnected, and my screen was dark. And if my heart ached as much as everything else did, that was because Hope touched all of me. Body and mind. Heart and soul. She touched it, and she took it.

She was mine, and I knew it. But the biggest surprise, the truly shocking development? I was hers just as much. And more.

an unexpected visitor

♡

Hemi

The bombshell my brand-new—and much more aggressive—New Zealand attorney had dropped into the midst of the Kiwi media three days earlier had probably had some effect there. I didn't know for sure, and I didn't care. Having it picked up by a few U.S. outlets, though, especially the fashion media—that had worked. The natives were growing much less restless both inside and outside the company.

I had this. A month ago, I'd felt the control slipping from me like sand through my fingers. Now, although the storm was still raging, I was driving my ship again. I had a steady hand on the tiller, and more importantly, a steady mind.

If Anika insisted on going to court after all, it wouldn't matter. It would cost me, but I was going to win. I knew it in my bones.

People called me lucky, but they didn't realize it wasn't

luck at all. It was preparation, and it was ruthlessness. If you were always willing to take it one step further than the other bloke, if you were willing to go to the mattresses and he knew it, if your reputation was that you hit first and hit hard, you became a much less attractive target.

Softness and indecision were the killers. That was why I didn't do them.

On the phone that Friday morning, Walter said, "I'm surprised they haven't made a settlement offer yet. We could approach them instead, though it wouldn't be my preference."

"No," I answered immediately. "The one who blinks first is the loser. I don't blink first. If Anika smells blood, she'll be in for the kill. There'll be no blood in this water but hers. Those stories won't have been fun for her whanau to read, and they won't have helped her anywhere else, either."

"In my experience," Walter said dryly, "people who do things like this aren't too worried about the reactions of their family."

"Ah," I said. "But then, you aren't Maori."

I'd been working even longer hours than usual these past few weeks, for the simple reason that I didn't enjoy coming home. Which was why a full twelve hours had passed since that early-morning conversation with Walter when I opened the door to the apartment.

I took off my shoes and slid them into their spot in the oversized entry closet. Hope's neat little five-and-a-halfs stood like soldiers in the back row, and Karen's larger shoes were just as meticulously arranged.

No mess anymore for Inez and Hope and me to barely keep on top of. No blaring television or godawful music to greet my arrival, no irritation to rise instantly, full-blown, the moment I stepped through the door. Order and silence, and that was all.

No Hope to keep me company on her kitchen stool while I ate dinner, with Karen adding her saucy contributions and making us both laugh. No sleepy lover to raise her arms to me from our bed, pull me in for a kiss, and let me know she'd welcome so much more. No sweet, soft body to wrap myself around as I fell asleep, and nobody to hold safe through the night. Nobody at all.

I stepped into the living room, dim in the gathering twilight, my hand going automatically to the rocker switch on the wall.

The hair rose on the back of my neck.

I didn't turn on the light. I backed up fast.

Home invasion. Get out.

I was already grabbing the handle of the front door when I heard it.

"Hemi. Wait."

♡♡♡

It wasn't a home invasion after all, except it was. It wasn't Hope, coming home because she'd missed me as much as I'd missed her, and she couldn't live without me anymore. It was Anika, and she was sitting on my couch.

I walked back into the living room showing no rush, no alarm, and flipped the light switch.

There she was, wearing a yellow-flowered wrap dress and high-heeled sandals, ankles crossed and hands folded in her lap, looking like the bloody Duchess of Cambridge.

"I'm sorry to startle you," she said. "And you're going to say I shouldn't be here,. I'm sorry about that, too. But you wouldn't have let me in, and I needed to see you."

"You're right." I read the slight widening in her eyes, the parting of her mouth, the indrawn breath of surprise and relief. And then I went on, standing absolutely solid, radiating the stillness and control that were my most potent weapons. "I wouldn't have let you in, and I'm going to say you shouldn't be here. Suppose you tell me how you got in and why you came."

"Please," she said, "sit down. I used to love you looming over me, but you're scaring me now."

"Good." I made no move to sit. She thought she could invite me to be at home in my own home? But then, Anika had never been short of confidence. "I'm still waiting. How?"

She sighed, her hands twisting together a bit more. "I had a mate call the front desk and be you. They don't know one Maori voice from another. And I was desperate."

I was going to have to set up a code word, I thought grimly. This had never occurred to me. Bloody stupid, especially with Hope and Karen living here, easy targets. I'd take care of that the minute I got Anika out of here. "They let you in because you were my . . ."

"Sister. I used my old passport with your name. I'm sorry, Hemi. I truly am. But I had to do it, don't you see? How else was I going to tell you what you've . . ." Her beautiful throat worked hard as she swallowed, and her mouth quivered. Even as I watched, a tear escaped one lustrous eye and traced a shining path over a sculpted cheekbone. "What you've done to me," she whispered. "How much it… hurts."

I shouldn't answer that. I did anyway. "You enjoy being hurt. You always have."

"Not like this. Never like this. You know the difference. You of all people. You always checked in. You always made sure I was all right. This time, you hit me so hard, and then you kept hitting. My job… my mum. My grandparents. My Koro… he cried, Hemi. He's *eighty*. He cried. He has to go to church tomorrow. He'll hold his head up, but he'll be dying inside knowing everybody's heard that, that they're talking about him, wondering what's wrong with our whanau that I turned out this way. And it hurts me to hurt him. It hurts like no whipping you ever gave me."

I told myself not to wince, and I even managed it. "I never did anything you didn't want."

"Except this. I didn't want this. You were *kind*. You were a gentleman, deep down, and I knew it. You made me feel safe. I used to laugh at you for it, I know, but underneath—I loved it. How could you have changed this much? How could you have turned into this man?"

"I warned you. Reckon you've found out why you shouldn't have done it."

"I can't help who I am. I can't help my tastes and my desires, just like you can't help yours. Do you have to punish me for them, too? Haven't you punished me enough?"

Breathe in. Breathe out. When I was sure I could do it calmly, I said, "That's not what I'm talking about, and you know it. Do you think I'd ever have talked about what you enjoyed, what we did together, what you did afterwards? Never. Especially not about the way you cheated. I could barely even tell Hope. If anyone else knew, it was because of what *you* said. You didn't care who knew. You didn't mind taunting that neighbor of yours, or telling Vi, knowing she'd tell me. That's why you told her, I'd bet, so she *would* tell me, to punish me for going to New York. You didn't mind sleeping with my bloody *roommate*. You say you hurt? How d'you think it felt to know all that? That you didn't love me enough to stay with me, and you were laughing behind your back at me with my mates? *Shagging* my mates? How many of them? How d'you imagine that felt? My *wife.*"

I wasn't making such a good fist of "cool" and "calm" anymore. I forced the dark rage down and said more quietly, "I didn't talk about you. I didn't do it this time, either. All I did was arrange a platform for all the people *you* talked to, all the people you shocked and hurt. I gave them a voice. The things you've done have come home to roost. I told you they would. I told you not to push me. You didn't believe me. More fool you."

"You're right. I've been such a fool. I've been so wrong." More tears were flowing now. Unlike Hope's, though, Anika's face didn't become blotchy when she cried. Her shoulders didn't heave, and her body didn't shake. She didn't lose it entirely when, with all her courage, she couldn't hold it in anymore, couldn't keep me from seeing her pain. No, Anika was a different animal entirely. A few silver streaks down her perfect skin, a quiver of her gorgeous mouth, and that was all.

She went on, a hitch in her voice. "All I've wanted was what was rightfully mine. Three years together means I get half. It's fair. It's the law. All I asked for was what was mine."

"No." I let the word hang there, flat and hard. "It wasn't three years, and you know it. You don't deserve a thing, and your tears won't work on me. Get out of my house."

"Hemi… please." She'd slipped off the couch, but she wasn't doing what I'd have expected. She wasn't coming to me and wrapping her arms around me, drawing me into the dark seduction that was her lush body, her twisted mind, her rich voice begging me, "Do it again, Hemi. Harder." Instead, to my horror, she was sinking to her knees.

"I'll do anything," she said. "Anything you say. I'll beg.

I'm begging now. Please stop. Let's settle. I'm in so much trouble. On the townhouse, the job, everything. I didn't want to tell you, because I know how you can't stand weakness. But I'm going to lose my house, and if you go on like this, I'm going to lose everything. My job. My whanau's good opinion. Everything. Please, Hemi. Give me something, and I'll leave you alone. Help me."

"No."

"Please. I'm begging you."

"I noticed. But you don't seem to realize the most important thing."

"What's that? Tell me, and I'll do it. Please."

"That I don't care."

sixteen going on thirty

♡

Hope

We developed a pattern, Hemi and I, after that first adventurous evening. During one call, we talked. Practicing our communication, and he was even willing to do it.

During the next call, we… went deeper. Call it "dinner" and "dessert." On the dessert nights, the date nights, we took turns sharing our fantasies, and I found myself saying things to him that I could never have imagined saying to a living soul. And let's just say he said more. He saw my bid and raised it, every single time.

I was a dirty girl, you bet I was, but Hemi put me to shame—in all sorts of ways. And whether I was talking or he was, I somehow always ended up performing for him. The combination worked like crazy, too. Well, for me, anyway.

Which was why, after our third date night, I spoke up. "I never get to watch you, though. When is it your turn?"

I got his real-deal smile for that. "Baby, it's always my turn. There's no way in the world that you could enjoy watching me as much as I love watching you."

"You may not know me as well as you think you do." I went for severe. Not easy when you're sprawled naked on your back across rumpled sheets, your body spelling out, "This woman has had several major orgasms!" on every inch of flushed skin. I did my best anyway, though. "When you're out here, I get a turn. That's a dealbreaker."

"It's a big ask," he said with a sigh, "but I may be willing."

I was smiling when I hung up. Hemi Te Mana, giving up control. How about that?

Saturday. Only four days to go, and then he was coming back after nearly four weeks apart. Back to pick up Karen, and back to see Koro.

And me, of course. And me.

Our communication was improving every day.

♡♡♡

On Friday morning, I woke up and reached a hand out for my chips, trying not to move so much as my head.

I was taking my first tentative nibble of ridged potato chip—yes, it's weird, but the salt helped the nausea—when it hit me.

Hey. I was barely sick. The nausea had been slowly improving over the past couple weeks, and this morning, instead of practically holding my breath while I sipped water and established my credentials for the World Championships of Slow Chip Consumption, I was inhaling my measly four chips and digestive biscuit and looking for more.

I wasn't sick, but I was *starving.* I'd lost six pounds in the past thirteen weeks, and I wanted those pounds *back*.

Fried chicken. That was what I wanted. Right the hell now.

No butler magically appeared to bring it to me, so I got out of bed, pulled on my robe, and went out to the kitchen. Eggs would do. Eggs and… spinach. And mushrooms. And *cheese*. Honey, this baby was going to be doing some growing, and so was I. When I'd taken my belly pictures this last week, I'd been able to inventory my entire rib cage, but that was about to change.

I was cooking a huge panful of eggs and vegetables, nibbling on a piece of cheese to tide me over for the next three minutes, when Karen showed up in the doorway.

"Hey," she said, blinking at me. "What is this? Dawn of the Walking Dead? You're dealing with food smells now? Pod person much?"

"We do it because we can. Suddenly." I tipped my eggs out onto a plate and added two pieces of toast that I buttered extravagantly. "Oh, sorry," I realized. "Want some?"

"Yeah," she said, and I suppressed a pang and divided my bounty onto two plates. Probably pushing my luck anyway, eating all that. The food had to stay down to do me any good.

"So how did it go last night?" I asked. "Have fun?" She'd gone to the movies in Tauranga with Tane's son Nikau, her sort-of-almost cousin, and some of his friends.

"Pretty good, but I still can't wait to go home." She focused on her eggs, and so did I. "This has been all right. I mean, Koro's great and all, but I miss my friends back home. Plus my laser surgery. Me with no glasses. Me *hot*. Imagine the intriguing possibilities."

I looked up from my own laser focus—on my plate—and studied her. She was chewing toast with honey with what I could swear was an innocent expression.

"Are you mad at me for not coming home for your surgery?" I asked, sticking one cautious toe into the water. Maybe, with all my self-improvement efforts and the endlessly distracting business of being pregnant, not to mention the looming figure of Hemi behind it all, I hadn't focused enough on her.

It had been such a relief to have all this extended family around. I hadn't realized the weight I'd carried until some of it had been lifted. All this past month, I'd had Koro here being her grandfather and Tane and June welcoming her into the fold as if she—we—really *were* their family. Not to have to be both mother and father to her, not to have to solo-parent a teenager when I'd barely stopped being one myself—it was different, and it was pretty great.

She waved her toast around as she chewed, which could have meant anything. "Nah," she finally said. "The recovery time for LASIK is a *day*. And, what? Your eyes sting? Compared to a brain tumor? Not even close. What was that thing you said? I'm either going to die, or it's an inconvenience. This is a *minor* inconvenience. This is a mosquito bite, and then I have perfect vision and no glasses. Yay."

"You remember that? What I said?" I didn't feel like quite such a bad parent-surrogate, suddenly.

"Sure I remember. You've always been there for me. I *get* that, Hope. You don't have to be there anymore. I'm sixteen. Plus, I'll be with Hemi, the world's most authoritative man. Born to boss. I don't need both of you doing it. Talk about overkill."

"Sixteen going on thirty," I said, and she grinned cheerfully at me and took another bite of eggs.

"So are we being hot for anybody in particular, or just on general principle?" I probed as lightly as I could manage, since we were having a Bonding Moment. "Noah, perhaps?" I didn't add "The Unattached Buddhist," Hemi's nickname for him. Hemi could keep the eagle eye on them and be the bad guy. He was tailor-made for it. It was my job to remain her confidante. That sharing-responsibility thing again.

"Could be," she said.

"You been emailing with him? Still an item?"

"Yeah. And this year, I'll be a sophomore. With hair. Also boobs and no glasses. And he'll be a senior, which is really hot, you know? Although last night, I'm telling you, this guy Michael? He'd totally have gone for it. And he's Maori, which is cool."

"Uh-huh." I did my best casual impression. "But you didn't?"

She heaved a martyred sigh. Whoops. Not casual enough. "No Aunt Bea. I exercised my freedom of one-hundred-percent choice and decided that I wasn't making out with a random guy who stared at my boobs, especially not when I was going home two days later and I sort of had a boyfriend. Plus," she added just as I was giving her major maturity points, "I swear Nikau told him to back off. Like—drew him aside and talked to him. What *is* it with the guys in this family?"

"Nightmare," I agreed solemnly. "Could be Nikau thought his friend wasn't good enough for you, what with the boob-staring and all."

"Which was totally my choice, not his. It's, like, 1902 around here. I'm not even his cousin, except that he thinks so. Nikau's pretty hot himself, if you didn't notice, but forget that, because I'm in the whanau now, so that's a no. And it goes way beyond that. It's like I'm, I don't know, precious or something. Off limits. Even Matiu's in love with you and never even *looks* at me. It's like I'm not here. I might as well go home."

I laughed in shock. "Wow. That's ridiculous. He is not." I'd known she had a crush. It would have been hard to miss. She was sassier than ever when Matiu was around. I'd seen Matiu be kind about it, too, which was nice of him—but then, I was sure he was used to it. But in love with *me?* Not hardly.

"Yeah, right," she said. "He is too. Anybody could see it. *Koro* can see it. Why do you think he told Matiu not to stay for dinner last night? Said he was too tired for company, like we'd believe that. He was practically hustling him out the door. And that wasn't because of me. He treats me like I'm twelve. I guess he's saving all his love for you."

I ignored the lump that had formed in the pit of my stomach. Too many eggs, that was all. "He's Hemi's cousin. You just said it. That possibility isn't on the table. And he's a huge flirt, too. It's habitual. Anyway, I'm not the kind of woman men long for. *You* will be, because you're tall. It's always tall women, isn't it? Also mysterious and sultry. I'm O-for-three here. Oh, and pregnant, too, by the way." I looked at her more closely. "Hey. You really *do* have a crush on him."

She shrugged, got up, and put another piece of bread in the toaster. "I'll live. You want one?"

"No, thanks."

"Well, anyway." She fidgeted around the toaster as if she could physically make it work faster. "I'm not mysterious and alluring *now,* so too bad for me. And I'm going home to live with Hemi. Yay."

I had to laugh. Karen would get over her crush, and whatever she thought, she *was* going to break some hearts. All you needed was attitude, and she sure had that. "Sorry, Miss Teenage Hormones. That doesn't seem like such a horrible thing to me. I was out there navigating the dating wilds all by myself, you know. Talk about overwhelming. I coped by backing away from everybody, until, of course, I jumped in with Hemi. Not exactly the kiddie pool. I'm not sure a little guidance would have been so horrible at sixteen. Or seventeen. Or twenty-four."

She came back over to the table and sat, pulling one leg beneath her before starting in on her toast. "So what did you have going on last night when I came home? Do you guys have phone sex or what?"

I stopped chewing, then carefully resumed, finally taking a sip of the ginger tea that had seemed like a reasonable precaution before I said, "Why do you ask?"

She sighed. "Hope. I live here. It's a small house."

I could feel the warmth rising straight up into my cheeks. What the heck was I supposed to say now? Parenting a teenager had been a whole lot easier before I'd hopped the train to Kinkytown. Hemi and I had started out being careful about noise, but we'd probably—*I'd* probably—lost the plot somewhere along the way. Which was awkward.

I believed in honesty and openness. I did. On the other hand, I also believed in the right to privacy. But I *also* believed in Karen. How was she going to be open with me if I didn't share anything with her?

Oh, man.

I was feeling my way here. "I miss him a lot. And he misses me. So… yeah. We get into it a little bit. He's a . . ." Studying my tea, now. "High-testosterone man, I guess you'd say. And I like that."

"Are you afraid that if you don't do what he wants, he'll cheat while you're gone? Or what?" She wasn't pretending to be interested in her toast anymore. She was looking right at me.

"No." I wasn't tentative anymore. I knew the answer. "Never. If Hemi isn't honorable, no man is. Everything we do is mutual. That's our deal. We don't do pressure. He doesn't put it on me, and even if he did, I wouldn't accept it. He knows that. And I miss him, too, you know. Goes both ways. Nothing two people do together, if they love each other and they both want to do it, is wrong. Including phone sex."

She studied me, and I willed my eyes not to drop. "You're turning really red," she informed me.

"What a shock. It's not an easy topic for me. It's personal. I'm telling you because I love you, and I want you to be able to talk to me about sex or anything else. I want you to feel like you can ask me, and that I might know the answers. But—yes. Hemi and me? I miss him like crazy, and he misses me. But we'll do our best to keep it down."

"When he shows up tomorrow," she said.

A flare of excitement at that. Near breathlessness, to be honest. "Yeah." It was a sigh.

She got up and, to my surprise, picked up my plate and silverware along with her own. Maybe Karen was growing up in more ways than one, now that she was looking after Koro instead of always being looked after herself.

"Note to self," she said. "Headphones."

what we have now

♡

Hope

Even the weather gods were cooperating on this Friday. It was only the second day of September, and spring hadn't sprung, but the ever-changing New Zealand climate was giving a good imitation of it. I rode my bike down the hill to town, then along to the café, under a sky so clear and bright, a breeze so fresh, I may have had to sing a little. "Oklahoma," which made no sense at all, except that it was upbeat, my mother had loved show tunes, and somehow, I *did* feel I belonged to this land, almost like I was a for-real Maori instead of an honorary one. Not to mention that the land I belonged to was grand. All of that.

Besides, if you couldn't sing out loud zipping down a New Zealand hill on your bike with the wind in your face, past fruit orchards, green fields dotted with sheep, and laundry flying like flags on clotheslines, with the wide Pacific spreading endlessly before you, when could you do it?

Plus, I wasn't sick, and I'd had to wear my yellow dress today when I hadn't been able to button any of my jeans. Because I was having a baby.

It was a quiet day at the café. Sunshine or not, it was a weekday in late August, the summer rush still far in the future.

"In fact, love," Sonya said at two o'clock, eyeing the lone couple lingering over coffees and a vanilla slice, "if you want to knock off a half hour early, I won't say no. You're jumping out of your skin today, and that's the truth. Something about those two days you're taking off?" It was easy to spot the teasing light in her eyes.

"Could be." I ran my thumb over the band of my engagement ring in a gesture that had become habitual. A reminder I needed.

She shook her head. "Hard to remember those days. My John's idea of a romantic gesture is pouring my beer into a glass instead of handing me the bottle."

"Well," I said, "a glass is good."

She laughed. "Go on, then. Get started on your holiday. But I'm not paying you for the time, mind," she hurried to add.

Kiwis. They could teach Scots a thing or two about pinching a penny. But I didn't care. I hopped on my bike again, pedaled to the pool, and put in my half hour.

I wasn't just paddling around anymore, either. I was doing *laps*. All right, slow ones, and not exactly a hundred of them, but they were laps. And, yes, before you ask—I'd learned to dive off the side, too, although the diving board and I were still unacquainted and would probably stay that way. There was no need to get all crazy about it.

Even putting in some extra time, though, I still left the pool twenty minutes before I was scheduled to meet Matiu. He was taking me to Countdown to do some shopping for the weekend, and to practice my driving, of course. Extra shopping because of that extra mouth we'd be feeding. Hemi's.

I'd even stopped dreading my driving lessons. Sometime over the past three weeks, sitting behind the wheel had gone from "white-knuckle exercise" to "transportation," and maybe even "personal power." I could parallel park, I could drive at a hundred kilometers an hour on narrow, winding New Zealand roads without needing CPR, and on two memorable occasions, I'd even done the motorway. Merging and everything. Karen might have more natural flair than I did, but as Matiu pointed out, one of us checked her mirrors every time, and it wasn't her.

Hemi would be surprised, that was for sure. I wondered how he'd feel about me driving *him.* In his car. That would be a true test of his evolution. He said I held his feet to the fire. I intended to do it, too, in the intervals when he wasn't holding mine there.

Down, girl. Time to take it to the sea, or I'd be jumping up and down and babbling like an idiot by the time Hemi showed up tomorrow. A little serenity here. A little perspective. I grabbed my bike again, rode three blocks, dumped it by a bench along with my bag, and headed across the broad stretch of sand.

The sea was relatively calm today, and the tide was out. I'd started noticing the movement of the tide, too. I was becoming an ocean person.

As always, the steadiness of the waves' endless pattern, sensed as much as seen, worked its magic on me. The sight of all that ruffled blue, glinting with a million diamonds where the sun hit each tiny wavelet—that was only one piece of it. It was the sound, as much hiss as roar, made up of so many component parts that you couldn't identify them all, except to say that the whole experience could never be anything but the sea. The clean salt smell, the space, and the emptiness. Nobody out here but a black-and-white dog racing along the shoreline toward its master, receding rapidly into the distance.

Sand, water, and sky, as far from Brooklyn and Manhattan as it was possible to get. The rush and hurry of the city replaced by the timelessness of water that would evaporate into the sky and fall again as rain, the cycle repeating as long as this great blue ball of ours kept spinning.

Our lives mattered, no matter how small and unimportant each of us was. Our lives were everything we had, all we could contribute to this complicated world. Sending the next generation on, giving it the best start you could—that mattered, too, but our legacy wasn't only in the genes we left behind, was it? It was in what we created, and maybe most of all in the kindness we showed. The understanding we demonstrated, the gesture that made somebody else's day fractionally better, the small acts whose effects spread like ripples in a pond.

Those ripples—maybe they were the true measure of what we'd offered the world. All the little ways we looked after each other, both the people we knew and loved and those we didn't. The million times we touched somebody else, that we shone a little light into somebody else's life.

An aged husband helping his wife of sixty years take her pills, his hand barely steadier than hers, the love of a lifetime on his wrinkled face. A baby putting a starfish hand on her father's cheek, and him turning his head to kiss that hand, however hard a man he might be otherwise, because she was his daughter and he loved her. And, after that, going out into his day that much softer, that much kinder, his heart that much more open.

A friend offering a shoulder to cry on, a willing ear, an entire evening spent sitting on a couch letting the tears fall without judgment when love went wrong. A teenager coming out of her preoccupation for a moment to let a young mother into line ahead of her at the grocery store because she had a toddler fussing in the cart. Or the group of four Maori girls I'd seen at the school bus stop this morning on my way to the café, bursting into song the same way I had on my way down the hill, their voices rising, strong and true, in the morning air. They'd been completely unselfconscious as they sang in their school uniforms, enjoying each other, the music, and the morning. Giving each other the gift of their joy, and giving it to me as well.

Joy. It was here, it was real, and it was mine. I was alive, and I was in love. In love with a man, a country, and two families that were about to become one. In love with my life.

I picked up the edge of my skirt in one hand and ran. I had to express my gratitude somehow, had to let that joy flow out through the fingers that stretched toward the sea, down through the soles of the bare feet that struck the sand, leaving footprints that would last only as long as the tide took to cover them up.

All things passed, the good and the bad, and so did everything on earth. Every bit of our lives was temporary, and that only made it more beautiful. All I had, all I knew for sure, was this moment. The past was gone, and the future was yet to be lived. I had now, and now was good. Now was enough.

I was still running, although slower—running wasn't actually my best thing, but what did it matter? Who was here to judge?—when the touch on my shoulder made me whirl. I had a hand on my chest, was laughing when I said, "Sorry. Talk about making you go out of your way. I lost track of time."

Matiu smiled down at me, his dark eyes lighting with his habitual amusement. "You were going along at a pretty good clip there."

"Carried away."

"Mm. Let's walk to the end before we turn around. I could use having my head cleared."

"Rough day?"

A pause before he answered. "A bit. Horror smash. Dad survived—the driver. Mum died, and one of the kids, too. On the table. Little fella. Those are the worst."

"Oh, no." I could feel his pain despite the matter-of-fact tone. "I'm so sorry."

He shrugged. "Can't let it get to you, or you'd quit the first year. You get a bit hardened, maybe. Detached, you could say. We all go sooner or later. It's my job to make it 'later,' but you can't work miracles."

I shivered, maybe with cold, but more like sympathy and horror. "I couldn't do it."

He laughed, the sound sudden and unexpected. "Nah, I don't reckon you could. Too much soft side, haven't you. But then, that's your charm."

Flirting again, and why did "soft side" always sound like "weak side"? And I knew Karen's idea was ridiculous, but still.

He was silent for a few minutes until he finally said, "Hemi's home tomorrow, eh. Visiting."

"Yes. He is."

"Taking Karen home with him, but not you."

"That's right. She's due back at school. I'll stay with Koro until his arm's out of the cast, anyway. Not too much of a hardship. I love it here."

"Are you sure that's all?"

I shot a look at him, and for once, he wasn't smiling. Instead, he was staring straight ahead, hard lines around the corners of his mouth that I hadn't seen before.

"What do you mean?" I asked.

"When people are sure," he said, "they stay together. Especially if they're have a baby on the way. And babies don't make things easier. They make them harder. If you're having problems now, they won't get better once you add that complication."

However soft he thought I was, I wasn't feeling that way now. "My relationship with Hemi isn't something I discuss."

"Could be you need to." He was looking at me now, I could tell, but I didn't return the favor. "Could be it'd help. He's a hard man, and everyone knows it. Too hard for you, I'd say. Too old for you as well. Too powerful. Too arrogant. I could add more. And 'pregnant' doesn't have to mean 'stuck.' I know you don't have family, but that doesn't mean there's nobody to step in and help."

"I don't need anyone to step in." My heart was tripping along in an agitated rhythm. This was going nowhere good. "I love Hemi."

"But does he love you? Does he love you enough?" His tone was gentle, but the words made me flinch. "Hemi doesn't compromise, and I'm guessing that's what you're trying to make him do. Anyone who doesn't toe his line is out of his life for good. We all saw him throw Anika under the bus this week. It would take a strong woman—a tough woman—to stand up to him."

"That's true." I kept my tone even. Matiu was Hemi's cousin, and that mattered. I wasn't burning bridges or driving wedges into Hemi's family. Not today, and not ever. "But you see, I *am* a strong woman. Stronger than you know. I'm strong enough to stand up to Hemi. I'm strong enough for anything. I know I am. I've had reason to know it."

I risked a glance at him. His eyes searched my face, no trace of amusement in them anymore. "If that changes," he said gently, "if you find you can't do it after all, you're not alone. You have somebody here for you. You have me."

He took my hand, swallowing it up. I tried to pull it out of his grasp, but he held it tight, and he was too strong.

"You're his cousin," I said. "This isn't all right." I didn't feel soft now. I was getting mad.

"It'd be rough," he said, "but it'd be possible. Hemi doesn't dwell on the past. He cuts his losses and moves on."

"No." This, I knew for sure. "He doesn't. Hemi holds hard, and he holds forever. You don't know him, and you don't know me. I love him, I always will, and I'm marrying him. And because I know how important his whanau is to him, I'm going to pretend this conversation never happened. I know what you're saying, and what you're not saying. Don't ever say it. I don't want to hear it."

"Hope," he said, "it doesn't work that way. Some things, you can't help."

"Maybe you can't help your feelings," I said, finally freeing my hand. "You can help your words and your actions, though. You can keep them to yourself."

My hands were shaking, I realized in disgust. I *was* strong. I knew it. But why did using my strength always have to take such a toll? Why did it have to feel so bad?

I didn't hear a thing. Nothing but the sea, nothing but my own harsh breathing in my ears. Until he was there, stepping in front of us. As hard as rock. As grim as iron.

"Hope," Hemi said. "Matiu."

a woman's heart

♡

Hemi

I hadn't been able to wait until Thursday night to leave New York.

Holiday weekends had always been an annoyance to me. All those days gone to waste, and you couldn't even expect your executives to put in a few hours, because it was meant to be family time.

I'd said something like that last Christmas, and Tane had laughed hard, caught June's eye, and they'd both laughed some more. Bloody annoying, I'd thought it.

"Cuz," Tane had said, wiping his eyes and heaving in an unsteady breath, "it's a good thing you've given up your New Zealand citizenship already, or they'd ask for it back. We've got a job to do to cut this tall poppy down, eh, Koro."

"Quality of life," June had added. "It's a thought, eh."

At the time, I'd thought, *That's why Kiwis never get anywhere.*

Too busy putting the boat in the water.

And what had I done? I'd not only planned to take off Friday plus the entire three-day weekend, one short month before the show that would launch a line I was more excited by than anything I'd done since my first year—I hadn't even been able to *wait* for Friday. By noon on Wednesday, I'd been ringing my pilot, and by Thursday morning, I'd been in the air. Which was why, nearly twenty-four hours and one international date line later, I was pulling into Koro's driveway, bounding out of it with a hurry I never showed, and seeing a delighted smile bloom on the old man's face.

He was outside with Karen, who'd been maneuvering a long-handled picker to get the first avocadoes from the tree under his supervision.

"Hemi," he said. "You're early. That's good, my son. That's good."

I knew he wasn't talking about the clock. He was talking about me losing my discipline, succumbing to impulsivity. The exact thing that scared me, even as I took his good hand, pressed my forehead gently to his, and said, "Eh, Koro. It's good to see you."

I gave Karen her own cuddle and kiss, and she said, "About time. Hope can stop going crazy now. I mean, love's great and all, but she's way over the line."

I laughed out loud, so happy to be here. Happy to leave behind the baking heat of Manhattan sidewalks wafting the scent of too many people and too many bad habits into the stale air. Here, a cool, moist breeze brought the crisp scents of bush and sea and trees bursting to leave winter behind and yield again. The sights and smells of home, and all of them were good.

Koro looked at me, his eyes wise in his lined old face.

"She's not here," he said. "Gone to work, then popping into Countdown afterwards, she said."

"So I can cook for everybody," Karen said with a sigh. "I have to say, the cooking thing isn't nearly as much fun when you *have* to do it. Every single day."

"Story of life," I said, but without my full attention. "How's she doing the shopping? Only got her learner's permit, eh."

"Matiu's taking her," Karen said. "Like always."

Something in her tone had my gaze sharpening. "Oh?"

"Matiu or Tane," Koro said calmly. "Lessons."

"Right," I said. "I'll go see if I can find her, then."

"You do that," Koro said. "Give her a surprise."

She *wasn't* at the cafe. The middle-aged woman I recognized from that last visit said, "Gone to the pool, love," then kept hauling a bag of rubbish out to the bin, sparing me a bright, curious glance along the way.

Hope wasn't at the pool, and she wasn't at Countdown, though I wandered every aisle searching for her.

I finally pulled the phone out of my pocket in defeat, then hesitated. I wanted that surprise. Home, then.

I'm not sure what made me look at the beach. Maybe just thinking about Hope dancing along by the water. Maybe wondering if she were as excited as I was about our being together again, and how she'd have to express that. How it may have had to spill over, because Hope had a hard time containing her joy.

Probably, though, it was just recognizing the sleek red Audi in the carpark. Not too many of those in Katikati. I was out of my own car again within seconds and over the berm.

I saw her instantly. Running, her skirt in her hand, wearing the yellow dress she'd worn for our second disastrous date, the one that made her look so pretty and sweet, you had to ache with it. And for some reason, she had Matiu running after her. She was barefoot, looking so happy even from a distance. Not running away, then. Running for joy, as I'd thought.

I took a minute to remove my own shoes and roll up my trouser legs. I was still in dress clothes, my usual dark trousers and white shirt, and now, I wondered why I hadn't changed to jeans on the plane. Because I'd wanted to appear strong, polished, in control, like always? Hope didn't care about that. She wanted to see me. She wanted me to hold her. That was why I hadn't been able to wait. That was why I was here: because she needed me to hold her, and I needed to do it.

It didn't even scare me. Instead, it gave me wings. I was running along the firm sand, careless of the occasional scallop of white-flecked water edging its way past its fellows and catching a bare foot. There was nothing to be careful of anymore.

That was why I was close enough to see it when Matiu took Hope's hand.

It hit me like an anvil in the chest. My steps slowed, then sped up again. The rage rose as quickly as the joy had, swamping it in a red tide.

Except that I saw something else, too. I saw her posture change, and his as well.

Every successful entrepreneur was a poker player, and I was one of the best. The rising of a pair of shoulders betraying tension that couldn't be hidden. A hand clenched too tightly, a body that couldn't stay relaxed.

I'd caught up to them before the thoughts had crystallized. The two of them had slowed, then stopped. The fury was still burning inside me, and more. And more.

"Hope," I said. "Matiu."

Hope's face worked, she gave a choked cry, and then she flung herself at me.

My arms went out to hold her. They would never do anything else. It wasn't possible. She didn't lift her face to be kissed, either. Instead, she buried it in my shirt and held on as if I were her life raft. As if I were her finish line, her resting place. Or her champion.

My eyes met Matiu's over Hope's head. Met and held.

"Maybe you'll explain," I said, with the steel in my voice I hadn't thought I'd need this weekend, "why you're grabbing my fiancée. Why she had to work that hard to get you to let her go."

My cousin was nearly ten years my junior. When I'd been a man, already hard beyond my years, he'd been a boy. Too good-looking even then, too easily charming, with a mother who doted on him and too smooth a path to walk.

He'd been intimidated by me then, and I'd known it. He didn't look intimidated now, although he ought to be. "I thought she might need my help," he said. "She told me she didn't. End of story."

"And that's meant to satisfy me."

Hope had unwound her arms from around me, though I still had my arm around her waist, her body pulled up tight to mine. I expected her to speak, to leap into the breach, but she didn't. She waited. Trusting me.

"It is," Matiu said. "I thought I knew what I saw. I took a chance and asked. Hope set me right."

"And?" I asked.

No sigh. No change at all in the eyes that stared steadily back into mine. "And I was wrong. Wrong conclusion. Wrong to ask. Wrong to put her in the position of having to tell me no. I let hope get the better of me, I reckon." His charming smile, now of all times, shocked me like a dash of ice water. "So to speak. She got the better of me, and she let me know that you did, too. If you're determined to make more of it than that, it's your choice."

"No." I knew my face and voice were sending a different message, but was wholly unable, for once, to control them. "I won't do that. Too much pain for Koro and everyone else, and there's been enough of that. Too much pain for Hope to think she did something wrong, when I'm guessing all she did was be herself. And maybe not pay enough attention."

"Probably," Hope said quietly. "And I'm sorry."

She apologized so easily, but somehow, it didn't make her weaker. She did it because she meant it, and she did it from the heart.

Something Eugene had told me after she'd left punched into me at that moment like one of his sneaky blows making its way over my guard and straight into my chest.

When I'd told him Hope was in New Zealand, that she was pregnant, he'd looked at me for a long moment, then sighed.

"And I know," I'd said. "You told me so. You don't need to say it again."

"Nope," he'd answered. "I don't. Guess you can see for yourself. Time to man up and admit it."

I'd tried not to wince, but had known he'd seen it in my eyes. "Yeah," he'd said. "She put you on the ropes a long time ago. This here, though—this here's a TKO."

I'd given it up. "That's it. Still can't figure out how it happened. I thought I was doing it right. Couldn't believe she'd go. Couldn't believe I'd follow her there like I did, or that I'd accept it. I still can't believe it, but it's true."

He'd shaken his head, showed me those missing teeth, and hit me in the shoulder with enough force that I'd had to brace against it. "Yeah. Ain't that a thing? Guess you found the only thing in the world stronger than a man's hard head."

I didn't ask, but he told me anyway. "That'd be a woman's heart."

mending the broken

♡

Hemi

Matiu turned around and walked away. I watched him go just to see the back of him, then looked down at Hope, still pressed up tight against my side.

Her gaze was steady, and her voice was, too. "You did good."

"So did he," I said. "Bugger."

She laughed, put her arms around me, and hugged me tight. Her voice was teasing, but a little husky, too, when she said, "I think there are a lot of men in your family who could give the world some lessons. One thing is completely clear—you're named Te Mana for a reason. That was *good.* On both your parts. Matiu's going to make some woman very lucky someday."

"He can make anybody lucky that he likes. Anybody except you."

"Mm. So, tough guy, how about kissing me? Since you're the one and only man for me, how about letting me know it?"

So I did, while the tide came in and foamed around our ankles and the sun dropped lower and hovered at the edge of the sea, here at the bottom of the world. And after a while, we walked back down the beach, I put her bike and bag in the back of the SUV, opened the passenger door for her, and said, "We're going to Countdown, eh. Quite the romantic evening we've got in store, it seems."

She didn't get in. Instead, she asked, "Do you mind if I drive?"

It took me a moment. It had never occurred to me. She sighed and said, "Yeah. I figured. Never mind. Baby steps."

"No," I said with some force.

She jerked back a little, then said, "I said, 'Never mind.'" There was an edge to her tone I almost never heard anymore. "I get it."

"No. You don't. Of course you can drive."

"Are you sure?"

I smiled. "Baby, here's that negotiation practice for you again. Don't ask me that. Just nod and say, 'Right,' walk around the car, and get behind the wheel as if you never had any doubt that I'd agree to your perfectly reasonable request."

"Oh. All right, then." She went to the boot for her bag, pulled out her learner plates, attached them, then came back, pulled herself up into the driver's seat, and said, "OK. Keys?"

I handed them over without a word, and she heaved in an audible breath, blew it out, and said, "I'm nervous. Do I get to say that by Te Mana negotiation standards? I'm worrying about what you'll think."

"Nah," I said. "No worries. It isn't my car, and I'm insured."

She laughed, and then she did it. She drove, and I was her passenger, and it wasn't all that bad. She wasn't going to be setting any land speed records, but she was conscientious, which was no surprise at all. That she was cautious—that wasn't front-page news, either.

Pushing the trolley in Countdown for her while she consulted her list wasn't terrible, and neither was looking at the way that yellow dress of hers couldn't conceal the bulge of her belly and knowing I'd be kissing that belly tonight, and so much more. In fact, I may have felt like the luckiest man in the world. It could be.

It took a while to get there, of course. Three hours later, I hadn't got any further than sitting on the couch watching telly with Koro while Hope sat on a footstool in front of him and gave him a hand massage.

When she moved on to his feet, I muted the advert blaring on the TV and said, "That's the royal treatment, eh, Koro. You're never going to give my girl back at this rate."

Hope looked up at me with that smile of hers. "Touch is good. It helps."

Karen said, "She did it for me when I was sick, too. When you hurt a lot, you kind of seize up, trying to hold the hurt part in so it doesn't hurt more, you know? When Hope would rub my hands and feet, it made at least part of me feel good, and I could let go for a few minutes. It was really nice."

"Could be more than that, too," Koro said. "Could be the feeling behind it, eh. Same way Hemi helped me with the bath tonight, even though I don't need it much anymore. Didn't mind me being a grumpy bugger about it, either. Course, could be he just didn't let on."

"Nah," I said. "You can be a grumpy bugger. I reckon I'd even rub your feet if I had to. If I'd ever thought of it, which

I didn't."

"Or it could be it's both," Hope said, rubbing cream into Koro's left foot and seeming perfectly content to do it. "The touch, and the feeling behind it. Of course you want to make somebody feel better if you love them. I did this for my mom when she got neuropathy in her feet from the treatments. I thought at least it'd be better than nothing, and it was. She said it was good. She said I had love in my hands."

Her voice had gone so quiet by the end, I almost couldn't hear her. Koro put out one gnarled hand to touch her soft hair, still a little tousled from her time at the beach. She bent her head, and I knew why.

Karen said, "Oh, great, Hope. Now everybody's going to cry. Way to go." Which made everybody laugh instead. Much better.

The program came on again, and when it was over, I said, "I should've been sending more flowers while I was gone, I'm thinking. A bit neglected in here, aren't you."

I'd been aiming for a smooth segue into a casual moment, but it didn't quite come off. Koro snorted and said, "Bordello. That's what this place has been."

"Doesn't have to be roses," I said. "Looked to me like your daffodils were already blooming. Made me think about your garden as well."

"Good," Koro said with satisfaction. "Maybe that means you'll till it for me tomorrow. Got a shed full of seedlings bursting out of themselves to get into the ground."

"I will," I said, mentally rearranging my timetable for the weekend. "But there's no time like the present." I stood up and handed the remote back to Koro, then said to Karen, "Come give me a hand."

She bounced up, not playing her part with nearly as much

nonchalance as she might have done. "Sure. I'll go get the flashlight."

Koro looked at me as if I'd lost my mind, as well he might. "The bath was enough. I don't need daffodils. Save it for the morning, at least."

"Nah." I headed off after Karen. "Seize the moment."

She was outside already, hopping about like a rabbit, the light of the torch making crazy patterns in the dark. "I thought you were *never* going to do it," she complained. "See, that would have been the *perfect* time, while Hope was massaging Koro's feet. And let's hope no guy ever thinks I'm going to massage *his* feet. I don't care what Hope says about love, that's just gross."

I laughed. "Nah. Knowing you, you'll have him massaging yours. Let's go, then. Light my way."

When we came back into the kitchen, Karen whispered theatrically, "I'll go get it."

"Right," I said, examining my bounty. Not too bad. Cheerful yellow daffodils and delicate paperwhites, their petals sending yet more fragrance into air that was still carrying the perfume of the steak and mushroom pie Karen had made for dinner. Koro might complain about the scent, but he wouldn't be complaining long, not when he'd seen what I'd done. I hoped.

Why was I thinking about Koro? I was nervous, that was why. Keyed up. Afraid Hope would appear in the kitchen before I was done, and trying to craft some sort of response that would get her out again. I should've taken Koro into my confidence instead, but I'd known Karen would love it, and… well, I hadn't.

Before I could spin myself up any more, Karen dashed back inside the room with a loaded laundry basket. "It was all

I could think of," she explained. "Hurry up, before Hope decides everybody needs a hot drink before bed or something. You know how she is."

I did. I made my preparations, took a deep breath, thought, *You know what to say. Harden up and do it,* and followed Karen out of the room with one hand behind my back.

Hope stood up at my entrance and said, "I'll go get ready for bed, I guess. Get in the shower before there's a crowd," and started toward the doorway into the hall. Which, considering that it wasn't even eight o'clock, I should have appreciated.

"Uh… can you hold that thought for a couple minutes?" I asked.

Karen gave a gusty sigh and said, "Remind me never to give you a surprise birthday party, Hope. Can't you see Hemi's trying to do something special?"

"Oh." Hope looked at me, back at Karen, sank down onto the edge of the recliner, and said, "OK. What?"

Koro's face was like some kind of carving. Representing benign ancestral power, maybe. I couldn't spare too much attention for him, though, as I pulled out the vase of flowers from behind my back and set it carefully on the coffee table.

"There," I said. "Much more cheerful."

Hope, unlike me, would never be a poker player. I could read the expressions on her face as easily as if they'd been written there. Surprise, confusion, incredulity, delight, one after the other. "Hemi," she said helplessly. "You found one exactly like it. How? That was *old.*"

"I didn't." My own eyes may have been misting up the tiniest bit. I sank to a knee in front of her and took her hand. "It's your mother's vase. It's the real thing."

She tumbled off the recliner and knelt beside me, her hand

stroking over the vase. "Where? I can't see . . ."

I touched first one meandering crack, then the second one, pointing out the barely visible seams in the basketweave pattern of the Irish vase. Green shamrocks on a white background. Hope's treasure, worth nothing but memory. Worth everything.

"Here," I said. "I mended it for you. That is, I had it mended. When I saw that you'd broken it and left the pieces on the counter, I thought, what could make Hope do that? What would she have to be feeling not to even try? It wasn't right to forget what your mum said, sweetheart. I thought maybe I could help you remember."

"She said . . ." Hope's hand was shaking on the vase as she traced the crack, stained with brown no longer.

"She said," I reminded her, the tenderness aching in my chest, "that a crack is just a place where something got loved extra hard, and somebody cared enough to mend it."

"You remembered." It was nearly a whisper.

"I did." I couldn't imagine why I'd been nervous about this. I knew how to make Hope happy. Nobody better at it, because nobody could possibly love her more. "A broken vase can be mended, and so can a broken heart. It just takes somebody who cares enough to do it."

♡♡♡

We took our shower together, in the end, because I didn't want to wait through two of them to go to bed with her, and I was pretty sure Karen and Koro weren't going to fall over with shock that we were retiring early. Afterwards, I took Hope's flower-scented lotion and rubbed it into her skin while she stood on the bath mat and let me do it.

At last, after weeks of wishing, I was touching that sweet swell of belly. I was smoothing lotion into the body that cradled my son or daughter, murmuring words to Hope that might embarrass me to remember in the morning, and completely unable to care. Telling her she was beautiful, body and soul. Telling her how lucky I was to have her, and how hard I was willing to work to keep her.

We made the quick journey to the bedroom to the welcome sound of the TV. Koro and Karen were watching an action film, and I hoped the explosions were loud and frequent. I closed the bedroom door behind us, pulled off my trousers and tossed them over a chair, dropped the rest of our clothes onto the rug, and went to Hope where she was pulling back the duvet on the bed.

She smiled over her shoulder at me, and then she was shrugging out of her dressing gown and kneeling naked on the bed to light the candles.

There would be no screen substituting for my presence tonight, or for hers. Tonight was all for us, and we took it.

We took our time, and we gave each other our very best. Long, slow, deep kisses and gentle, stroking hands, hers exactly as avid as mine. Sighs and murmurs, sweet words that we both needed to hear. And more.

The catch in her breath when I touched her breast, and the shock it gave me, as sharp a pleasure as any boundary I'd ever pushed. The look in her eyes when she shoved me gently over to my back, the soft touch of her lips working their way down my body with her hands following behind. The softness of her cornsilk hair between my fingers, and the dark, nearly desperate thrill of her lips and tongue finding me at last, pleasuring me every bit as well as I'd ever pleasured her, and more. The helpless surrender when I abandoned all effort at control, and the astonishing absence of fear, of uncertainty, of pride.

Nothing about loving Hope could scare me, not anymore. It wasn't possible.

And, finally, after she'd pleased me and I'd pleased her, after we'd slaked the first desperate hunger of nearly four weeks without each other… that final slow, sweet slide into her willing body. The way she closed around me, my perfect fit. The choked, gasping cry she gave when I began to move, the eager way her legs came up to wrap around my back, the hunger in the hands clutching at my shoulders. As if she couldn't get close enough. As if she needed all of me inside her, as if she cradled my very soul. The bliss of rocking her to slow, sweet fulfillment, taking care of her every single step of the way.

Watching her underneath me, listening to her sighs, her moans, inhaling her scent, taking all of her and feeling her take all of me. Flowers and softness and strength. A willow, not an oak. The strength to bend without breaking, to hold without grabbing.

The strength to love a man who was too hard to love. The endless patience to fit my broken pieces together again and make me whole. Hope, my unlikely, incompatible, perfect match.

And when she was crying out beneath me, completely unable to keep herself from doing it… in that last second where I could still form a thought, I gave thanks for the thing I'd never dared to believe in. For the impossible.

That Hope had brought me to this place. And that I'd been willing to go.

the te mana school of negotiation

♡

Hope

Some men are good at loving. Others are *great* at it.

Hemi and I made love twice more that night, and by the time we finally got out of bed the next morning, we may almost have been satisfied. Body and soul, because, wow—Hemi did "love talk" almost as well as he did dirty talk. I'd known there was a reason he was so successful. He was one fast learner, and he was nothing if not devoted to his work.

I say "almost satisfied," though, because we weren't permitted to find out how long we'd have stayed in the too-small bed that had become a world in itself. Instead, I was jolted awake from sleep by somebody banging on the door.

"Hey, you guys," I heard while I was still coming out of the fog. "I'll mow and everything, but I'm not rototilling. I mean, Koro says I'm not. He says rattle your dags, Hemi."

"Ugh," I moaned, rolling over. "Is it morning?"

"Sleep," Hemi ordered, proving that Command Central was up and running again. "You don't need to do this."

I climbed out of bed, and if my legs were still a little wobbly—well, yours would be, too, if you'd been through what I had during the past—I checked my phone. Whoops. Twelve hours.

"Nope," I said. "I'm all good, see? Ready to be a hardworking Kiwi. All set to till the soil."

I didn't do that much tilling, though, and neither did Karen. Surprise. Karen did mow the lawn as she'd been doing since the first week, when Matiu had shown her how. Hemi, meanwhile, moved Koro's chair under a huge old apple tree so he could supervise, then worked a huge, unbelievably noisy cultivating machine in satisfactory agricultural fashion, tramping up and down while he turned over a sizeable patch of dirt until the muscles stood out on his arms and his T-shirt clung damply to his back.

Not that I was looking. Well, peeking, maybe, in between trips to the shed to bring out the endless sets of filled egg cartons that were Koro's seed trays, which Karen and I had helped him plant, water, and nurse into proud little leaf-bearing seedlings over the past few weeks.

"This is, like, *score,*" Karen had said happily when the first hopeful green shoots had poked up. "Much nature. Maybe I'm not going to die on the desert island after all."

"As long as you've got vegetable seeds in your pockets," I'd said.

"Way to rain on my Earth Girl parade," she'd said, making me laugh. "Better be nice to me. You're going to need me on our island. I've got way more skills than you." Which was sadly true.

Here on our much bigger island, meanwhile, Hemi

finished tilling, cleaned the machine and put it away, then started breaking up dirt clods with a hoe as if he weren't a very rich man with a very large staff. After watching him for a minute—there's only so long it takes a person to carry trays—I went to the shed, found a second hoe, and came out to join him.

It smelled suitably rich and loamy out there, although the agricultural peace was somewhat spoiled by the dull roar of Karen's lawnmower in the distance. Still, the sun felt good, and the teamwork wasn't bad, either.

Of course, the second I had that thought, Hemi looked up and said, "No."

I didn't stop. It was oddly satisfying to watch the heavy clumps of black dirt break up under my hoe. "Yes," I said without looking up. "I've been riding my bike and swimming like you wouldn't believe. You wait until Eugene feels my bicep next time. I'm going to get a gold star."

Hemi was beside me just that fast, reaching out to grab the handle of the hoe. "No. This is too hard."

He expected me to let go, but I didn't. I hung on until *he* let go.

"Ha," I said. "I knew you weren't about to jerk me off my feet. You're too easy to read. And I can do this. If I get too tired, I'll stop. Trust me to know my own body, OK?"

He wasn't happy, it was obvious. In fact, he opened his mouth at least twice and then shut it again both times.

I said, "Good job suppressing that," and got his best hard stare for my pains, then a reluctant almost-smile. But he didn't grab the hoe again.

I was pretty tired, I'll admit, by the time we had the whole plot smoothed out and half of it planted. Karen came to help once she finished mowing, and even Koro got out of his chair to crouch in the dirt, scatter seeds, and ease seedlings as tenderly into the dirt as if he'd been tucking babies into bed. *He* didn't listen to Hemi telling him not to do it, either.

"Poor you," I told Hemi when he'd given up yet again. "You're going to have to go back to all those people whose paychecks you sign to get your own way."

"Why did I ever want a saucy girl?" he muttered. "That's what I'm asking myself."

"You can tell *me* to stop," Karen said. "I mowed. I deserve a break."

"Nah," he said. "It's good for you."

"Nice," she said.

Koro looked thoroughly satisfied, but all he said was, "Go get us some water, Karen."

She gave a huff. "See, Hemi? *Koro* cares about me. *He* sees I need a break. Do I want to go home with you? That's what *I'm* asking myself."

"Yeh," Hemi said. "You do. Because you want your LASIK surgery."

"Fine," she said. "Bribe me."

"Thanks," Hemi said. "I will. Meanwhile, go get your sister and Koro a glass of water."

It wasn't too much longer, though, before I stood up, put a hand on my back, carefully did *not* sway on my feet, and said, "You know what? I think I'm done," and saw Hemi blow out a breath. "Congratulations on holding back, though," I told him. "You encourage me strangely."

"Pushing," Karen muttered, and I laughed and said, "Always," and Hemi shot a look at me that told me that was exactly what I was doing.

As for me? I went into the house, took a much-needed shower, lay down for a nap, and thought, before I fell asleep,

That's how you do it, girlfriend. And that's what Hemi gets for sending you to the Te Mana School of Negotiation.

♡♡♡

That night, we had a hangi at June and Tane's: an entire meal slow-roasted for hours under burlap sacking in an earthen pit without which any Maori home apparently would be incomplete. Well, any Maori home except one in Manhattan. I mostly spent my time tucking into succulent lamb and chicken, silken potatoes, kumara, and pumpkin, and thought how grateful I was not to be sick anymore. Meanwhile, Hemi talked to an incredible number of relatives, the "big whanau" that gave "extended family" a whole new meaning, Koro looked happy, Karen flirted with cousins she knew and cousins she didn't and glanced sideways at Matiu too much, and Matiu didn't come anywhere remotely close to Hemi or me. Which could have been the "she's-mine" way Hemi's hand kept going to the back of my neck, the alpha male testosterone waves that were practically pouring off him, or simply Matiu's good sense. However it was achieved, family harmony was preserved and Koro was happy, which was what mattered.

The next morning, things took another turn. Hemi looked at me over breakfast and said, "Time to buy you some jeans you can button, I reckon, which means we're shopping today. In Auckland."

"Oh?" I took another hopefully-dainty bite of pancakes, caramelized bananas, and maple syrup, as a woman does who's trying not to turn off her beloved for good by putting her face down onto the plate and shoveling everything in. "I'd say something snippy about your high-handed ways, but as it happens, I'd really like some jeans I can button. Plus, you're much less restrained than I am, and I admit to some reprehensible pleasure of my own along those lines."

"Which is a roundabout way of saying," Hemi told Koro, "that Hope loves it when I buy her pretty things and spend too much money on her, but she reckons she shouldn't."

"Concussion's all better, my son," Koro said with a twinkle in his eye. "I don't need you to explain what she said."

"Ha," Karen said with satisfaction. "Owned."

"Are you OK staying here?" I asked Karen. "It's your last day, so maybe you'd rather come to Auckland with us. We could get Tane or June to bring Koro his dinner."

"No, we couldn't," Hemi said. "We're going out to dinner as well, and then we're staying over. It's you and me today. Or mostly, because I invited Violet to have dinner with us. But I'm not leaving you tomorrow without knowing that I can look after you and that you'll let me do it."

"Sounds like a non-negotiable deal," I said, attempting to find something wrong with his plan and failing completely. Violet? I'd love the chance to say "thanks" to Violet for that newspaper quote, not to mention pumping her about Anika. In the ladies' room, maybe…

"That would be because it is," Hemi said. "You said I took you for granted once I had you in my… apartment, and you were right. I'm not taking you for granted anymore, though. If you want me to set aside time for you, you'd better let me show you that I'm willing to do it, or I'm likely to fall back into old habits. That starts today."

"Very forceful," Karen said. "Very manly. Notice how I'm not acting all hurt that you don't want my company, Hemi. Probably because being with you guys while you're in makeup mode isn't exactly my favorite thing. That'd be some fun day for me."

"Probably," I said, thinking once again how much my life had changed in a single short year. "Too bad I've got a fatal weakness for forceful and manly. And yes," I told Hemi. "Oddly enough, I find that I'd be willing to go to Auckland and be hopelessly spoiled. Thank you for thinking of it."

Koro didn't say anything. He just did his benevolent-ancestor look and ate his pancakes.

♡♡♡

I drove all three hours to Auckland, and Hemi let me do it. He didn't even grab the armrest or press his foot obviously into the floor as if there might be an extra brake pedal there. Instead, he asked, once we were on the highway, "What kind of feedback do you want?"

I shot a lightning-quick glance at him, then resumed my Death Stare on the road. "That wasn't what I thought I'd hear."

"Reckon you may not know as much about me as you think you do. No point in my letting you drive if I put you off while you do it. Tell me your expectations, and I'll tell you if they're acceptable to me. If they're not," he said, anticipating my next question, "we negotiate."

"All right, then. I slowed for a logging truck ahead of me and thought with a flutter of nerves about overtaking. "I'd like you to tell me if you think I'm doing something wrong, or not doing something I should. Like if I should be going faster, you can say, 'Speed limit's a hundred,' or whatever. Calm, the way you do. If I should be in a different lane, you can say, 'You can move over now.' Just don't yell at me and make me nervous. What do you think?"

"I think I can do that," he said. And he did. I was sure he'd had to exercise some powerful self-control, but then, Hemi *had* some powerful self-control. All the same, when I pulled into the parking garage in Auckland's Newmarket district after the most harrowing driving I'd ever done and inched the SUV into a spot that I'd have sworn was too small for it but Hemi said wasn't, I turned off the car, handed Hemi the keys, put my face against the steering wheel, and had to take a moment.

"All right?" Hemi's hand was on my back.

I nodded without lifting my head, he said, "Eh, sweetheart," and I sat up and tried to laugh.

"One more checked off the list," I said. "And next time will be easier."

"You were brilliant," he said. "The motorway, Auckland, and all. Ready for New York, I'd say."

I laughed for real this time, though it still wasn't quite steady. "Admit it. You were two seconds away from telling me to pull off and let you drive."

"Could be. But I stayed two seconds away. And you've got courage to burn."

"OK." I reached into the back for my purse. "Please take me to buy clothes and keep saying nice things to me. In another hour or two, I might stop shaking. And thank you."

"For what?"

"For loving me enough to keep your mouth shut."

After that, it was lunch, during which I calmed down, and then it was shopping. Hemi took me first to EGG Maternity, which he'd clearly checked out already. At least, he seemed to know exactly what would work for me, because he went through the place like a Bloomingdale's after-Christmas sale shopper on steroids, handing item after item to the bemused clerk, who looked as if she didn't know what to make of him. Within an hour, I was outfitted as well as I could be, at least for this stage of the affair.

"We'll do it again at six months," Hemi informed me, watching, his eyes full of pure satisfaction, as I modeled a filmy blouse printed with camellias—a blouse I wanted to wear right *now,* because it made me feel pretty instead of pudgy, and graceful instead of awkward and off-balance. "This is the in-between stage."

"Let me guess," I teased. "Josh has become a pregnancy expert."

"Nah. I have. Google is my friend."

I stopped in the act of pulling on a stretchy red tee that promised to show off my growing bump in an entirely satisfactory fashion. "Really? You've been looking things up?"

"I have. I may have mentioned that I wanted this baby, and that I wanted you. If I haven't, let me mention it now."

"Huh." It was a thought I could live with.

I wore my favorite outfit out of there—the flowered blouse and skinny jeans, though I craved kicky ankle boots to an unhealthy degree—and felt all the thrill of actually needing maternity clothes and wearing them, and of knowing that Hemi was just about as excited about it as I was.

"Next stop, lingerie," he said. "Save the best for last, eh."

"I have to admit," I said, "that's necessary. I don't have anything left that's pretty and fits. We're in crisis mode."

One second, I was talking to him. The next, I was talking to the air. I turned around, and he was staring at a store window. I had the only man in existence who window-shopped more than I did.

It was a high-end boutique, and *not* a maternity one.

"What?" I asked, circling around back to him. "You get inspired again?"

"Nah." Just like that, he had my hand and was pulling me into the shop. "Or yeh. One or the other."

"What?" I was still saying, but Hemi was already approaching the sales clerk.

"That dress in the window," he told her, and within two minutes, I was in a fitting room again, with Hemi zipping up the back of the most non-maternity dress you could imagine.

A beaded, sleeveless sheath in peacock blue, to be exact, ending in a scalloped hem four inches above my knee and with no room whatsoever for any future growth in the belly area.

"This would be fine," I said, "for about two more weeks." All the same, I couldn't help running a hand over the iridescent beads that were laid out in a pattern as intricate as lace. "Although I'll admit that I feel most deliciously mermaid-like."

"Mm," Hemi said. "Right, then." Just like that, he was unzipping me again, and I couldn't help a pang of disappointment. My beautiful mermaid tail, disappearing off me just because I happened to be growing an extra person. Well, it was over eight hundred dollars, and it was ridiculous.

I know you've guessed already. He bought it. Yes, he did. I didn't get a vote. "I don't have shoes, though," I objected weakly as he pulled out his credit card yet again and I tried to be bothered by that. "I didn't bring anything nearly dressy enough to New Zealand, clearly."

"I'll do the shoes." He didn't look up from the card slip he was signing in his black, forceful scrawl. "You do the lingerie. Bendon, about six doors down. I'll meet you there. High heels OK, or will they bother you? Balance and all?"

Oh, man. High *heels*. I'd been bicycling to work and wearing jeans for weeks. Now I had a mermaid dress, and I was getting spectacular shoes, too. I just knew it. "Unless you're making me walk," I said, "they won't bother me. If we're talking about me feeling do-me-right-now-please-sir sexy, and you looking at me and thinking the same thing, they *really* won't bother me."

His gaze heated up by about ten degrees. "That's what we're talking about."

"Then," I said, trying and failing to keep my breath from coming faster, "high heels work."

He didn't smile. He just gave me his best dark smolder and said, "Go buy lingerie, then. Make it good."

mermaid out of water

♡

Hemi

If I'd been the man I was at twenty-two, I'd have spent half that afternoon thinking about what I was going to be doing to Hope tonight, and the other half wondering how I was going to leave her again tomorrow.

I wasn't that man anymore, though, and I didn't waste time thinking about things that hadn't happened yet. I moved on, knowing I would be doing whatever it took to get what I wanted. The hardest thing of all was waiting, your future out of your hands. I'd done hard things before, though, and I'd do this.

For right now, I bought shoes and thought of Hope choosing lingerie to fit her new shape, and about taking her out in that blue dress and taking her home again. I rang the Langham Hotel and made a few special requests. And then I went to find her, paid for her purchases without looking at them after she whispered, "I want to surprise you" and blushed pink, and took her to the hotel.

She walked into the suite on the tenth floor, took in the vase of red roses and bowl of strawberries on the coffee table, looked out the enormous wall of windows at the park, the city, and the Sky Tower, and said, "Somehow, I'm not even surprised. Very nice, Mr. Te Mana."

"We'll meet Violet at seven-thirty," I said. "Time off from me until then."

"Because you have some work to do. Which is fine," she went on when I would have said something. What, I wasn't sure. I *did* have to work. Work paid for the suite, and the dress, and the shoes. Work paid for everything, and beyond that—I couldn't be somebody I wasn't.

When I didn't answer, she plucked a strawberry out of the bowl and said, "You spent all day yesterday with us, and most of today with me. I needed some time and attention from you, and you've given it to me. I don't need all your focus all the time. For one thing, it'd be exhausting."

"Well," I said, "there's that."

"So I'm going swimming. They have a pool, did you know? And I have a new suit. You just bought it. I'm telling you as a matter of information." She went into the bedroom, where the bellman had stashed our luggage and purchases. "In case you wanted to know."

"That's nice," I said, keeping it bland. "There are some different herbal teas in the kitchen there as well. I had them stock up for you."

Did I go down to the pool and swim with her in her new suit, the way she expected me to? I did not. I did have work to do, and besides—not taking the bait would make her wonder. It would keep her on edge, and that wasn't a bad thing.

Last night had been for reconnection, for tenderness and love and everything we needed to say to each other. Tonight was for everything else I needed from her, and everything she needed from me. And tonight had started the moment we'd bought that dress.

She left the room quietly, and she came back in quietly. There was nothing spiky or punishing about her silence, though, no angry sighs or jerky movements. She took a shower, made her tea, went into the bedroom, and shut the door. And if I opened that door quietly a couple hours later and found her lying on her side, fast asleep with her book beside her? If I had to cover her with a blanket, ease the book out from under her hand, and set it on the bedside table—well, I had to do heaps of things.

She appeared in the doorway to the lounge at six-thirty, blinking, her hair in a wild cloud around her head.

"I'd ask what happened," she said, still sounding fuzzy, "but I think I know. Worn out on the luxury of spending your money. How long do I have to get beautiful?"

"Forty-five minutes."

She sighed, tugged at the sash of the hotel dressing gown that was swallowing her up, and said, "Then I hope you don't need it, because that bathroom is going to be occupied for the next forty-four minutes and thirty seconds. I've got a long way to go."

"No worries," I said. "I get beautiful with very little effort. Already almost done."

She punched my shoulder as if I'd been her mate Nathan, laughed at me, and flounced off with as much attitude as a petite blonde in an enormous terry dressing gown could manage. And I smiled and went back to work and guessed she'd be worth the wait.

The woman who walked with me into the Sugar Club an hour later wasn't wearing a dressing gown. Instead, she was carrying off a deliciously short beaded dress with a demure neckline in front and a keyhole back that showed a devastating amount of silky bare skin, and doing it in style. I had my hand resting lightly on the small of her back, guiding her or putting my stamp on her, whichever way you wanted to look at it, and she was as aware of that hand as if she were already lying underneath me. Her hips were swaying with all the rhythm inspired by four-inch heels with the most wicked ankle straps that ever set a man's imagination alight, her hair was up in a clip that exposed the nape of her neck and left a few tendrils floating free, and all I could think about was where I wanted to bite her first.

I couldn't even be sorry we were meeting Violet for dinner. Some of my best times with Hope had come after torturously long restaurant meals during which I'd watched her pupils dilate and her color rise and had pretended I wasn't seeing it. There was something to be said for waiting, and tonight? Hope was going to be waiting, and I was going to be enjoying making her do it.

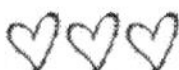

Hope

I walked, slightly in front of Hemi, into an intimate space decorated in sumptuous Art Deco style and full of sumptuously decorated people. We were on the fifty-third floor of the Sky Tower, in a circular room that was nothing but windows from floor to ceiling. Below us, the lights of the city provided a glittering panorama, while the velvety black of the harbor was punctuated by the swooping arcs of the Harbour Bridge. Way above my pay grade, as usual.

Part of me thought, *No way am I sitting by that window with a pane of glass between me and fifty-three stories down,* and the other part felt Hemi's hand on my back, knew why he had to touch me, and put a little work into my walk. Not hard to do when you're wearing killer heels and a mermaid gown.

I'd never been the kind of woman men turned to look at. What I'd told Karen was true: that sort of thing was reserved for the tall and striking. But tonight, men were looking. Maybe it was Hemi's magnetism, because that force radiated darker and more powerfully than ever from him tonight. He'd complemented his usual tailored black jacket and trousers with a dark gray shirt and black tie, and let's just say it worked. He looked like the Lord of the Underworld, and I'd bet that any woman who got the benefit of that smoldering stare tonight would be willing to go right there with him. I knew I was.

Or it might not be Hemi at all. It could be the way I was filling out this rockin' dress. A 32-almost-D makes a powerful statement of its own, I was discovering, and tonight, it was making it loud and clear.

Or maybe, just maybe, it was confidence. That was the thought that had me working it even harder. Maybe it was a woman who'd driven in city traffic today and was going to be doing it again, whose bare arms were firm and toned from swimming, and who could give Hemi Te Mana as good as she got.

Like when I'd opened the bag from the shoe store in the bathroom an hour earlier, for example, and had poked my head out the door again and said, "OK. No fair."

"Pardon?" It was said with all his usual calm, but I could see the smile he was suppressing.

I held up the low brown boots, all buckles, studs, and Western tooling. I wanted to put them on right *now*, except that I had some even better shoes here. "Dirty play, buddy, reading my mind."

"Mm. Using too many of your forty-five minutes, though. Wouldn't want to keep me waiting."

"Now, see, that's where you're wrong." He got my best wide-open eyes. "I'd *love* to keep you waiting. And then knock your socks off. In fact, that's what I plan to do. You wait."

In the end, of course, he knocked *mine* off. When I opened the door at last and swayed my way over to him, putting everything I had into it, he shut his laptop, looked me over from head to toe, sighed, and said, "Oh, yeh. That's my beautiful girl." And then he upped the stakes. He reached for something on the chair beside him, said, "You left this behind," and opened a velvet box to reveal the bracelet he'd bought me nine months earlier.

A cuff of sapphires and diamonds in endless undulating waves, all the glory of the sea in their sparkle. My 'I love you' present, which I hadn't wanted to bring with me to New Zealand, because it would have hurt too much to see it. And besides, it wasn't the sort of thing you wore waitressing or digging the garden.

I was clearly going to be wearing it tonight, because Hemi pulled me to stand between his legs, fastened the bracelet around my wrist, and said, "Still needs something, though."

"Oh, yeah, because this isn't enough." I tried my best for nonchalance and couldn't pull it off, so I abandoned the effort and went for sincerity instead. "Thank you for bringing it. And by the way—I love you."

That lightening of his eyes, and he was pulling out *another* box and opening that.

"Hemi," I said helplessly as he pulled me down onto his knee.

"Nice, eh."

"Nice" didn't begin to cover it. Four separate lozenge-shaped diamonds had been placed with their points touching to form the petal that made up each glittering stud of the earrings, while a single large sapphire fell in a teardrop below. They were stunning, they were spectacular, and they were entirely over the top. Exactly like Hemi.

"They're flowers," I said.

"They are. Just like you." He fastened them in my earlobes, then stood up, dislodging me, gave me a little swat on the bottom, and said, "Let's go."

He definitely did *not* play fair.

But you see why I might have been feeling pretty when I walked over to join Violet, who was already seated at a table and looking me over appraisingly. Perils of hanging around with fashion designers, but this time, I'd been dressed by Hemi Te Mana, and nobody was going to find anything wrong with that.

Hemi was embracing Violet, kissing her cheek, and the maître d' was pulling out a chair for me, but I said, "I'd rather not sit by the window, thanks."

He didn't react, just pulled out the chair on the aisle, but Hemi said, "Surely you'd like the view."

"No, thank you." I seated myself and set my tiny black clutch down on the table beside me. "I wouldn't. Too much glass, and too far down. Hi, Violet. It's great to see you. In fact, you're one of my very favorite people right now. Awesome hatchet job."

She was smiling. "A bit of a change in this one since the last time I saw her, eh, Hemi."

"Sadly," he said, making me gasp. "She's got even stroppier, as you see. Talks back, tells me what she will and won't do, runs off to En Zed without me, takes over my granddad and twists him round her finger. The list goes on."

"Mm," Violet said. "Sounds like wife material to me. When's the divorce?"

"Two and a half weeks. Still got her dress?"

"Too right I have, and Karen's as well. Looks like I'm going to have to let Hope's out, though, if you don't get your skates on and marry her fast. And if that's just the benefit of too much Kiwi cooking," she told me, "sorry about that. I never did have any tact. But those aren't the measurements we took."

"Could be you'll be doing that." Hemi's hand was on my shoulder, his thumb stroking over the back of my neck. "Congratulate me, Vi. I'm going to be a father."

So all that was very nice, and so was the tiny, perfect steak that my knife went through like butter, and the carrots with a hazelnut crumb, and the velvety-smooth baked aubergine with yoghurt and feta and mango that made me have to close my eyes to appreciate it fully. All the good things, and, boy, was I enjoying them. My potato days were behind me for sure.

I wasn't even left out of the conversation, to my surprise. I'd have thought Hemi and Violet would talk shop, but the one time she said, "So. Lots of rumors going round about your Paris show," Hemi looked at her blandly, said, "Always rumors," and changed the subject. He really *didn't* talk outside the company, then. To anybody but me.

They talked about their families instead, which was why I

was in the midst of describing Koro directing Hemi's garden labor to a much-amused Violet when a woman walked up to our table, the energy field pulsed, and I stopped cold.

Hemi got still for a split second, then stood up, his face its hardest, coldest mask. Violet said, "Anika. What a not at all pleasant surprise."

Hemi said nothing. He and Anika stood there looking at each other, the connection between them as strong and dark as if they were fighting some internal duel, all the more powerful for being invisible.

She didn't look like her pictures. She looked better. *Stunning* didn't begin to cover it. She was wearing a red jersey dress, cut low in front and slit nearly to the hip on one side. As high as my heels were, hers were higher. And if somebody had wanted to create a woman that men *would* turn their heads to look at, surely he'd have created Anika. Long, lustrous dark hair falling to the center of her back, aristocratic bone structure that could slice a man in two, velvet-brown eyes, and a mouth that promised everything. And let's not talk about her figure, because it's too depressing.

I could see why Hemi had been attracted. More than that—I could see why he'd been bewitched. Because it was more than her looks.

Confidence. Attitude. Presence. Those were the words. If Hemi sucked the air out of a room, Anika did that and more. The two of them together—that was serious wattage. That was blow-a-fuse power.

Anika spoke first, in the end. But then, Hemi could outwait anybody.

"If you're going to go into half the shops in Newmarket," she said, "I'm going to hear about it."

"You could hear about it," Hemi said, "without turning

up. Can't imagine why you'd make the journey, or go to all the trouble of discovering where I'd booked, either."

Anika didn't answer that. She looked instead at me. One quick scan up and down, and I was summed up and dismissed. Her eyes flicked back to Hemi's. "You're joking."

Hemi hadn't moved. Now, he got even more still, pulling all his power into his body in a way that was truly intimidating to watch.

"Are you going to ask me to sit down?" Anika asked.

"No," Hemi said.

She smiled, something purely feline. And then she pulled out the chair beside Violet, sank gracefully into it, and said conversationally, "It's very nearly a crime."

Hemi sat again himself, but Anika didn't look at him. She was still looking at me. "How old are you, darling? Nineteen?"

I said, "No," and left it there. I might not be able to manage scary, but I didn't have to do cowed.

She glanced at my water glass. "Not old enough to drink, either? Or maybe you think the innocent bit will keep him enraptured." She leaned forward slightly, compelling me to do the same, a compulsion I resisted even as I felt her hypnotic power trying to draw me in. "It won't," she told me, dropping her voice so low, I had to strain to hear it. "He's trying to tell himself he wants this, that he wants to lose the dark side, that if he could only leave his demons behind, he'd be happy. He can't, and he won't. Some demons are too strong to be defeated. You don't know what you're getting into."

"Yes," I said. "I do."

Hemi said, "You need to leave. Now."

The tone of his voice would have had anybody else

scurrying for the exit. It practically did it to *me*. Anika paid it exactly no attention. Instead, she held a hand across the table to me and turned it over, flexing her palm so the underside of her wrist was fully visible.

Maybe I was supposed to notice the fineness of her bones, or the graceful, tapering length of her fingers. Except that she said, "Do you see the scar?"

I did. A faint white line interrupting the perfect bronze of her skin. She held out the other hand, then, and showed that to me, too. "Do you know how I got these?"

Hemi was on his feet again. "No."

Anika ignored him. "Ask your fiancé," she told me. "Ask him what kind of a husband ties his wife so tightly and for so long that he leaves permanent scars. Ask him what else he did to me that night. Ask me why I loved him anyway. Ask yourself why you do, and how he sucked you in. Why he chose you, a woman without a family to look after her, to ask inconvenient questions, to give her somewhere to run. Ask yourself if that's the life you want."

All the nausea I'd been spared for the past week was roiling inside me. The blood had left my head, and I felt so faint, all I wanted was to put my head between my knees. And my hands over my ears.

I didn't do either thing. I said, "I know who Hemi is. I know everything he is."

"Do you?" she asked. "Do you really? Do you know I came to see him just a couple weeks ago? Do you know that I begged? Did he tell you that?" She must have seen the involuntary widening of my eyes, because she smiled, a tinge of sadness to it, and said, "Thought not. He had me on my knees. His favorite position for a woman, but then, you know that. He made me beg, and then he laughed at me and turfed me out. Deserted me one more time."

"Shock," Violet said. "Considering how you treated him."

I expected Anika to turn on her, to strike like a cobra. Instead, she said, "But then, Vi, all you knew was what Hemi told you. That's all anybody knew. Nobody was in that apartment but the two of us—unless Hemi issued invitations—and if I was damaged afterwards, if I acted out? I had my reasons. Not all my scars are on the outside. And I *will* show them. If I've asked Hemi for help, it's because he's owed it to me for years. Before, I had no way of getting it. Now I do. Call it justice."

I asked, "Are you finished?" My voice, somehow, was ice-cold, even though I was a quaking mess inside.

"I'm finished. I've done what I could." She stood up, looked at me a moment more, and then, before I could react, bent and kissed my cheek, her perfume, all Oriental topnotes on a musky base, swirling down inside me, overwhelming the light floral scent I wore. "Be careful," she told me, straightening up again and touching my face, a soft caress.

I was on my feet, too, standing as if pulled by a string. My feet weren't my own, and my hand wasn't, either. It was rising as if somebody else were in control of it, drawing back.

It didn't land. Hemi's iron fingers closed around my wrist instead, so quickly I didn't even notice him moving.

Anika said, "My. The kitten has claws. Maybe you'll last longer than I think. Take my advice, though. Get a very good attorney. I wish I had."

With that, she turned on one graceful heel and walked away. And every man in the room watched her go.

how forever feels

♡

Hemi

I was shutting down. I didn't want to do it, but I couldn't stop it happening, like the hatches slamming closed on a submarine before it dove. Preparing to go underwater, to run silent and deep.

"Well," Violet said, "that was special. Bitch."

Hope laughed, nothing but an angry puff of air. Not the reaction I'd been expecting. "Why didn't you let me hit her?" she asked me. "I was *dying* to hit her."

When I didn't answer, she said in a completely different voice, "Pay the check and take me home."

Vi's head went up, and so did mine. I stared a Hope for a long second, and she stared straight back at me. Then I lifted a hand for the waiter.

The long ride down in the lift was a silent affair. Out on the street again, I hailed a taxi and told Vi, "Yours." My voice sounded rusty, and I realized it was the first thing I'd said in some time.

Vi reached up, took my face in her two hands, and said, "Trust comes hard. Don't I know it. Trust Hope, mate. You can do it."

When I didn't answer, she sighed, turned to Hope, gave her a hug and kiss, and said, "Awesome, that's all. I want you on my team."

"You've already got me there," Hope said. "Thanks for everything."

Vi nodded. "Anytime you want that dress. And I mean *any* time. But I want to watch you wearing it."

"I want that, too," Hope said. "I'll let you know."

Vi got into her taxi, and as it pulled away, Hope looked at me and said, "That's enough."

"Pardon?" Another thing I hadn't expected to hear.

"Brooding's one thing. This is something else. I'm starting to get insulted. You've got things to tell me, and you need to start."

I didn't. I couldn't. She said, "Right, then. I'm mad. Six months ago—*three* months ago—I'd have stomped off. I'm not doing that tonight. I'm going to stand right here on the sidewalk and let you know that if you think there's anything you can tell me about your past that's going to make me believe I don't know the man I see, you're wrong. And what's worse, you're insulting my perception and my judgment and my commitment and so many other things, I don't even want to list them, because it'll just make me madder. So tell me."

"Anika already did."

Hope snorted. "I know what 'manipulative' means. Let me guess. She has many faces. Tonight, I got to see the vulnerable, wounded one, because that woman will do and say whatever she thinks will work. You aren't just ashamed because of something you did. You're ashamed because you fell for her, and because you let her twist you around. You feel wrong and sick and dark because she wanted you to lose control over yourself, and as soon as you did, she was the one controlling you. That scared you to death. And by the way, you didn't tell me she'd showed up recently. That's another thing I'm mad about. So you pick. Start somewhere. Start off by telling me about her showing up, maybe. That'll be easier."

I ran a hand over my hair. Every muscle in my body felt stiff. "You're getting cold. You're not wearing enough to have this talk here."

"So have the valet bring your car around, get me nice and warm, and then tell me."

I did. I started as soon as we pulled out of the SkyCity drive onto Hobson Street. I didn't put off unpleasant things, and I didn't duck reality. Not anymore.

"She turned up," I said. "A couple weeks ago. She did what you saw tonight. She was wounded. Hurting. She did get on her knees, begging me to settle, begging me to give her something. Anything. I didn't believe her, and I didn't do it."

"And you didn't tell me." Hope's voice was matter of fact, not angry.

"I was planning to. Tomorrow morning, maybe, on the drive home. I didn't want to spoil it. She's like . . ."

"Poison. Or battery acid. Eating away at all the beautiful things, the sweet things, making you think you can't trust anything or anybody, including yourself."

"Yeh." I felt exhausted, suddenly. "She wants my money. She thinks she has a right."

"Except that it wasn't three years."

"No. It wasn't. But maybe she thinks she has a right

anyway." There. I'd admitted it, or close.

"Or maybe *you* think she does." She picked up on it straight away, of course. "Tell me why."

I was stopped at a red light, and I sat staring at it, not wanting to see Hope's face. "She always wanted to push it further," I said reluctantly. "But maybe that's just my excuse."

"You make the fewest excuses of any man I've ever known. Tell me."

The light changed, and I drove. "The night she got those scars." I forced the words out, dragging the memory from its locked box, pushing and shoving it ruthlessly to the surface. "She wanted me to . . ." I stopped, breathed, and said it. "Share her. It was the last thing I wanted to do, but she said it was her fantasy. She pushed for weeks. And finally, I did it. Maybe I thought I'd lose her otherwise. That was how it felt. But I never should have done it. Never."

"How many guys?" She sounded sick, which was exactly the way I felt.

"Two." I pulled into the hotel garage, parked, and turned the car off, but I didn't get out, and neither did Hope. "People she'd met online, she said, but now I wonder if it was more than that. It got… out of hand so fast, and I didn't stop it nearly soon enough. I didn't know if I should, and I was excited, too. That's the truth." The hard truth. The sick truth.

"And what did she say the next day?" Hope asked, which, again, wasn't the question I'd expected.

"Said it hurt, and it scared her, and it was too much, and she wanted to do it again. Later. When she… felt better. She had her wrists bandaged for a week, and every time I saw those bandages… seeing those scars tonight . . ." I didn't go on. I couldn't.

"And you never did it again."

"Bloody hell." I scrubbed my hands over my face as if I could scrub the memory clean. The worst night of my life, when I'd let myself down, and worse. When I'd let my wife down. When I'd done things no man should do. "No, I never did it again. Three weeks later, I heard that I'd got the internship in the States, and from then on, it was all rows, and then I left. When she stopped writing, though, when she didn't come… I thought—of course that happened. Of course she didn't trust me anymore. Of course she didn't want me."

"No. She was wrong."

"So was I." I'd never said it. I said it now.

"All right. So were you. And after that, you said you could never lose control again. Because you were terrified of what you'd do."

I didn't have to answer that. Hope knew it already.

"Did she tell you to stop?" she asked next. "That night? Did she ask you to make it stop?"

"No. But I should've known."

"Did you tie the ropes?"

I didn't want to go back to this. I wanted to lock that box again and throw away the key. "No. But I let it happen."

"Do you want to know what I think?"

I laughed, though it wasn't funny. "No. Yes. And you're going to tell me anyway."

"I am." She sat straight as a soldier and did it. "I think you found out that you enjoyed domination, but you don't enjoy pain. Not real, hard-core pain. I think she does. I think she craves it, and she thought she'd get it from you, and when she didn't, she told you it was because you weren't man enough. I think she went way further than you wanted to go, and since she knew she could use that to hurt you, she brought it up tonight. I'll bet somebody's doing those things to her now, and I'll bet you know it."

"Yeh. I do. She said as much, that night I went to see her."

"And she tried to get you to go down that path again, because it had hurt you to go before."

I didn't answer, and Hope said, "And did you?"

"No." The word was an explosion. "No."

"That's right. You came home to me, and you needed it sweet. You needed it gentle. You needed to remind yourself that you weren't that man anymore. You wanted to tell yourself that you were hard, but you weren't brutal. You wanted to believe that you could love somebody. That you could protect her from anything, even from yourself."

I was wrung out. I was shattered. "How do you know?"

"Hemi." She'd turned in her seat to face me, her face as urgent as the hand she put on my cheek. "I know because I know you. I know because I see you. I know because I love you."

♡♡♡

Hope

The evening didn't end up the way I'd thought it would. It was so much more.

When we went into the hotel, Hemi had his arm around me, and I had both of mine around him, not caring who saw or what they thought of us. And when we got into our room, he grabbed me.

The kiss was hot and wild, out of control from the second his mouth closed over mine. There was no calculation in the way he devoured me, or any control at all in the way he shoved a hand up under my skirt and got hold of my hip.

His fingers dug in, and I didn't complain. I had my hands around his head, pulling him into me, but despite his urgency, his own hand was behind my head when he backed me straight up against the wall.

And there was absolutely nothing civilized about the way he ripped off the black underwear I'd chosen so carefully, or the way he spun me around.

His fingers were in my hair, unfastening the clip, and a metallic *ting* told me it had landed on the stone floor. My hair was falling out of its knot, and then his hands were at the back of my neck, unfastening the hooks holding my dress closed. And controlled, deliberate Hemi Te Mana's hands were fumbling.

"Shit." It was nothing more than an explosion of breath. I felt the release of the fabric collar at my nape, then the coolness on my skin as he yanked the zipper down, and I shivered. His hands were shoving the delicate fabric roughly down and over my hips, and I didn't care. Not about the dress, and not about anything else. He needed this, and so did I.

Hemi talked during sex. Always. Now, he was silent, his ragged breath and my own the only sounds in the quiet room. My bra fell to the floor, and his hands were all over me.

I had my forearms against the wall, and I was surrendering, falling down, falling deep. One of his hands was between my legs, the other one on my breast, not rough even now. He was remembering how sensitive I was, taking care of me even in the midst of his nearly unbearable excitement. But the second his fingers gently pinched my nipple, a dark shock ran straight to my core, my back was arching, and I was moaning.

"Shit," he said again. "You're so wet. I have to… I have to …"

"Do it. Please. *Now.*" It was almost a sob.

He spun me again, and my back hit the wall. His hands were at his belt, fumbling again, and I was there, helping him. I was naked, dressed only in black fuck-me-now heels and a barbaric display of jewelry, and Hemi was fully dressed, and I didn't care. There was only one thing that mattered.

One hand went under my bottom and lifted me straight off my feet, and the other was in my hair, tugging my head back. I wrapped my legs around his waist, put a hand down, and helped guide him inside me.

He entered me in one hard thrust, and I let out a choked cry. I'd been expecting it, and still, it was nearly too much.

He stopped dead. I could sense his pulsing energy, his unbearable tension, as clearly as if I'd been in his skin. "Hurting you," he said hoarsely.

"No." The need clawed at me. "Never. Do it. Hard."

He groaned, and then he did it. Hard, and strong, and savage. There was nothing but ferocity in the hips that pumped against mine, and no control at all in the hand that pulled at my hair.

He didn't kiss me. He didn't say a word. But he told me everything. How desperately he desired me, how frantically he'd needed to be inside me. How only I could fix this, could soothe the hurt burning in him. He took me hard and deep, and I took him the same way, and when my orgasm came on me with the force of a locomotive, I honestly thought I wasn't going to be able to stand it.

When it hit me, it felt exactly like that train. Like a shock wave, slamming into me, knocking me senseless. And Hemi doing the same thing.

Too much. Too hard. Too deep. Everything.

♡♡♡

Hemi

I thought I was going to pass out. I was sure Hope was. I shouldn't have done it, and I couldn't have helped it.

Afterwards, I stayed where I was for a long time, and she stayed with me, her hands on my shoulders, holding me close, not asking for a thing. At last, though, my arm relaxed, and I supported her as she slid down the wall.

And still I held her. Even after her feet hit the floor, I didn't let her go. I couldn't. I stood, still pressing her between my body and the wall, while my head came to rest against my forearm and I trembled and shook, while I tried to stop it and couldn't. I needed to move, to let her move as well, but I couldn't.

It ended, of course. Every moment did. Life moved on, whether you wished it wouldn't or you couldn't wait for it to happen. In the end, it was Hope who took off my jacket and tie, Hope who unbuttoned my shirt and pulled it off, then dealt with the rest of my clothes. She unfastened her own shoes and left them where they lay, then stripped off her bracelet and earrings and dropped them onto the hall table. And when we were both naked, she took my hand and led me into the bedroom, pulled back the duvet, drew me down with her, and wrapped her arms around me.

"This is how I love you," she told me, and if I'd ever thought a gentle woman couldn't be fierce, I'd been wrong. "This is how I hold you, and this is the way I'll be holding you forever. In my arms when I can, and in my heart always. *Always*. You'll never lose me, because I'll never let go."

I did my best to control myself. When my chest began to tighten, I called on the self-discipline of a lifetime. When the tears pricked behind my eyelids, I did my utmost to shut them down. That was what I did. That was who I was.

I failed. My chest heaved, and a ragged, ugly sound came out. I sobbed once, and again. Twice more, and then I was rolling away, onto my back, away from her. I was breathing hard, squeezing my eyes shut against the tears, and feeling them trickling, hot, shameful, and unstoppable, down my temples.

"It's all right. You're all right." Hope's voice was soft and sure, her hand was stroking over my hair, and she was kissing my cheeks, my eyelids. Kissing the tears away, taking them into herself. Sharing my pain, accepting my burden, letting me know that she would help me carry it. Now and forever.

I'd always been alone. I'd known that was the way it had to be. But I wasn't alone anymore.

I'd have died for Hope. I knew it as deeply and as surely as I'd ever known anything. I'd have killed for her, too. I'd have done anything it took to keep her safe.

But the thing I'd never expected, that I'd never dreamed could be possible…

She'd have done the same for me.

attitude adjustments

♡

Hemi

Anybody would have thought that I'd have flown back to New York with Hope at my side. I know I'd thought it. The only problem was, she wouldn't go.

"Too bloody right I don't understand," I said. We were driving to Katikati the next morning, and nobody could have called me cool today. "You said I didn't share. I've shared now, and you can't say I haven't. You said you weren't strong enough to stand up to me, that I wanted to keep you weak. Here you are, though, driving to Auckland and driving us home, and here I am in the bloody passenger seat letting you do it. There you were last night as well. All of that."

I didn't go into detail, because some of those details were more than embarrassing to recall. A general summation would have to do. "You can't tell me now that you don't know you're strong enough. You have to know I realize you are. You know you've got me wrapped around your finger, too. Ask Koro if you doubt it. I know he'd be happy to tell you. So why the hell not? What in the world are you waiting for? What are you making *me* wait for?"

"You're yelling," she said, her hands tightening on the wheel.

That brought me up short. I didn't yell. Well, maybe.

"Right," I said after a moment and a couple deep breaths. "I've stopped. Why not?"

Her eyes didn't leave the road. "I love you more than ever, and *you* know *that.* But I told Sonya I'd stay at least three more weeks."

"Bugger Sonya."

"Best boss I've ever had. The most confidence I've ever had, too. And, yes, I know I'm a waitress, but you have to start somewhere. I know Karen needs me, too, but . . ."

"No," I was forced to admit, "I don't think so, not in the way you think. Could be good for her to be without you for a few weeks. Takes you for granted, doesn't she. Besides, she needs to know she can count on me, and listen to me, too. I'm tougher than you are, and she needs that. You may be good at holding my feet to the fire. You aren't good at holding hers."

She took a moment to answer. "I'm going to concede that you could be right. And, yes, I get that this is what you were saying not very long ago. That I needed to let go of some of that control myself and learn to rely on somebody else. You aren't the only one with those issues. That's what *I've* learned, maybe. Or at least I'm learning it. Not easy to change. We both know that. That's why I'm here working on it. But there's Koro, too."

I didn't answer, because I didn't have an answer to that,

and after a minute, she went on. "He's old, Hemi. I know he seems so strong, but he's not going to be around forever."

"I know that." I debated telling her that she could overtake the tourist driver ahead of us, then abandoned the idea. Why, so we could get home two minutes faster, and I could leave her two minutes sooner? "But you aren't the only one who can look after him, and I need you, too."

She didn't seem to realize the immensity of that statement, because all she said was, "And I need *you.* And, yes, I know I'm not the only one available to help him—far from it—and I'm not part of your family yet. But with me, don't you see—he feels useful. He's helping *me,* and he knows it. He's a teacher, and a mentor, and a… privilege."

"You were born to be Maori. You do realize that."

That surprised a laugh from her. "What?"

"Only a Maori would say that looking after her granddad was a privilege. A pakeha? No."

"Maybe you just haven't known any pakeha well enough."

"Could be." I was losing, I could tell. "But using Koro? And you say *I* play dirty."

She sobered. "I'm not playing. And if you told me it was do or die, that I had to come home or forget it, I'd do it, even though I'd know I shouldn't. I hope you won't tell me that. It's a few more weeks, and then Koro gets his cast off, and I'll know I did everything I could and so did you, and I'll come home. Besides, I just keep feeling that it's… right. That it's necessary."

It wasn't defeat, I told myself. It was just a change of tactics. "Then I'll see you when I come back for the divorce. Only about two weeks to go, and this time, I'm going to be there to watch it happen. To make *sure* it happens."

"I'd say that's a great idea." She was clearly relieved to be moving on. "And I'll also say that I'll be counting the days until then."

"I'd like you to go with me." Something I wouldn't have said a week ago. Something I wouldn't even have *thought.* I'd wanted to keep everything to do with Anika in that locked box, but like it or not, the box was open. Time to face it.

Hope took her eyes off the road for a split second, then hastily resumed her laser focus on the sparse traffic. "Really? Oh, wait, this is some more of my negotiation practice. Here I go, then. I'd love to be there with you. I'd love to watch your marriage end and help you put the 'Done' stamp on it. And if Anika shows up, I'd *especially* love it. You might have to hold me back, though, because I could jump her. Fair warning."

"Like I said. Born to be Maori."

♡♡♡

All too soon, I was on the jet with Karen, trying to move on from thoughts of Hope and Koro, from the way Hope had kissed me goodbye and how she'd clung to me for those final seconds.

That was enough of that. I needed to get stuck into my work now, but I had something else to do first. Multitasking wasn't my best skill, but it was time I started developing it.

Karen was stretched out on a couch in the rear of the jet, watching a movie. When I stood over her and tapped my own ear, she paused the film, tugged her headphones off, and swung herself up to sit. "What?"

I sat down at the other end of the couch. "Ground rules."

She heaved a sigh. "How did I guess. Chastity belts are illegal, you know."

"Since you've gone straight there," I said, "what's important isn't whether or not you have sex. It's whether you're safe doing it. In all ways."

Her eyes narrowed. "Yeah, right. You hate the whole idea. So does Hope. There is nothing morally superior about virginity. That's paternalism."

I chose to leave the lofty debate for another time. When Hope was here to have it, preferably. "Reckon we'd better talk about birth control and STDs as well, then," I said instead, going for the part I had some expertise in, "because if you're counting on him to take care of those things, you're counting wrong. Condoms."

"Great." She'd wrapped her arms around herself. Not as confident as she wanted me to believe. I knew all about that, too. "How about embarrassing me a little more?"

Seemed I hadn't forgotten everything about being sixteen after all. "If you're too embarrassed to say the word 'condom,' or to buy them, or to discuss them with him beforehand, you're not ready to have sex, full stop. And if he says he won't wear one, run away. Which would lead to the point. What we *hate* is you doing something you're not ready for, or feeling pressured to do it."

Geez, I sounded like a dad. Not like *my* dad, of course. Somebody else's.

"Maybe I'd be pressuring *him,*" she said. "Did you think of that?"

"How would that be any better?"

That one took her aback, I saw with satisfaction. She finally rallied enough to ask, "Did you win the gold medal in Debate Club or what?"

"More or less. Right, then. Concrete details. You want to go out with somebody? Hope says you're allowed, and it's her call. A group thing, or a date."

"Nobody has a *date* anymore. You just go out."

"Fine. You go out. I want you to bring him to meet me first, Charles will be driving you, and you're to tell Inez or me where you're going and what you're doing."

She snorted. "Wow, how spontaneous can you get?"

I didn't smile, but I came close. "Not spontaneous at all. Three more years, though, and you'll be at University. Something to cling to, eh. Meanwhile, you can take it or leave it."

Her eyes definitely rolled. "What a hard choice."

"On to something you'll like better, then. You've never had your friends at the apartment. You're free to do that, you know. It's your house, too. A girlfriend to… sleep over, or whatever you call it. Friends after school. All of that." At home, where Inez or I would be around.

I got some serious side-eye. "You sure about that? They could eat on the coffee table, you know. They could turn up the volume on the TV. They could take off their shoes in an unapproved area. All sorts of evil deeds."

"They could. And as you'd be the hostess, I imagine you'd like to make sure the state of your room doesn't embarrass you, and that you clean up after your guests and help make them comfortable. More Maori rules for you. Hospitality, and the state of your home when you offer it. Most people are more comfortable knowing what the rules are, too. And do not tell me Inez can do the cleaning up," I added. "It's not her job."

"Hey. *I'm* not the one with servants. *I'm* not the rich person."

"No, you're just the one who was acting like it until you went to help Koro and looked after him so well. I'm thinking that could've felt better to you and made you feel more at home there, but you tell me."

She was silent for so long, I thought she was going to give me the cold shoulder entirely. Finally, she said, "I get why you're so good at business and everything. What am I supposed to say?"

I smiled. That was enough of that. "Want a secret for when you'll be making your way to the top?"

"Well, yeah. Obviously."

"You don't have to get the other person to say that you're right and they're wrong. You don't even have to get them to admit it to themselves. Nobody wants to lose face like that. You just have to get them to do what you think is best."

She considered that. "Huh. Kind of manipulative."

"You could say that, or you could call it human nature. Besides, you aren't going to be focusing on what you want personally. It's not about you, it's about the best outcome, and that may not even be an idea you came up with. Could be somebody else's idea entirely, in fact. Take what I just said. Some of that came from Hope, some from Inez, and some from me. And where were we all trying to get? Not to have you cleaning up after yourself, because Inez *could* do that. She could do it more easily than we'll be able to get you to do it. So why should we bother at all? We're trying to keep you taking responsibility, to be somebody who cares about other people and what *they* need. We're trying to help you succeed. Business, friends, life. Everywhere. The rules aren't that different, eh. Something to consider."

"You know," she said, "I'm carefully not mentioning, while you're giving me all this life advice, that Hope ran away from you, and that she's still gone. I mean, you're great at business, sure, but otherwise? That all sounds super wise, like something Koro would say, or maybe Hope, but, you know… it's you."

"Ah. Well. Call it my own lifelong learning." I stood up again. "I'm going to be working. If you want a snack or help getting your bed ready, ask Annette."

"Fine." She bounced straight back, as usual. "But maybe my lessons on not being an entitled rich person shouldn't come from somebody with a personal flight attendant. I'm just saying."

"I'm entitled to a flight attendant. I pay her wages." I gave her hair a rumple. "I'm not entitled to think I'm better than my flight attendant because she works for me. There you are. Two lessons in one day. Just imagine how much you'll learn after a few weeks of this."

"Plus," she said, "LASIK. Tomorrow, I stop being blind."

♡♡♡

Of course, it took me about twenty-four hours to stuff up.

I'd scheduled a session in the gym with Eugene for the next day. It had been a week since I'd worked out, and I was sure I'd be hearing from him. I just hadn't anticipated *what* I'd be hearing from him.

He walked into my home gym at eight that evening, dropped his bag, looked me over with the critical eye I'd fully expected, and asked, "What's goin' on out there with Karen? She's been crying for sure, and that ain't like her. Hope didn't come home with you two? Why not? Don't tell me you screwed up again there."

What had that taken? Five seconds? "Nothing's wrong with her, and she's not crying." I was on the bike already, warming up. "She had laser surgery on her eyes today, and they're irritated. They'll be better tomorrow. And Hope's staying with my grandfather for a few more weeks, helping out there. And before you ask—the two of us are all good." I wasn't going to share the state of my heart with the whole bloody world. I'd told Hope, and I'd told Koro. Two more people than I normally confided in, and two were enough.

"Huh." Eugene's weathered face looked even more skeptical than usual, but he pulled out his clipboard and started shuffling pages. "Well, all I got to say is, maybe that surgery was a big deal and maybe it wasn't, but it must've scared Karen good, 'cause I sure never seen her like that. No, sir. No sass in her at all."

"Inez said she came through it fine. Probably just tired. And I know it's a blow for you not having Hope to lecture me about, but I can live without you starting in on me about Karen. Her eyes will water for a day or two, that's all. She's not out there having a cry."

Eugene looked up fast, and I didn't have to be a poker player to read his expression. "You telling me you didn't take her? Left it for Inez to do, like she was droppin' off your shirts?"

"I wasn't aware that I was telling you anything. It's a simple procedure." I upped the resistance on the bike. "And I'm not paying you for life coaching."

His hands were on his hips. "Ain't that just too bad, 'cause that's what you're gonna get. You let that child go have that done all by *herself?* Her sister ain't here, and you thought that was fine, no need for you to go along, give her a hug, tell tell her she'd be OK? Be there when she got out? After she been through *brain* surgery? Ain't you learned one single damn thing all this time?"

Losing my temper wouldn't solve anything, so I pedaled

faster instead and said, "She did have somebody there. Inez waited with her, if you need to know. Have you ever *talked* to Karen? She *did* go through brain surgery, and she came out of it, too. She's probably tougher than anybody you've ever coached, and I'm including the boxers in that. She told me she'd be fine, and she was. Hope rang her, too. Before *and* after. She was fine."

Eugene stared at me for a long moment. "Man, I can't believe I got to tell you this again, but I guess I do. Listen up, hard head. You love somebody, you're *there*. That's not some extra thing, something nice to do. That's *the* thing. And no, you don't got to tell me you had meetings, 'cause I already know. You got your work, oh, yeah. Big, important things to do. Big man. So here's what you do, big man. You take that laptop of yours and do your work while you sit on the chair and wait for her to be done. And then she comes out and you put the work away, 'cause she's more important, and she needs to know it. You bring her home, you get her comfortable, you tell her she can call you anytime she needs you, and if she does, you'll be comin' right back home. And *then* you leave her with Inez and go back to work."

I would've protested, but I didn't have much answer for that. "Right," I finally said. "Could be."

Did he let it go? Of course he didn't. "'Could be,' hell. You keep screwing up like this, you ain't going to keep getting chances. You could think about something else, too, if you can ever get your mind in the unique spot of you not being right every single time. You could think about how you're going to go about letting them two into your life more, and how you're planning to get to know that baby. And I don't want to hear about no quality time. That didn't work so good for you before, I noticed. I want to hear about *time*

time."

"I've told you. I've told Hope. I don't have that kind of time, and she knows it. She said she needed more attention, and I'm paying more attention."

Looking impressed had never been Eugene's specialty, and nothing had changed. "Well, congratulations, that's all I got to say." It wasn't. "I'd say you got yourself set up to get all the time you want, because pretty soon, you won't have no family at all. *Again.* And when that baby of yours gets a little bigger and asks about daddy and how come he ain't around, his mama can talk about daddy's big job and explain how it was more important. If that sounds good to you, that's just fine, 'cause you're right on track to get it. If it don't sound so great, then maybe for once you could try learning one single solitary thing without doing it the hard way. Might be easier on you, and it'd be a *whole* lot easier on that family you're tryin' to make. Specially on that woman you love, 'cause that's what love is. Making it easier on her."

I tried to think of an answer, but I couldn't come up with much. I'd achieved exactly one thing so far that evening. My heart rate was up.

Eugene shook his grizzled head. "For a smart guy, you sure can be dumb. Get off that bike and hit the bag, then. Might as well do you some good somehow, seeing as I hauled my bony ass all the way over here."

right speech

♡

Hemi

I'd done it wrong, so I tried harder. That was the only possible response. I started coming home in time to eat dinner with Karen most nights, and I did encourage her to have her friends over, exactly as I'd promised.

That bit wasn't too bad. Her time in New Zealand seemed to have helped along those lines. I wouldn't call my home "pristine" anymore, but at least she was making her bed and putting her dishes in the dishwasher, and her shoes generally got left in the entryway. The rest of it, I could live with.

I made the supreme sacrifice, too. Two weeks after school started, I suggested that Karen invite Noah the Unattached Buddhist to join us for dinner on Saturday night, since he didn't seem to be going away. That would give me a chance to meet him, and it would give Karen a chance to cook and to be a real hostess in her home. I was fairly proud of thinking of it, actually.

As for Noah… I wasn't sure what I'd expected, but it had probably involved more listening and definitely more deference, the kind I'd have got from a nephew. Unfortunately, Noah wasn't Maori, and I wasn't too sure about the Buddhist bit, either.

He turned out to be good-looking in a soulful-WASP sort of way. Tall and lean and beach-and-ski-slope tanned, with dark hair that fell over his collar and tended to drop into one dark-lashed gray eye. I'd have bet he played the guitar, and that he'd look into a girl's eyes while he sang her a song.

You could say that I met him and hated him and not be too far off, but I did my best. I asked him about his plans for university and the future, for example, which made Karen sigh and say, "Old-fashioned much, Hemi? I mean, for Question *One?*"

I just looked at her. None of the responses I could have made seemed particularly helpful. Noah didn't seem fazed, though. He said, "I'm going into medicine."

"That what your dad does?" I asked.

He looked at me pityingly. It wasn't a look I got very often, and I wasn't enjoying it now. "Both of my parents, actually. Women can be doctors, too, you know."

"Mm," I said, not rising to the bait. "Takes a bit of doing, medicine."

"If you mean I'll have to go to med school, well, yes, obviously."

"Takes getting in as well," I said dryly. "A few stages of that, I reckon."

"Noah's in the top twenty percent in his class," Karen put in. "He's built houses for the poor in Central America. He's got an amazing resume."

"Aren't you in the top ten percent?" I asked her.

"It's a lot easier as a freshman," Noah said. "Before most of your class gets serious."

I'd had practice controlling my temper, and I called on it now. "Not too easy with a brain tumor, though. And I've thought at times that universities might want to look a bit more at students who've been poor themselves and less at ones who've built houses for them. Two different experiences, eh."

"I never said Karen didn't work hard," Noah said, not sounding quite so Buddhist. "Admissions committees take family circumstances into account, too. Maybe too much. The scholarship students I know are some of the best prepared in the school. Lemuel Sanderson—he'll probably be our valedictorian. He's African-American, and everyone knows he's on scholarship. Here's another way to look at it. I've had more temptations and distractions than some people, and I've stayed focused anyway. Or maybe we should ask somebody who actually *is* poor and see what they say."

Before I could tell him that "more temptations and distractions equals hardship" was the stupidest thing I'd ever heard in a lifetime of listening, Karen said, "Of course being poor is harder, Noah. I mean, geez. You don't have any idea." Which told me she hadn't gone all the way over to the dark side. "Hemi knows that, too. *He* was poor, and so was I. That's just *lame.*"

"I'm just saying," Noah said, digging himself in deeper, "that people should study the admissions criteria before they judge, like I have, and consider all the factors. I do realize I've had advantages. That's why I plan to do some good in my practice."

"Planning to work in the inner city, are you?" I asked. I'd

bet not.

"No," he said. "Cardiologist. My parents are dermatologists. I'm not going to spend *my* life making rich people's wrinkles and zits go away. I want to fix real problems."

I considered saying that there was another kind of problem that could be even more real. Things like untreated diabetes and high blood pressure, mums who sat in the emergency room for hours with their feverish babies. Or young women who couldn't get anyone to order the tests that would diagnose their little sisters' disabling headaches.

While I was working to set that aside, Noah said, "I've got a question for you, too."

"Go ahead," I said. Hope would have told me not to put Noah's back up, or Karen's, either, so I took another bite of Karen's chicken and made an attempt to keep an open mind. Not easy. My mind tended to make a decision fast and stick with it, and that decision had already been made.

"Why isn't Karen allowed to swear?" he asked. "She says it's because of you. Don't you think that's an outdated vestige of the patriarchy?"

"No, but you do, clearly." Maybe this kid was book-smart, but that was where it stopped. I reckoned "pathologist" would be a better career choice. That way, his patients would be dead already. He might have enough bedside manner for that.

"Women aren't delicate flowers who need protection, though, are they?" he said, cheerfully going on to dig his grave. "Men who say they're protecting women by treating them differently—aren't they just holding them back, keeping them from full participation and equality? You could call it a virtual burkha."

I wondered if he'd thought that one up all by himself. I'd have bet not. I looked at Karen. "Right, then. Participate fully. You don't need Noah to speak for you. Tell me what you think."

She was looking particularly pretty tonight. She hadn't quite grown into her slightly oversized mouth and eyes, but once she did, she would be a striking woman. And a woman who deserved better than this bloke.

For once, she didn't rush into speech. "I don't know. I mean, I thought so before, that you and Hope were ridiculous. But I noticed that my cousins—I mean, not my cousins, but, you know, the cousins—they don't swear around their parents, either. And *nobody* swears around Koro."

"Why do you imagine that is?" I asked, keeping it calm. Keeping it deliberate.

"Well, a Maori thing, obviously," Karen said. "And maybe a respect thing? You know, respect for your elders and all that. Which Maori are super big on," she told Noah.

"Words are just words," he said as if he'd invented that idea, too. "And people should meet each other on an equal playing field, not with all that status attached to them. Money, power, age, gender, race—it's all the same thing. Artificial distinctions so people can feel superior." Which would have made me laugh if he hadn't been pissing me off so much. If anybody had ever felt more superior than this kid, I hadn't met him.

I didn't laugh. I said, "Right thought leads to right speech, which leads to right action. Seems to me I heard that somewhere. Seems to me it was Buddhist, too."

"That isn't what it means," Noah said. "It means not saying hurtful things. It's not about whether you swear or not.

It's definitely not saying you shouldn't speak up and make your point directly instead of being all polite and passive-aggressive about it. Saying 'fuck' or 'shit' isn't any different from the word Karen uses instead. 'Geez.' How's that different? It would be one thing if you were calling a woman a cunt, but unless it's a racial or sexual slur, a word only has power if you give it power."

I didn't say anything. I couldn't think of anything better than, "Right, you. Out of my house now," and I didn't think that would meet Hope's test.

Finally, Karen said, not sounding happy, "Hemi means it's his house, so he gets to decide." Which told me Karen was heaps smarter than Noah, but then, I'd already figured that out.

"It's *our* house," I said. "But you don't make the rules in it, and neither does Noah. Hope and I do, and she's in nobody's burkha. Telling the truth doesn't require bad language, and 'respect' and 'politeness' aren't four-letter words."

It wasn't a brilliant evening, no, and Karen didn't have much to say about it afterwards. But I might have made her think a bit.

Speaking the truth was only half the battle. The other half was giving it time to sink in.

something that you do

♡

Hope

You could have called Hemi's divorce three weeks after our meeting with Anika an anticlimax, if it hadn't been for the undercurrents.

I'd driven up to Auckland—yes, *I'd* driven, and in a blowing rain, too—together with Koro and Tane to meet Hemi, who'd flown straight there. Koro had come because he'd wanted to be there almost as much as I did, and Tane had come because he would be driving Koro home again. It couldn't be me, because Hemi and I had someplace else to go afterward, somewhere we'd need to fly to reach in time. I'd had to schedule it for today, since Hemi wasn't even staying overnight.

I wanted him to hang around longer, you bet I did. But being apart had been my idea, not his, and he had important things to do. Some parts of our life could change, but not every part. I was realistic enough to know that. At least I hoped I was, because otherwise, I was setting myself up for a lifetime of disappointment. I'd have him today, and today counted. Today was important.

He was waiting for us under the protective overhang in front of the Auckland District Court, mere blocks from the lingerie shop where I'd first discovered he'd been married before, when all of this had begun. But then, Auckland wasn't very big.

My mind was skittering off to that insignificant detail because I was nervous. Not for me—for him.

Do you think he looked nervous, though? Of course he didn't. He looked as cool and controlled as ever in his usual black suit and white shirt. Tailored and barbered to perfection, and betraying his emotions by not so much as a muscle twitch in his set face.

Until he saw us approaching under our umbrellas, that is. Then his face changed and he was coming forward fast, greeting Koro with a hongi, the Maori salutation that was both hug and kiss. A meeting of forehead and nose, a grasp of a shoulder. After that, he put his arms around me for a too-brief moment before shaking his cousin's hand. He kept his arm around me, though, as if he needed to hold me. Which was good, because I certainly needed to hold him.

That was about as exciting as it got for a good two hours. We sat in a half-empty courtroom and watched a judge run through one civil case after another, a fair percentage of them divorces. None of the other marital parties seemed to be in attendance, or if they were, they didn't do anything. An attorney presented the case, the judge ruled the marriage dissolved, and it was done. No testimony and no arguments, just two people's once-bright hopes and dreams becoming their past.

The weight of it sank more and more deeply into me the longer it went on. This was meant to be a positive occasion for the two of us, wiping Hemi's slate clean so we could start again. Instead, it felt dark and cold, and I could tell from Hemi's face that it was exactly the same for him. He was remembering what it had felt like when his parents had been divorced, probably, and the blow when Anika had told him she wasn't joining him in New York. He was thinking about his mum and his wife telling him he wasn't worth keeping, so they were setting him aside. Letting him go.

He'd never say that, but he didn't have to. I held his hand and tried to let him know his new truth, doing my best to send the message from my body into his.

That was then, and this is now. This is us, and it's forever.

At last, his name was being read out. His and Anika's. And in less than five minutes, it was over. The judge's gavel hit the bench with the sharp *crack* of finality, he said, "Next case," Hemi's New Zealand attorney turned to leave, and Hemi stood up so fast, I nearly stumbled getting to my own feet.

The rain hadn't abated one bit in the past two hours, either, I found when we were back in the lobby. It was blowing straight across the windows as Hemi shook hands with his lawyer, who headed off again at once. Job done, bill to come.

Tane watched him go, then asked, "How much did he charge you for two hours of sitting and five minutes of standing? Too much, I reckon."

Hemi cracked his first smile of the morning. "Let's say it was worth it."

"Well, congrats, cuz," Tane said. "I wouldn't normally say that to a bloke about his divorce, but I'm saying it about this one. I'm saying, break out the bubbly. Or maybe I'll say what June did. 'Good riddance to bad rubbish.'"

Koro said, sharply for him, "You don't celebrate misfortunes and endings. You know better, my son."

"Probably right," Tane said. "Sorry. Time for lunch, eh. Wash the taste away."

"We don't have time, unfortunately," I put in. "We're on a schedule here."

"She tell you yet what her surprise is, mate?" Tane asked Hemi.

"Nah." Hemi still looked shut down, and no wonder. "Only that we need to fly to Tauranga for it, and that it wasn't at Koro's."

Tane looked smug at that. Koro looked satisfied himself, but all he said was, "Go on, then. You don't want to be late."

Hemi hesitated. "Wish I could stay the night, but . . ."

Koro waved his good hand. "Never mind. You'll be back."

The flight to Tauranga was mercifully brief, because the little jet bucked and pitched through the storm in a way that recalled all too vividly my arrival in New Zealand. I held Hemi's hand again, but this time, I was receiving rather than giving comfort.

It *wasn't* an omen. There was no such thing. There was no terrible surprise waiting on the other end. There couldn't be. It would be too unfair.

When has life been fair? my treacherous brain mocked.

This mattered too much, though. This mattered more than anything. To me, and to Hemi. He was the best thing that had ever happened to me, and he'd told me I was that for him. Our bad luck was *over*. It had to be.

I breathed a little easier when we were on the ground

again. And when we were in the car, which I was once again driving—"Part of the surprise," I'd said, trying to sound cheerful and perky—Hemi started talking a little more, which meant that he must be breathing more easily himself.

"Karen wanted to come," he said. "I said no."

"I know." I pulled cautiously out onto the main road from the Tauranga airport, my windshield wipers slapping furiously at the sheets of water, my headlights probing the murky gray. "I've been getting blow-by-blow details. I was glad you said no. No way she should miss two days of school to watch you get divorced. It would probably have scarred her for life, as depressing as that was. Anyway, I texted her that it was done."

"I wondered," he said. "And since you always say this, it's probably my turn. Good job letting go of the control and letting me make that decision."

"Oh," I said, taken aback. "Huh. I never even thought of it that way. All right, then. You're welcome." I turned onto Bethlehem Road, then into the drive of Mills Reef.

Hemi studied the curving, elegant sweep of the low, modern building, the warm golden light glowing in the windows against the bleakness of the day, then glanced at me quizzically. "This my surprise?"

"First part of it." I felt more certain, suddenly, as I pulled beneath the portico, hopped out, and handed my keys to the valet. We walked through glass doors into a foyer that smelled like flowers and good food, and I breathed in the aromas and said, "I was afraid we were going to miss our booking when I saw that everybody else in New Zealand was getting divorced before you did, but here we are. And this is *my* treat, by the way. This is my present."

"I've been here before, you know," he said. "If we're

having lunch, it's likely to mean a day's wages for you, or even more."

"Fortunately, my future husband is both rich and indulgent." I took his arm. "Which means I get to spend my meager earnings on whatever I want. Come on. I have a baby to feed, and it's getting cranky. Or maybe that's me."

I got his second smile of the day for that, and in another minute, we were seated in a cozy spot in the corner of the wine estate's sumptuous dining room, its white tablecloths and glittering modern chandeliers offering welcome cheer on this dreary day. And five minutes after *that,* Hemi had been served a glass of red wine and I hadn't, and he was saying, "Koro said you don't celebrate misfortune, but I'm celebrating this one all the same. Not saying that was fun, but I'm free, and I reckon both of us can celebrate that."

"We can." I lifted my water glass and touched it to his. "Congratulations. It was bad, but now we're moving on."

"Together." He lifted his glass and drank. When he put it down again, though, he pulled out his phone.

I couldn't help it. My heart sank. He had to check his messages *now?*

Apparently not, because what he said was, "I've got a couple surprises of my own for you, and here's the first one." And with that, he handed the phone to me.

It took me a few seconds to understand what I was seeing. The stone floor of Hemi's terrace, the planters filled with roses around the edges, and something else. Something new.

"It's not glass." First came my smile, and then a laugh. "*Hemi.* The walls aren't glass anymore. You did this? Did you do it for me?"

He looked proud, he looked pleased, and he wasn't trying to hide either thing. "Yeh. Talked it over with Karen, and we worked out the design together. Concrete to three feet up, glass above that for another eighteen inches. So you can feel safe going up to the edge and cutting your own roses, and we can have the baby out there without making you nervous. I thought we could do a sandpit, and maybe a wee play structure as well. I was looking at a few."

You could say I was surprised. You could say that. "Hemi Te Mana," I teased, the tears there behind my eyes, "king of the sandbox. Are you going to sit on the edge and help him or her build castles?"

"Could be. And that's the other bit of my surprise."

We were interrupted at that inopportune moment with our lunches. Well, not so inopportune, because I *was* starved, and I'd ordered a salmon salad that I wanted to start eating right *now.*

Hemi must have seen the haste with which I seized my fork, because he commanded, "You eat and I'll talk. The surprise is this. I've worked out a timetable for when you're back, and for when the baby arrives. For all of that."

I finished my absolutely delicious bite of fresh, buttery fish and crunchy, tangy greens, then said, trying not to be disappointed, "Babies don't run on timetables, though. They're hard to schedule. That's how I remember Karen, and what I've read, too."

He didn't look the least bit abashed. Instead he looked smug. "Ah. But you see, this isn't a timetable for the baby. It's a timetable for me. I'm coming home in time to eat dinner with all of you every evening from here on out."

"You are?" I may have been sitting there, stupefied. It's possible. "What about work?"

"Got a home office, haven't I. I can work there after dinner, after I've heard about everybody's day, told you about mine, and helped put my baby to bed, maybe. Dunno why I haven't been doing that all along, except that change doesn't come easily to me. It's come now, though. What do you reckon?"

"I reckon that's a pretty great idea. I reckon I'm pretty happy to hear that." An hour or so a day wasn't exactly Mr. Mom territory, but it was more than I'd expected, for sure.

"But here's the big one," he said. "Ready?"

"Oh, yeah." My heart had started to beat faster. It was the way he looked, maybe. Brimming with expectancy and pleasure, exactly the opposite of the shut-down man in that courtroom.

"Sundays," he said. "They're for you, and for my family. They're for us. No calls, no meetings, no email. Nothing. From the day you come back home, Sundays are for you, and so are Women's Wednesdays, except that they'll be Family Wednesdays now."

"Or maybe," I said, "Whanau Wednesdays."

He smiled, and it was so sweet, I could barely stand it. "Even better. Though I'm keeping our date night as well."

"You'd better," I said. "That one's sacred."

The amusement left his face, and he put out a hand and grasped mine. "Something Eugene told me a long time ago. I may have forgotten it for a while, but I won't be forgetting it again. He told me that love isn't something you say. It's something you do. I'm going to be doing it, and so are you."

"That's some surprise," I said, the happiness threatening to overpower me. "That's… that's a *change.*"

"You told me people could change. You said you could learn to put your hand on me and tell me that you needed my time and attention, and I could learn to give them to you. I reckon it's better if you don't have to put your hand on me.

It's better if we know we have that time and attention coming. For both of us."

All I could do was nod. If I tried to talk, I was very much afraid I was going to cry. And then I thought of something.

"What if Anika gets what she wants?" I asked. "What if you do have to start again from halfway down, rebuilding? Are you sure you won't be thinking that you need your Sundays? That you'll need every bit of time you have to do that?"

"That's why they're called priorities. Because they're what matters most."

I knew my smile was too wide, and that it was completely foolish. "I thought you'd given me some good presents before, but, Hemi… this is the best. It's the *best.*"

"Not much I wouldn't do for you," he said, and his eyes were so warm, the hand around mine so firm. "Time to prove it. You've given me your surprise, and now I've given you mine. And I'm going to marry you as soon as we can manage it. I'd call this a good day. I'd call it almost the best, except that what's coming is going to be even better."

I smiled again, but this time, it was slow and secret and special. He had no idea what kind of day this was going to be. "Oh," I told him, "this isn't the surprise. Finish your lunch. There's someplace we need to be."

a different view

♡

Hemi

When Hope pulled into the carpark of a medical building, I thought I knew what her surprise was.

"I'm going to your check with you," I said. "I didn't realize it was today."

"I made sure it was." She looked excited, and a little shy, too. "I thought we might need something positive to even the scales. I thought it might help."

"It does." The rain had stopped at last while we'd been at lunch, and even as we crossed the carpark, the sun came out from behind the clouds. Hope's hand was in mine, and we were looking at a mass of billowing clouds that glowed around the edges where the sun was making its presence felt, and at a wide beam of sunlight that shone down out of them, blessing the earth after the storm. As poignant—and as trite—as any religious painting you could hope to see.

I'd never have designed anything that obvious, but it didn't matter. It worked. "Rain for sorrow and rebirth," I said. "Sun for joy."

Hope touched the pendant at her throat. It was the manaia carved from South Island greenstone that I'd given her, the protective spirit of an ancestor looking after her soul. She'd worn it today for strength and connection. I knew that without her telling me.

She didn't say anything, and I thought she might not trust herself to speak. So I did it for her. "Yeh," I said. '"That feeling you have—it's your mum, guarding your spirit through all of this. Maybe guarding our baby, too. That's her grandchild, eh. That matters."

She stopped where she was, on the pavement outside the building. Her face worked, and she tried to say something, but all that came out was a choked sound.

I did what I hadn't done yet today, what I hadn't done for weeks. I gathered her in my arms, held her tight and close, and said the words. "I love you, and I always will. We're going to be all good, you'll see. Everything your mum could have wished for you, that's what you're going to have. You and Karen both. Everything I can give you."

She gasped once before burying her face in my jacket. Her shoulders shook, and I held her, rubbed a hand over her back, and thought, *That's my promise to you, Rose Sinclair. I'm holding onto your daughters and your grandchild, and I'll keep holding on forever. I'm keeping them whole. I'm mending the cracks.*

"No fair," Hope said at last, her voice shaky. She stepped back, wiped her fingers under her cheeks, then searched in her purse, pulled out a tissue, and began putting herself to rights. She laughed, unsteady and sweet as a baby's first steps. "The midwife's going to think we've been having a fight."

♡♡♡

The midwife didn't seem to think so, as it turned out. When she came into an exam room to find Hope sitting on the table, swinging her feet with obvious nerves, and me in a chair in the corner, all she did was shake hands with me and say, "Always good to see the dad here, especially on this visit. Gillian Wright."

"Hemi Te Mana," I said. "Pleasure."

The assessing look she gave me told me she knew who I was, but she just washed and dried her hands, then turned to Hope and said, "Well, my darling, let's see how you measure up. You've gained over a kilo and a half, I see. Working your way back up to the positive side of the ledger."

"I'm eating like crazy," Hope assured her. "I'm going to have to be careful not to overdo it if I keep this up."

"Mm. Still got a ways to go, I'd say. Keep an eye on the scale and the guidelines, and you'll be good." She pulled up Hope's deep-blue sweater, tugged her leggings a bit lower on her belly, took a tape measure out of her pocket, and did some checking. "Very nice."

Hope let out a breath. "Good?"

"Looks good to me. But then, that's what we're going to find out today, aren't we?" She took hold of the bell of a stethoscope, ran it over Hope's belly, and frowned.

Five seconds. Ten. Hope was holding her breath, her eyes widening with fear. I could tell that was what it was, but I wasn't sure why. The midwife was listening for a heartbeat, obviously. That was what stethoscopes were for. But how would Hope know whether she heard it?

At that moment, I heard it myself, amplified so loudly that

it made me jump. Not a heartbeat, not the way I was used to thinking of it. More of a gallop. The heartbeat of something very small.

A hummingbird. Or a baby.

Hope was hauling in breath as if she couldn't get enough and turning her head to look at me, the smile on her face as wide as the sky.

"Baby," she said.

I took her hand, said, "Yeh. Baby," and thought I might float away.

I had time to compose myself as Gillian chatted with Hope. Diet and exercise and sleep and vitamins, and I tried to focus, and to listen. I needed to know this, too.

Finally, Gillian said, "And this is the visit when I tell you not to lie on your back from here on out. You don't want the weight of your uterus cutting off blood flow to your heart, or to baby. And since dad's here, I'll anticipate him and say, yes, that includes during sex. Propped up's OK, if he's strong enough to keep *his* weight off your tummy. Flat on your back isn't."

"Oh," Hope said faintly. "Is there anything, um, else about that? Anything we should know?" She was turning pink, and I couldn't help but be amused. And interested. And, yeh, I was strong enough.

"Not really," Gillian said cheerfully. "As long as you want to do it and it feels good, feel free." She glanced at me. "Which means as long as *she* wants to do it, and any way that's comfortable and feels good to *her,* except on her back. Check in, and experiment. Sitting up's good, facing each other. Spoon fashion's another. Or from behind, hands and knees. That's easy on the woman, and no belly to get in the way. You get the picture. License to be inventive, eh. And, yes, oral sex is all good as well, long as you don't blow into her vagina. We have to say that, though I've never heard of anyone doing it. Why on earth would he?"

Hope had a hand over her eyes by now, and I had to laugh. "I think I've got it," I said. "Cheers. I knew there was a reason I'd come."

"Oh?" Gillian asked. "Don't want to see your baby?"

My heart knocked against my chest so hard, you might have seen it jump. "Pardon?"

"Ah." Gillian looked at Hope again. "Are we surprising dad?"

"Yes." Hope had lost the embarrassment, but she was breathless again. "That's the idea."

"Awesome. Off you go, then."

♡♡♡

We could walk to this one, because it was next door. I was quiet, but Hope was quieter. And by the time she was lying on another table, in a paper gown this time and covered by yet more crackling blue paper, she'd gone absolutely silent and still.

I knew what that meant when I did it. It meant I was feeling too much, so I was gathering all my energy into myself, pulling it inward so I couldn't betray it. The more I felt, the quieter I got. But Hope didn't have to protect herself. Not here. Not with me. That was my job.

"What is it?" I asked. I took her hand, and it was beyond cold. It was frozen. "Baby, what?"

"What if . . ." She was forcing the words out through tightened lips, a constricted throat. "What if something's wrong? Everything's been so good. What if my life can't go this way after all? What if it's too much to . . ." She swallowed. "To expect?"

I had hold of both her hands now, and the helplessness, the tenderness—they were making my chest ache. "No," I told her. "Nothing's too much to expect. Nothing's too much to want. Love, babies, work to do that makes you happy. You've given so much to Karen, to your mum. To Koro. You've rubbed his ugly old *feet.*" As I'd hoped, that made her smile, even though I knew the tears weren't far away. "And to me. What you've given to me alone—it's going to take a lifetime to pay that back."

"But what if… I haven't taken good enough care of it?" It was a whisper. "What if I haven't eaten enough? What if I've hurt it?"

I made my voice, my face as firm as I could manage. That was what she needed, so that was what I was going to do. "You know better than that. You've taken the best care you could. You've never done anything less, and you never will. It's not in your nature. It's not possible. And if something *is* wrong? We'll deal with it, you and me. We'll do it together. You think you couldn't bear it alone? You could, but you won't have to, and neither will I. We'll only have to bear half. Less than half, because we'd both take more than half off the other. We can get through anything if we're doing it together."

The tears were running down her temples, into her hair. Her eyes were squeezed shut against them, her lips pulled back in her effort to suppress the sobs, her chest heaving. If anything had ever hurt me more to see, I don't know what it could have been.

That was the moment when the tech walked in. Her scrubs were printed with bright balloons, her hair pulled back in a swinging high ponytail. A greater contrast to the suffering woman on the table beside me you couldn't have imagined.

"We having a bit of an emotional moment?" she asked cheerfully, plucking a box of tissues off the table and holding them out for Hope, who took them with a choked gasp. "Never mind. Happens all the time. Let's take a wee look and see what we see, and after that, the waterworks can *really* let loose."

Endless fiddling followed. The tech typed into the keyboard of a huge machine, then spread some thick, clear stuff from a plastic bottle onto Hope's firm little belly that made Hope jump and say, "Oh. Cold."

One minute, the machine's screen was showing a rectangle of black with white block letters in a corner. The next, the tech was moving a paddle over Hope's belly, her eyes on the screen, and the black background was covered with specks and swirls of white that were… nothing I could sort out, try as I might.

"Keep breathing normally," the tech said. Hope was probably holding her breath again. I took her hand, held it, and watched the screen along with her. And still had absolutely no idea what I was seeing.

Just like that, it was there. A pulsing white blob, and movement beyond it.

"Ah," the tech said with satisfaction. "There's our baby."

"Is that the heart?" I asked over my own racing heartbeat. That was a person, and it was *mine?*

"It is," she said. "And we're kicking. See that? Those are legs. Lively, eh. One second. Let me get through the business end." She was moving her paddle, measuring, clicking, stopping to type onto the keyboard. Minute after minute, while Hope stared at the screen and I held her hand and stared with her.

Finally, when I could tell that Hope couldn't last another moment without knowing, the technician said, "That's that done. Now comes the fun bit. Want to meet your baby?"

"Yes," Hope and I said together.

"Right, then." She moved her paddle, and a cursor on the screen moved with it. "Head, nose, chin. See?"

I did. I saw. A face, in profile. A baby's face. I was having trouble with my chest. With my breath.

"Arms," the tech went on as the cursor moved. "Fingers. You see?"

Hope said, "Oh. They're moving. She—he—they're waving."

"Kicking as well, still. Active, and that's good. Do we want to know the sex?"

Hope turned her head, her eyes searching mine. "Do we?"

"Do *you?*" I knew how I felt, but I wasn't the most important person here. I was number three, in fact.

"Yes." It wasn't tentative. It was sure.

"Yes," I told the tech, and she smiled and said, "Here we are, then."

More movement of the cursor, and she said, "Legs, and here we are between them."

"I can't see anything," I said.

"That's because," she said, "you're having a girl."

Hope

We were in a café again, Hemi with a coffee and me with yet another herbal tea. Not because we needed them, but because we needed more time. Our hands were linked across the table, his fingers threaded through mine.

Somehow, I was going to have to let him go. Somehow. He left for Paris in a week, and Koro had a cast to get removed, and anyway, that was the plan. Karen was in school, Hemi seemed to be doing a fantastic job with her, and I needed that relationship to be cemented.

When he came home from Paris, though, I'd be there. *We'd* be there.

"What do you think?" I finally managed to ask. "About a little girl? A daughter?" I was pretty sure I knew the answer. I asked anyway.

"I think," he said, "that I'm over the moon. I think I can't wait. I think I love you. What do *you* think about names?"

I hesitated. I'd thought about them, of course, but I hadn't dared to think quite enough, to take it all the way. Somehow, it still hadn't seemed real. Now, it did. So real, I was overwhelmed by it. "I wondered," I said slowly, "about Maori names. I wondered if you'd want that. I wondered if you'd want to choose."

How had I ever thought this man was hard? There was nothing but happiness in the face opposite me, nothing but warmth and strength in the hand holding mine. And I'd been right, that day all the way back in the Auckland airport, when I'd imagined how fiercely he'd protect us, how tenderly he'd hold us. Our daughter and me, and Karen, too. All of us.

"I have a name," he said. "Came to me when I saw her, as soon as I knew she was a girl. It came into my head, and it's been there ever since. I'm hoping you like it, because to me, it's her name."

"What is it?" I asked, praying that I *would* like it, that it wouldn't be something strange and hard to pronounce.

"Aroha Rose Te Mana," he said. "That's our daughter's name. I hope."

"Aroha," I said. "Love. And Rose, my mother's name. Hemi, that's perfect. That's beautiful."

"This is when I ask you," he said, "whether you want to change your name. And remind myself that it's your choice."

"You'd really say that?" I had to tease a little. There was too much happiness in me not to. "You really wouldn't wage a subtle and not-so-subtle campaign to get me to change my mind?"

"Not answering that," he said promptly. "Let's hear it."

"Then, yes. I want to change my name. I want to be my own person, but I want to do it with your name. I have my mother's, because my dad took off. Aroha is going to have her dad with her all the way, though, and she's going to have his name. And I want us all to have the same one."

"Hope Te Mana," he said.

Something went through me, strong and bright as silver, leaping from his hand to mine. "Hope Te Mana," I said. "Very soon."

It didn't matter that Anika was still out there. She couldn't hurt Hemi, and she couldn't hurt me. She could take his money, but that wasn't what we were about. That wasn't it at all. We were so much more.

right choice

♡

Hemi

Once again, I'd had to leave Hope behind. This time, it was harder, and it was easier. Easier because I was divorced now, and even though the specter of Anika still loomed over the company, still threatened everything I'd spent fourteen years building, it didn't threaten Hope and me anymore. That was what Hope had done. She'd convinced me.

I could cope with anything. Coping was my life story. With anything except losing her.

It was easier, too, because it was only for a couple weeks. Then I'd be flying to Paris, and when I came home, she'd be there. That had been her promise, and Hope kept her promises.

Harder, now—"harder" was getting a photo that next week showing her belly a tiny bit bigger, and not being there to feel my baby girl under my palm or to hold her mother.

"Harder" was talking to Hope on the phone in the early morning, then having to ring off and start my day without her. "Harder" was coming home to an apartment without her in it.

And tonight, on a Friday night a week after my divorce and two days before I left for Paris, I came home to an apartment with *nobody* in it, because Karen had gone off to the first school dance of the year.

She'd decided to get ready at her friend Mandy's house in Brooklyn, close to school. That had sounded good to me, considering that Noah the Unfortunate Buddhist was driving her. He'd be picking her up in the Porsche Boxster his parents had given him for his eighteenth birthday, Karen had told me, and if I'd had Josh arrange some unauthorized checking of his driving record, I wasn't going to apologize for it. Parking tickets appeared to be his specialty, though he'd had a speeding ticket a year ago as well. Which didn't make me happy, but wasn't enough to forbid Karen to drive with him. Unfortunately.

She was spending the night at Mandy's as well, but I wasn't worried about that. I'd rung up and had a chat with Mandy's mum, and I was confident that Karen would be in good hands.

Once she got there.

At eight, I got a group text that eased my mind. A shot of Karen and Mandy in their pretty dresses, Noah and another bloke in suits, with a roomful of other students behind them. They'd made it, then. And Karen had sent that text to both Hope and me, which was good as well.

I texted back, *Pretty girls. Have fun,* then went back to work.

I was deep into it, part of me relishing the chance to have an entire uninterrupted evening, when my phone chimed with a text. I picked it up and glanced at the screen.

Could Charles come get me?

I was out of my chair before I'd finished reading. It was just after ten, I saw as I texted back, *I'll come. Leaving now. Where are you? Safe?*

School, I read. *I'm OK. I just need to come home.*

City traffic had never seemed slower, but finally, I was outside Brooklyn Friends, double-parking and out onto the pavement in an instant.

I didn't realize how worried I'd been until I saw her sitting at the top of the steps in front of the building, her arms wrapped around herself against the night air. I slowed from my near-run and said, "Eh, sweetheart."

She stood up, not looking at me, and said, "Thanks for coming. I thought you'd send Charles. I mean, I know you were working." Her voice was tight, not sounding like my easy-breezy Karen at all.

"Nah." I put my arm around her and tugged her against me as we headed down the steps again. "Always happy to come get my girl. Any time."

Her breath was a bit ragged, and I said, "Whatever happened—he's a fool, and not worth your time or your worry."

She gave a half-laugh and said, "You don't even know anything about it yet."

"Call me prejudiced. Both ways." I popped the locks on the door, and she slid into the passenger seat. "I like you, and I don't like him."

I began to drive home, and she was silent for a long couple of minutes. I waited as long as I could before I said, "You can tell me, you know. I doubt I'll be surprised. I wasn't even surprised that you weren't crying."

"I want to." There was a catch in her voice now. "But I don't want to give him the satisfaction, you know?"

I had to smile at that. "Nobody better. Of course you don't."

"You can probably guess anyway. Big surprise. He wanted to have sex. We've been, you know, making out."

I relaxed my hands deliberately on the steering wheel. "And when you said you didn't want to, he said you were… what? A little girl?"

"Yeah. And stuck in the past, like virginity was some special thing I'd give to the right man, like it was some big deal, instead of sex being something you started doing when you were old enough, like when you were old enough to start riding a bike. Which *sounds* right," she burst out, "but it doesn't *feel* right, you know?"

"Why would you want to sleep with somebody who thought you were no big deal?" I still sounded calm. Somehow.

"See?" It was an explosion. "See? That's what *I* said! I said—if I wasn't special, what was the *point?* And he said I was *scared.* I'm not scared! Maybe I just want somebody to *care.* What's wrong with that? And then he said I wasn't… I wasn't . . ." Her voice wobbled for the first time.

"That you weren't that good anyway," I said. "Not that pretty. Not that exciting. That he'd have been doing you a favor."

"He said if I didn't want to, we could just… I could just . . ." She was crying, finally. Tears of anger, and I was glad to hear them. "You know. Oral."

"Right." I swung into a bus zone and stopped the car. "We're going to his house. Right now. The little bastard. I'm going to rip his head off."

"I don't . . ." Karen's voice was shaking. "I just… I wish Hope was here. I tried to call her, but she didn't answer, and I… I *wish*… I just wanted to *talk* to her, you know? She's always… she . . ."

Her voice was breaking, and so was my heart. I said helplessly, "Eh, sweetheart. No," reached out, and pulled her into my arms. Which was when she started to sob.

For the next few minutes, she tried to talk and kept trailing off, and I held her tight, ran my hand over her hair, said, "Shh," and "Never mind," and "It's all right," and wished I could think of something better. I wished Hope were here, too. Never more so. But she wasn't, which meant it was down to me to harden up and do my best.

When she pulled back at last and started wiping at her face, I said, "Listen to me. Listen hard, now. You're a beautiful girl with spirit and fire and strength that any man would want. Any *man*. Not any entitled boy who thinks he's doing a girl a favor. What I told you on the jet—that's the truth, and you need to remember it, no matter what your body's telling you. If he cares about you, he's not going to push you, and if he pushes you, he doesn't care about you. Something else, too. Nothing about having sex or not having it makes you any more or less of a woman, so there's no point in doing it until you're sure you're having it with somebody who cares more about you than he does about himself. And if he's talking about you performing on him in his car," I finished grimly, "he doesn't care a bit, and the only answer is to slap his face."

"Did anybody ever slap yours? Any girl?" She was still sniffling, but she didn't sound broken anymore.

"One woman. Your sister."

"Oh. Wow. But I mean… I don't have to say no, do I?

For a guy to respect me? Why? Why *shouldn't* a woman say yes?"

"She should. When she can't stand *not* to have sex with that man, and she knows for sure that he's a man she wants to have it with. When it's her choice."

"Because that virgin thing *is* dumb," she said. "And wrong, and… and sexist, and *everything*. I still think so."

"You can think so and still not have sex with any Noahs. That, I know. You wait. And any time you wonder if he's the right one, you ask me."

"Or invite him to dinner." I thought she might be smiling a little now, even through the remains of her tears. "So you can tell me. He was kind of a jerk that night. I just didn't want to admit that you and Hope were right."

"No 'kind of' about it," I said. "He was a jerk, full stop. You can do better, and you will. You concentrate on being awesome, and on finding somebody as awesome as you that you don't have to make excuses for. You concentrate on making *your* choice."

"Like Hope did."

"Yeh. Exactly like Hope did."

Silence for another moment, and then the night was split by the blast of a horn, light flooded the car, I leaped in my seat, and Karen shrieked.

I pulled out of the bus zone, ignoring the angry final hoot behind me, and Karen said, "Wow. I don't think I've ever seen you doing anything, you know, awkward."

"Because you're seeing me now that I'm not sixteen anymore," I told her. "You wait. You're going to make all kinds of right choices. You've already started. You're going to have poise. You're going to have confidence. You're going to be a woman to reckon with. It's going to take a strong man to match you, and you're going to find him. You'll see."

naked ambition

♡

Hope

On a rainy Friday afternoon more than a week after Hemi had left, I finished drying off in a shower stall at the Katikati pool, grabbed my things, and headed to my locker.

The midwife had said that I'd find myself slowing down when I reached the third trimester, but that gave me ten weeks more to feel great, and that was how I felt. I'd swum thirty laps today, in fact, which was a new record.

Swimming in the rain was exciting, too. An adventure, and for the first time in my life, adventures didn't scare me. Maybe because I wasn't out on the edge anymore, knowing that one push or one wrong step could send both Karen and me into the abyss. I had the luxury of enjoying a challenge. Like today. I'd be walking up the hill in the rain, but I could cope with that. And in one more week, I was going home.

I'd had a thought out there doing those laps, too. A *work*

thought, which meant I was moving out of the now-zone and into the future-zone, and, boy, was *that* exciting. I could ask—

The thought left my head just like that. There was somebody sitting on a bench right smack in the middle of the room, as if she owned it. Her elegant legs were crossed at the knee, and she didn't look dressed to swim.

Anika didn't say anything. She just sat there with her beautiful face, her shiny hair, and her glorious figure and smiled at me. It wasn't a sad smile like before. Or a nice one.

I made my feet move again, and I kept my voice level. "What a surprise." I headed for my locker. She thought she could come here and intimidate me? She could think again. "Well, I guess it's a free country."

I nodded to Gemma and Roberta, two older ladies who often swam around the same time I did. Unfortunately, they were heading out, leaving only their curious glances behind. And leaving me alone with Viper Woman.

Deal with it. I channeled Hemi, spun the dial of my combination lock, and opened my locker. I didn't bother to cover up with my towel, either. This woman wasn't Hemi's wife anymore, she had no power over me, and I wasn't ashamed of how I looked. She had a killer body, but I had her man.

I know what you're thinking. That's a lovely evolved thought. No, it isn't, but too bad. I ignored her, stuck my head into my locker, and rummaged through my bag.

I heard her voice from behind me, rich with amusement. "All this time, I've been wondering what on earth Hemi could see in you. Insipid little blondes aren't much in his line, especially not when they've got a bit of pudge. Hemi's never settled for less than a ten. What was he doing with a six? It was a puzzle."

I turned around and began smoothing lotion into my skin, controlling my breathing with a pretty heroic effort. "Well, I don't know. I guess people change, because here this six is with a three-carat rock on her finger. How's *your* life going?" I could play in the Bitch Wars, too.

"But then," Anika said, totally ignoring what I'd said, "until Ana told me, I didn't realize you were pregnant. Oldest trick in the world, but still effective, eh. If you can find a susceptible man, that is. And there Hemi is, aching to be somebody's hero, dying to be told he's lovable after Mummy didn't want him, and neither did I. Ana said none of them were impressed by you, but I don't know that I agree. You may be more clever than they realize. If you call getting pregnant and playing the helpless card 'clever,' that is."

"I don't know how Ana would know, seeing as I've never met her." I shoved back my emotion at the rest of it. Throwing a man's vulnerability back in his face? Using his family against him?

"Oh, she's heard reports. Let's say I'm not the only one surprised at his choice."

I pulled on my underwear, keeping my movements as smooth as I could manage. Hemi had told me, in one of his coaching moments, "The winner is the one who needs it less." Well, Anika sure needed to talk to me more than I needed to talk to her, because I wouldn't have crossed the street to have this conversation.

I let her wait, then sat on the bench, began to put on my pants, and finally said, "So you're surprised. So what? If Hemi likes me enough to marry me, what do I care what you or his sister think?"

Another smile. "You shouldn't. But you should care about

what I can do to him. And what I can do to you, although of course"—the smile turned mocking—"you care more about Hemi than about yourself. Or should I say—you care about his money more?"

"I think you're mixing me up with you," I said sweetly. "And if that's the best you've got, I can't imagine why you bothered to come all this way."

She smiled, faint and contemptuous, and I told myself, *No hitting,* and went back into my locker for my bra and top.

"I came because I have a present for you," she said.

"Let me guess. An acid bath. Oh, wait. You already gave us that." Hey. That had been *good.*

"Oh, darling, I've hardly got started." With that, she reached into her slouchy black bag, and I froze for a second, then whirled.

My baby. That was the only thought making it through. *Run.*

I'd barely taken two steps when she said, her dark voice full of amusement, "Don't be a fool. I'm more subtle than that. Besides, if you go out there topless, Katikati will be talking for weeks, and you wouldn't want that."

She wasn't holding a gun, or a knife, or whatever I could have imagined. She was holding her phone, pressing and clicking, and I heard Hemi's voice. His bedroom voice.

"Touch yourself. Because I'm touching you. Tying your ankles now, putting a pillow under your hips so you're all the way open for me. All the way helpless. Ready for anything I want to do to you."

My voice, then. A whimper, a moan. I stood there, halfway dressed, halfway to the door, listening to Hemi. And to me. And burning.

"Nice," Anika said. "But too tame. Now, let's see . . ." She clicked around a bit and said, "This one's a bit better. See what you think."

Hemi again. *"I'm going to turn you over, tie you down on your stomach. Wrists and ankles, so you're spread-eagled on the bed, and you're already begging me to stop. Going to shove a wedge up under you, get you ready for me. And now I'm shoving that vibrator up your pretty little arse, stretching you wider and wider while you squirm and beg. Until you start to howl. Because tonight's the night you're going to give it to me, and I'm going to fuck it hard. I'm going to fuck it till you scream."*

My breath was coming fast. I was half-naked and vulnerable. Helpless. And Anika kept playing that… tape?

"How . . ." I found myself saying despite my best intentions.

Another smile, and Hemi's voice mercifully stopped. "Did you and Hemi really think I flew all the way to New York to beg? Without a backup plan? That's why he'll never get as far as he thinks. He assumes everybody's as soft as he is. He doesn't think outside the box. Or maybe he doesn't think outside *yours*. You've cost him his edge, and that's just sad. He wants to live in a kinder, gentler world, but he should know better. It doesn't exist. Getting soft means getting screwed. But then, you know all about that, don't you? That's your specialty."

"What the hell are you talking about?" I wasn't horrified anymore. I was back at my locker, pulling out the rest of my clothes, dressing myself. Arming myself. "What you're doing doesn't have a thing to do with Hemi's character, or with mine. It's all about you, and it's all about money. You planted something on him somehow, or you hacked into his computer so you could hear our calls. Whatever it was, you eavesdropped on our private conversations, and that's illegal."

"Not that private, were they, if one little bug in the bedroom could pick them all up, and I heard them that many times? Sorry, darling, but he recorded everything he said to you, and everything you said, too. You're a noisy girl, aren't you? Oh, I'll bet he loves that. Think how much everybody else will."

The light was dawning. "No," I said, and put every bit of horror I could muster into it. "He wouldn't."

She sighed. "Hemi didn't tell you that he likes to share, did he? I told you that you were in over your head. And now you'll be shared even more. Hemi gets to share you with the whole wide world. Isn't that nice? A little leak, but that's all right, because you have a sharing fantasy of your own, don't you? I know all about it. You really shouldn't talk so much."

"What do you want?" I asked, not trying to hide my fear anymore.

"Oh, darling," she said reproachfully. "I'm disappointed. I thought you were smarter than that. What I've wanted all along. Money. We can make all of this go away. I'm not greedy. Ten million dollars. It has a lovely ring to it, doesn't it? U.S., of course. Hemi can raise that without breaking a sweat. No lawyers, no courts, and the happy couple gets married and has their pretty little baby, and nobody ever, ever has to know what kinds of dirty things they get up to when they're alone. Nobody has to hear their nasty secrets. That would be so… ugly, wouldn't it? If Hemi couldn't protect his little girl? *Either* of his little girls?"

I sank down onto the bench. "Why are you telling me? Why aren't you taking this to him? You're right. He *does* want to protect me. But why tell me? I don't have any money. I can't make it happen."

"You really aren't a very clever girl, are you? Come on,

little Hope. Use that blonde brain of yours a teensy bit."

"You think he'd play chicken with you." My voice was too breathy, too shallow. "His anger would get the better of his protectiveness, and it would end up as a showdown. You could end up with nothing at all to show for all your efforts, because he could refuse to play. But you knew I'd be scared. You knew I'd beg him. You want me to do it for you. You want me to work him, because you know I can. You know I will, and you know he'll give in."

I got her predator's smile for that. "Very good. He thinks he's hard, but he's got such a soft spot, doesn't he, if it's touched just right? You should know, because that's exactly what you've been doing. He's so determined to play the protector and provider. He knows he failed me. It's been eating at him for fourteen years. He won't be able to bear it if he fails you, too. So come on, little Hope. Help me help you. Ten million dollars and it all goes away, and you can be sweet and innocent again, and . . ." She leaned forward, suddenly, put an index finger under my chin, and lifted it. "And nobody will ever have to know. Our secret."

With that, she leaned forward and *kissed* me. On the mouth.

I scrambled away and stood, shaking with rage, and she gave a faint smile, picked up her bag, and stood.

"Very nice," she purred. "Very sweet. Pity Hemi doesn't want to play anymore, really. There are so many things you've never done, aren't there? Five days, darling. After that, it's twenty million for another five days. And after *that?* I'll see you both in court."

maori mana

♡

Hemi

"That's what we've got," Henry Delacroix, my marketing director, was telling the group. It was five o'clock in Paris, the show that would launch my most ambitious line was happening tomorrow, and I needed to get out of this meeting and start on the latest round of cocktail parties in and around the Louvre convention center, the epicenter of the earthquake that was Paris Fashion Week. During which the most important action, as always, happened at the bar.

Or maybe I just needed to get out and move. I had myself under control, but the effort was getting harder every day.

You didn't create buzz by doing the same old thing, I reminded myself, and in the "risk and reward" equation, the risk was the hard part. Most people couldn't cope with it, but I could. I did. Somebody had said once that life was either a daring adventure or nothing at all, and I reckoned that was about right.

Helen Keller. She'd said that, and she'd been blind and deaf. Nothing left to lose, and everything to dare. Who wanted to live scared? There was no "later." There was only now.

"Right," I said. "I want to see the final seating chart after you make those changes, and the final press list as well. Have those to me by morning."

Henry nodded, but didn't answer, and neither did Hope's friend Nathan, in charge of the press for this event. Instead, they were staring into space.

I suppressed a pang of irritation. My temper was all over the shop this week.

I didn't do mood swings. They were unprofitable. I'd been having them anyway. There was so much riding on all of this. The show. Hope. The baby. The new line. Hope.

I was swiveling in my chair on the thought, following the direction of everybody's gaze, and there she was. Walking into the room—no, *striding*. Pulling her suitcase behind her and looking fresh, breathless, and absolutely vibrant in a swingy chocolate-brown cashmere cardigan, fawn trousers, and boots, all of which I'd bought her on that day in Auckland. We'd chosen well, too, because she looked fantastic.

She'd come to see my show. She'd come to be with me.

I was standing, opening my mouth to speak, but she got there first. "I need to talk to you," she said, her body all but quivering. "Right now."

The electricity was prickling in my arms, the blood roaring in my veins. *Fight or flight.* It was going to be "fight." It was always "fight." Especially now. This would be "fight" to the end.

"Meeting's over," I told the group, and somehow, my voice was still level.

The group filed out, and I caught the curious look Nathan cast Hope. The curious looks they were *all* casting her. And me, of course. None of which mattered.

I was shutting the door on them, then turning to Hope. "Right, then. Sit down and tell me." My voice, my body went through the motions while the rest of me tried to separate, tried to escape from this reality, even as I forced them back.

Face it. Deal with it. I could take anything and come out on top. Hadn't I proved it, over and over?

Not this. Not Hope. Anybody but Hope. Anything but this.

She didn't sit down. She pulled her phone out of her purse, slapped it onto the table, and said, "*You* sit down."

I didn't. But I listened. No choice. I listened, and the blood left my head.

Anika, then Hope. Anika baiting, taunting. Then my voice, and if the adrenaline had flowed before? Now, it was flooding me. Drowning me. The hot rage was there, impossible to control, and I spun away and said, "No. Like *hell.*"

"Shh," Hope said, and her hand was on my arm, pulling me back. The excitement was still thrumming almost visibly inside her, and she was *smiling.* "Wait."

Anika asking for ten million dollars. Anika threatening, and Hope sounding cowed. Sounding scared. Sounding beaten.

It ended at last, and Hope allowed the silence to fill the air for a few seconds before she said, "Call Walter and tell him to take that prenuptial agreement I know he's still yapping at you about and shove it where the sun doesn't shine, because your future wife just saved you ten million dollars. Twenty million dollars. A *hundred* million dollars. Tell him she just used your credit card on a last-minute first-class plane ticket from New Zealand to Paris, and she isn't sorry. And that she's going to be buying new furniture for our apartment, furniture she *likes,* because she's earned it. And while you're at it? Tell him to stick a fork in Anika, because she's done. Her lawsuit is going to be *gone.* She can leak all the tapes she wants, but she'll be on her way to prison for extortion and revenge porn and burglary and perjury and everything else Walter can think of. She can tell the world about us, and I don't care. Every man who heard that would be jealous of you, and just about every woman would wish she were me. And *I. Do. Not. Care.* Yes, we had kinky phone sex. Yes, we talked about our fantasies. It was great, and it's the twenty-first century, and we don't live in New Zealand. I'm nobody's innocent little doll, and I'm not going to die whimpering."

I was still so angry, the top of my skull was ready to blow off. And I was laughing, too. Both of them together. For once, I wasn't under control. Not one bit. "Sweetheart. Slow down and tell me. How did you do that?'

"If you're going to attack a naked woman in a locker room," she said, her smile starting to bloom, "if you're going to play your illegal recordings for her, you might want to check whether she's recording *you* when she keeps going to her locker. Of course, to do that, you might have to consider that she could be smarter than you. She could be tougher than you, too, even if she's little and blonde. Even if she's a six and you're a ten. You might have to consider that nice girls can fight. You might even have to believe that nice girls can *win.* And we do. You bet we do. Nice girls kick butt."

"Kick ass." I took her in my arms. There was nothing else I could possibly have done. "Nice girls kick ass. Yes, they do."

♡♡♡

The next day, Hope stood in the wings with me. She didn't touch me, and she didn't say a word, but I could feel the excitement in her tense body as clearly as I could feel my own.

When the lights dimmed and the haunting notes of a Maori bone flute filled the room, the audience stilled. I'd let the music go seconds longer than normal, and it worked. It was a whisper, not a shout.

You can whisper, Hope had said. What happened when somebody whispered? People listened harder.

The first model walked out, a tall, full-figured, bronze-skinned woman with her dark hair tied back in its Maori knot. The rich orange dress was caught on one shapely hip, gathered around her lush body, flattering and emphasizing her curves.

There was a murmur from the crowd, but I couldn't tell. When a model-slim blonde followed, though, her short dress falling to the middle of one thigh defined by muscle and another leg that ended in a prosthesis, the murmur got louder. She turned at the bottom of the catwalk with all the poise and confidence of a fashion veteran—or just a veteran—and revealed the tattoo on her bare left shoulder.

Army Strong.

That was when the applause took on a different quality.

On they came, tall and short, curvy and slim, black and brown and yellow and white. A rainbow of women radiating strength and confidence and feminine pride, all of them lending their beauty to the clothes they wore.

My clothes. My line. Soft fabrics cut to flatter and

enhance, to embrace every curve of a woman's body, in the colors of my homeland. The soft creams and browns of the earth and the beach, the vibrant red of a pohutukawa blossom, the orange of a bird of paradise flower. And running through, around, behind everything, the endless shades of green of the New Zealand bush and the ever-changing, variegated blues of the sea. As subtle and as bold, as shy and as spectacular as a woman.

And the footwear, the funky, rocker-chick shoes and boots Hope had inspired me to add. The hard against the soft, the unexpected punch of a bold statement coming from a gentle woman. The courage to give when it was hardest, the strength to bend without breaking.

The clapping turned to whistles, and I could feel the energy pulsing back from the barely-seen crowd as clearly as if I could measure it. It was new. It was different. It was working.

It wasn't just me, either. Not anymore. It was everybody standing in the wings behind me, and everybody who wasn't here today. The entire entity that was Te Mana.

He waka eke noa. A canoe we are all in with no exception. The canoe we were all paddling together.

Our show, which had taken so many months and person-hours and thinking and changing and arguing, all the late nights and moments of despair, and the renewed determination that kept you going when you wanted to give up—it passed in a flash. In a heartbeat. It seemed like five minutes later when the petite blonde, her curves as subtle as Hope's, came on stage wearing the final piece, and the crowd fell silent again for one glorious moment.

The wedding gown was unlike anything I'd ever designed. Unabashedly romantic and undeniably fragile, from the form-fitting, barely-there underdress to the white-on-white flowers embroidered onto the fabric of the sheer gauze overskirt that clung to below the waist, then billowed out below. The delicate fabric that embraced the model's arms and bodice spoke of softness and tenderness, and that full overskirt promised a bride who would dance in your arms and make you want to hold her forever. It was a dress to make a woman feel treasured and precious and perfect, a dress that was special enough for the most important commitment two people could make.

Hope hadn't seen this one. I'd meant it to be my surprise. Now, she looked at me at last, her eyes shining, and said, "Oh, Hemi."

That was all. I couldn't have heard more anyway. The room was erupting in applause, in cheers and whistles. The model was coming off again, and I needed to go out there. I said, "Thank you," and then I went out to meet the audience.

Hope

I was still reeling from the effects of the show. I hadn't been to many of these, only a handful the previous year, glimpsed from the back of the room, but surely—*surely*—I'd never seen one get that reaction. Or one that wonderful.

It had been Hemi's designs, of course, but it had been everything else, too, coming together to make a unified whole that was more than the sum of its parts. It had been the music and the models, the boots and the leather jackets.

And that dress. That *dress.* A dress that Hemi hadn't put on a tall, willowy brunette, but on a petite blonde. Because that was who he'd designed it for.

He was out there now, talking, taking his moment. Looking as commanding as only he could, as strong and confident as any woman could possibly desire. Behind him, a huge screen projected a twice-life-sized image of a group of models of all colors and sizes standing in the endless green of the New Zealand bush, their arms around each other, laughing, looking happy, looking glorious. Looking real.

He finished his short statement, thanking the audience, thanking his staff, talking about a team effort, about everyone behind the scenes, sounding every inch a Kiwi and not at all like an arrogant designer.

Then the music started up again, the bone flute whistling softly, slowly, and the lighting faded away until all was darkness except the spotlight on the tall, imposing figure in sharply tailored black and white.

"I am Maori," he said as the music faded. "And being Maori isn't about a tattoo or a strong body or a jade pendant. Being Maori is a way of life, a way of fitting into the world and living with everything in it instead of asking the world to fit around you."

The audience was silent, wondering where he was going. He told them. "There's a concept every Maori knows, that every Maori man and woman aspires to. Mana. Mana is honor. It is dignity. Mana is the prestige and respect that comes from the way a man walks the earth, the person a woman is when all the trappings are stripped away. You can't buy it, you can't take it, and if you announce that you have it, everyone knows you don't. Which brings me to somebody I'd like to bring out here. Hope, would you please come join me?"

My first thought was, *I should have dressed much better for this.*

My second thought was, *I'm there.* I walked out into the spotlight, not looking at the audience, and went straight to Hemi.

He wasn't looking at them. He was looking at me. He took my hand and said, "There's a time to be reserved, and there's a time to open up and tell the world. This is that time for me. I'd like to introduce you to Hope Sinclair, who has more mana than anybody I've ever known. This is a woman who tells the truth no matter what it costs her, because the truth needs to be spoken. Hope sat in my conference room some months ago, knowing nobody wanted to hear from her, knowing she wasn't supposed to say anything, and said this."

Behind me, I could see the picture change. The models went away, and a block of text filled the screen with letters six inches high. Hemi waited a moment, then read it aloud.

"What's the alternative to a token? I'll tell you. It's everybody looking exactly the same. It's everything staying the same. It's starved teenage girls with their clothes hanging off them like all they are is clothes hangers. It's women looking at that picture and thinking, how would this dress look on a real person? How would it look on me? And not having a clue, because they can't tell. If the campaign is focused on the clothes being wearable, then show that. Call it… call it 'For Every Body.'"

"If I've done something different today," Hemi said, his hand so strong around mine, "if I'll be doing something different from now on, it's because Hope showed me the way and told me the truth. My future wife, the mother of a daughter I know will have her mother's strength and heart, because she'll have her mother to show her how to do it. My shining star, my lodestone, and my inspiration. Hope Sinclair."

threads of silver

♡

Hope

It was the day after Thanksgiving, and I hadn't had any turkey. I was in New Zealand, I was nearly six months pregnant, and I was getting married tomorrow.

It wasn't like any wedding I'd ever imagined for myself, not even the one I'd thought I'd be having six months ago. There was nothing rushed about it this time, and no uncertainty, either. We both knew what we were getting into, and we knew that it was what we wanted.

We'd even had time to invite guests, and they felt as much mine as Hemi's. Eugene and his wife Debra, Inez and her family, my former coworker Nathan and his girlfriend Gabrielle from New York. It looked like Nathan was settling down. But then, it happened to the best of men.

Some of the group had been taken out fishing by Tane and Matiu today. I couldn't wait to hear what Nathan had to say about that. Nathan wasn't exactly an outdoorsman.

Violet, who'd brought Karen's bridesmaid's dress down from Auckland but had left mine behind, wasn't among the group. "Not possible, darling," she'd said when Hemi had offered the fishing outing. "Not that I want to. Glad to have the excuse, to be honest. I *do* have a bride to fit, though, and it's not easy. Changes every week, doesn't she."

Violet had been given the considerable task of altering Hemi's design to accommodate my twenty-five-week belly. "Not quite kosher, darling," she'd told me when I'd asked her to do it. "If the groom isn't meant to see the dress beforehand, he surely isn't meant to design it."

"Hemi and I," I'd told her serenely, "make our own rules. He hasn't seen me *in* the dress, and that's good enough for me."

"You know," she'd said, "when I first met you, I thought, 'Hemi, mate, you can't be serious.' And now, I think, 'Hemi, mate, I only hope you can keep up.'"

So, yes, those were all people I counted as my friends, too. And then there were all the people I could count as my family.

Koro, of course. Tane and June and their kids, and Matiu as well, despite the laughter in his eyes every time he encountered Hemi and me, as if he knew Hemi was watching him every moment, waiting for him to slip up and declare his undying love. All the other cousins and aunties and uncles and babies that made up a Maori whanau. And the few whose arrival would be greeted warily by all. Hemi's father, who'd continued to stay clean—and who'd be borrowing money throughout the reception. His mother and sister, whom I hadn't met yet and wasn't excited to see.

Tane had told Hemi the day before, when we'd all been at

their house eating dinner and discussing wedding plans, "And before you say anything—if somebody needs to chuck your mum out or drive her back to her hotel, it'll be me. You're not the only man in this whanau who can take charge. Time you learned that."

"Could even be me," June had said with her usual cheerful laugh. "Since I'm more likely to be fit to drive than you, Tane, and you know it."

"Right, then," he'd said. "We'll do it together. You're not to worry, mate, and neither is Hope. We'll get it sorted. You two focus on each other. That's what it's all about."

Soon enough, Hemi would be headed over to Tane's, where he'd be sleeping tonight while Karen and I stayed at Koro's. But right now, on a glorious early-summer afternoon, all fresh breeze, impossibly blue sky, and light striking diamonds off the water, he was taking me for a drive.

"Soothe the wedding nerves, eh," he'd said, looking decidedly un-Hemi-like in shorts, a T-shirt, and jandals, the ubiquitous flip-flops that were mandatory attire in this most casual of countries.

"Speak for yourself," I'd answered. "I don't have wedding nerves. Somebody's got to make an honest woman of me, and it had better happen soon, because I'm not getting any less pregnant here."

"Compliant," he'd said, that hint of a smile in his dark eyes. "That's what I thought when I first saw you. Obedient. Sweet."

"Good thing you were wrong," I'd said—yes, sweetly. "How boring would *that* have been?" And this time, I'd been rewarded with the laugh that I, more easily than anybody else on earth, could coax from him.

Oh—I know you're wondering. Yes, I had a job, and no, it

wasn't working for Hemi. So what was I doing? I had the job of my dreams, maybe the job of a lot of women's dreams. I was thinking about, talking about, dreaming about, and writing about—shoes.

Funky shoes. Rocker-girl shoes. Skedixx Footwear, to be exact, the company whose designs Hemi had chosen for his show. When I'd seen the shots, I'd known that was something I had to be part of. And when I'd proposed the idea to Hemi, right there in Paris, in the afterglow of his triumph, he'd said yes.

After that, I'd done the work. I'd made the call to the president, a fast-talking, whip-thin woman with the dirtiest mouth I'd ever heard, a woman who would have intimidated me to the point of silence a year earlier. But when I'd called her, introduced myself, and told her that Hemi was interested in using her company as an exclusive supplier and that I'd like to be the liaison in their joint venture? You could say she'd leaped at the idea.

Maternity leave? Flexible hours? No problem. And I had my dream job. All it had taken was a little confidence and a lot of Te Mana. The difference was—this time, I knew I had something to offer. I wouldn't be a token, and I wouldn't be a figurehead. I'd be working, and I'd be contributing. I'd already started, in fact, and I loved it.

And Anika? That's the other thing you're wondering about. Anika wasn't going to prison, at least not now.

Walter had paid her an unexpected visit on the day after the Paris show, together with Hemi's New Zealand attorney. Let's just say that Anika had dropped her suit in record time, and that if she ever *did* share those recordings, she'd pay a price she hadn't seemed one bit eager to experience. The spider had gone back into her hole, and she seemed likely to stay there.

If she didn't? What I'd told Hemi was true. I didn't care. Sex scandals were a dime a dozen, and a husband talking dirty to his wife wasn't going to be front-page news.

"Nice here," I said now, a little sleepily. We were driving along Seaforth Road in Waihi Beach, just north of Katikati, past a row of houses, some modest, some grand, located to catch the best possible views of one of the endless stretches of spectacular shoreline that were New Zealand's specialty.

"It is," Hemi agreed. He turned onto a side street that ended at the beach itself and pulled to a stop. A path led through scrubby grass onto the sand. Public, like every beach in the country.

I could have walked and run on these wide-open spaces forever. Or even, maybe, swum. I'd tried a swim in the ocean with Hemi that morning, and it had been different, a little scary but exhilarating all the same, the water clear enough that I'd seen live sand dollars half-burrowed into the sand beneath me, a flash of blue that had surely been a fish.

"This house is for sale," I said idly, looking at the elegant, modern building beside us. A pristine white, its entire front—the part that faced the beach—was domed. Arched, you might say. In order to allow more window space, I guessed, and to get more view. "That's a nice one."

"Would you like to have a look?" Hemi asked.

I stopped in my tracks. "Do not tell me. You bought a house."

"No," he said. "I didn't."

I suppressed the pang of disappointment. What, I expected him to buy me a *house* now? Redecorating his entire apartment and rearranging his entire life hadn't been enough?

"But," he said, "I could do."

I stopped again. "Tell me. Right now."

He pulled a key from his pocket and dangled it from his fingers. "Borrowed it, that's all. Come see. Just in case, eh."

When we went inside, I stood in front of that window wall and said, "Oh, yeah," and Hemi smiled and started folding glass doors back. On and on, until they stood wide open and I was in an indoor/outdoor area that stretched from the modern kitchen behind me to a spacious, airy lounge, then all the way out until the stone-flagged patio ended in a low concrete wall. Beyond that was the beach, and the sea, and the sky. It was pretty good. Scratch that. It was *great*.

"Three bedrooms in here," Hemi said. "And something Americans care about even more, eh. Two baths."

We walked around the downstairs and looked at all of it. It was modern, but it was so light, so breezy, so cheerful. And I was in love.

Then we went upstairs, and it was even better. The top part of that huge curved window gave an uninterrupted view of the sea, an overhanging deck provided more of that indoor/outdoor space, and an enormous bed sat against the far wall from which to take it all in.

"You'd see stars at night," I said dreamily. "I'll bet."

"You would. If you were, for example, here on a visit. Say, three or four times a year. If you had excellent satellite reception so you could work while you let yourself be inspired by space and light and color, that is. It could be someplace where you could spend the odd evening having a barbecue with your whanau, let your Koro spend time with his mokopuna. You could take your kids out on a boat, teach them to fish and to swim and to be Kiwis, and to be Maori. For example."

I stopped where I was, in front of those windows. "I am

very pregnant," I told him. "Don't mess with me. Don't tease me if you don't mean it."

He took my hand. "Don't you know yet that I love to tease you, but I always mean it?"

I knew my eyes must be shining like stars, and that everything I felt was there to read in my face. "Tell me."

"It's your wedding present, if you want it. I wanted you to see it first. If you don't like it, no worries, we'll find another."

"I don't want another one," I said at once. "I want *this* one. I even like the way it's decorated, although of course I know that won't stay."

"It can do. I can get it turnkey if I like. We could change it up gradually, maybe. Add some art, things we found over here. Make it ours."

"Bright things," I said. "Pretty things."

"Pretty things," he agreed solemnly.

I had to laugh. "I can see you now, terrified I'll buy some tacky flower picture or a corny saying painted onto a board that'll make you wince every time you walk past it. Veto power on either side. How's that?"

"Works for me." He took out the key again and jingled it. "Say the word, and you've got your honeymoon suite."

"You're kidding. For tomorrow?"

"Yeh. For tomorrow. Can't think of anything I'd rather do than spend the next three days and nights here with you."

It would be a short honeymoon. It had to be, because Hemi had to get back to work. But that was all right, because we were coming again for a week at Christmas. And every Sunday was mine.

"Then, yes," I said. "Yes, please. I want a house for my wedding present. I want time in New Zealand every year for a wedding present. And I *definitely* want a baby who'll learn to be a Maori and a Kiwi for a wedding present."

"Then," Hemi said, "that's what you're going to get."

Hemi

It could be that a man gets born twice. Once when he takes his first breath of life, and the second time when he finally realizes what that life is all about.

It had taken me longer than most, maybe. I was thirty-seven years old on the day I stood beside my cousin Tane and watched a vibrant Karen walk down the aisle of the wharenui in a yellow dress, carrying a bouquet of yellow roses that stood for her health and our friendship.

I was about to be her brother-in-law, but that wasn't all. I was her guardian as well, the court having made it official only a week earlier. I'd be responsible for her from here on out, and that bothered me not one bit.

I managed a smile for her, and she smiled happily back at me. She looked disconcertingly older than sixteen today, and too beautiful for my complete comfort. Being her guardian was going to be a challenge. But then, I'd always been able to handle a challenge.

The thought entered my head and left it again. I didn't have room for it, not now. Not with my bride coming down the aisle to me on my grandfather's arm.

I'd designed her dress, and I'd thought of her during every minute of the process. But I'd never anticipated the way it would affect me to see her wearing it, and to know she was wearing it for me.

The gossamer fabric seemed to glow around her. She

appeared smaller than ever beside Koro's bulk, her pregnancy the only substantial thing about her, but nobody standing to watch her pass could have looked away. That was how brightly she shone.

The two of them came to a stop before me. Koro bent and kissed her cheek, and she put a hand on his shoulder and whispered something in his ear that might have been, "Thank you," or "I love you." Probably the latter, from the shine in the old man's eyes. She handed her bouquet of white and lavender roses to her sister, and then Koro was joining our hands.

I could swear that something passed between us at that moment, leaping from her hand to mine. The same spark I'd felt that very first day in the photography studio, when I'd touched the cheek of an overworked assistant with a coffee stain on her T-shirt and blue eyes too big for her face and had known I wanted her.

I'd known that spark was sexual attraction. I hadn't realized it could also have been her heart calling to mine, and I couldn't possibly have anticipated the silver threads that had begun to twine around us from that moment, binding us together in a way that would become impossible to resist.

Not that I was resisting. Not anymore.

When I put the circlet embedded with tiny diamonds like stars onto her slim finger, I felt that current pass between us again, stronger than ever. And when she held my hand and slid the platinum band onto my own finger, I knew the circuit was complete.

I didn't need the man to say the words, but he did anyway. And when he told me I could kiss her, I didn't, not right away. First, I twined my fingers through hers, and our rings were touching when I lifted her hand to mine and kissed it.

After that, I kissed my bride, then lifted her off her feet and kissed her again.

Hope Sinclair Te Mana. The girl who had stolen my heart. The woman who had given me back my soul.

threads of gold

♡

Hope

How many honeymoons can a woman have in four months? I'd had three.

Well, it had *felt* like three, anyway. First had been the all-too-few days and nights in our new house, during which Hemi *hadn't* tied me to the bed… well, all right, he had once, but not the whole time or anything like that.

I'd tied *him* there once myself, too. That had been fun.

In the intervals, we'd cooked and eaten and walked on the beach and swum and talked and even lain around together reading and listening to music. We'd relaxed, and it had been wonderful. The least eventful honeymoon you could imagine, especially since we'd already made me pregnant.

We'd come back for Christmas the next month, and it had been a major relief to have our own house to escape to along with Karen when Hemi's parents and sister got to be too much.

"No offense, Hemi," Karen had said on Christmas night, while she and I had been engaged in an unofficial tiny-mince-pie-eating competition.

Hemi and I had looked at each other and smiled. Karen's "no offense" always preceded something special—and usually offensive.

"You sort of had to marry Hope and get pregnant and get me in the deal," Karen went on. "You know, build a new family? Because your birth family kind of sucks."

Hemi and I *had* laughed, then. We'd laughed until I'd gotten the hiccups and had had to drink out of the wrong side of the glass and had felt the giggles creeping up some more.

"Terms for you to learn," Hemi had finally told Karen. "Big whanau, small whanau. My small whanau *definitely* sucks. My big whanau, though… that's all right, eh."

"Mm." Karen had reached for another mince pie, then decided it would be even better with a giant dollop of custard on it. "Especially Matiu. Still yum."

"Except that you're saving yourself for a duke," Hemi had said.

"I am broadening my horizons," Karen had announced loftily. "I can make my own success. I will marry for love and love alone."

"Oh, no," Hemi had groaned. "I foresee a starving artist. A musician, maybe."

"Could be," Karen had said serenely. "Sweet as."

Now, we were finishing up the *third* honeymoon, which had also included Karen. Hemi had finally delivered on his promise to take us to the Great Barrier Reef, now that we'd both learned to swim. He'd had to order a special maternity wetsuit for me, or maybe Josh had. I was coming to believe that Josh had superpowers.

We'd taken off for Karen's spring break, since it would be our last chance before the baby came, and had spent it in Australia's Whitsundays, a group of islands off the coast of Queensland where the sea was blue, the sun was warm, and the living was very, very easy. We'd kayaked past enormous sea turtles swimming along the sandy bottom of crystal-clear waters, had sailed in the sunshine, and, most of all, had snorkeled to our hearts' content. I'd seen corals and fish and anemones and sea stars of every size and shape and color. I'd explored a lush undersea garden with my two favorite people in the world, and then had sat in the tropical Australian dusk and watched entire flocks of cockatoos and parrots wheeling and screaming before they came to roost in the trees.

It had been the adventure of a lifetime, and it was just beginning.

Now, we were flying home, six hours into our journey with eighteen or so to go. Both Australia and New Zealand were behind us, and the next stop would be Hawaii, for refueling. Just the… seven of us. Hemi's pilots, the flight attendant, Hemi, Karen, and me. And the doctor.

Yes. He'd brought a *doctor* along for the whole trip. Dr. Melody Simmons, to be exact, a New York obstetrician who'd been delighted to accept an all-expenses-paid luxury vacation to Australia in return for being Hemi's peace of mind on the plane.

"I'll only be eight months pregnant," I'd told him when he'd brought it up. "And Australia isn't exactly a third-world country."

"Checking you over," he'd said. "And for the flights as well. You'll be thirty-seven weeks by the time we're done. No airline in the world would let you fly, and neither will I. Not without a doctor on board."

"Fine," I'd said, sounding like Karen. I may have been a little grumpy. It's possible. My maternity leave from work had begun when we'd left on the trip, and even though I knew women all over the world worked until they had their babies, I was—all right, I was tired. Especially today. I was too short and small-framed to make carrying an already-seven-pound baby anything but uncomfortable, and I'd probably overdone it a little on our last day. Swimming in warm, salty water looking at fish was about the most blissful thing a pregnant woman could do. Except, of course, having sex, and I'd done that, too. *That* was what I'd probably overdone, in fact.

But then, it *had* been a honeymoon. Of sorts. And Hemi didn't need much excuse.

I shifted in my seat, and Hemi looked up from his laptop. "Need something?"

"No," I said. "Go back to work. Geez. I'm fine."

See? Grumpy. I sighed. "Sorry. But I'm fine. Just tired. I'm going to go lie down for a while."

He'd upgraded his jet. Apparently, the one he'd had before had been insufficiently grand. Now, we had a bedroom in the back, complete with double bed made up fresh for the trip.

I propped myself up against the pillows, turned on the overhead TV, found a movie mindless enough for my current state—*Frozen,* because sister-love was good, and so were strong women—and prepared to while away some time. Aroha squirmed, pushing off my diaphragm and shoving her head down harder onto my cervix, and I put my hand over her and said absently, "Good job exercising, sweetheart, but could you give the leg lifts a rest?"

In answer, she kicked me under the ribs and punched me

in the kidney. Right, then. Maybe not.

I don't know how long it took me to realize that I wasn't just uncomfortable. All of *Frozen*, anyway. Anna had thawed, I'd wiped away my tears, and we were into the epilogue when my abdomen began to tighten again, harder than ever, and I thought, *Hey. Wait,* and realized that the contractions were getting pretty strong.

I lay there, one hand on my distended abdomen, and waited some more, trying not to hold my breath. And sure enough, in a few minutes, there it was again.

Braxton-Hicks, I told myself, but… I *was* up here in the air, hours from land and getting farther away every minute. And there *was* a doctor on board. I'd just check. Quietly.

Ha. Small chance of that. As soon as I waddled up front and asked Melody, "Could you come talk to me a second?" Hemi was up.

"What?" he asked.

The pressure came again, tightening around my belly like a band, and I put a hand onto the seatback beside me and breathed my way through it. Melody had a palm there, too, a look of concentration on her face. And, I thought wildly, if Hemi took that expression into a poker game, he'd lose his shirt.

"Let's go on back and have a look," Melody said, switching, from one second to the next, from a carefree adventure-sports enthusiast into a take-charge professional.

Hemi came, too, and Karen was pulling off her headphones and saying, "What? What's happening?"

I wanted to laugh, it all seemed like such an overreaction. "Nothing," I said. "Probably just looking to create some drama to liven up the trip." But I said it to the air, since Melody was guiding me toward the back of the plane.

And after that, it *really* got exciting.

♡♡♡

Hemi

I was swearing at myself, and I was bargaining with God. Neither of which would do any good.

Why did you risk it, you bloody fool? You knew it could happen. What the hell were you thinking?

And, in the next second, *Please. Just let her be all right. Just let the baby be all right. I'll do anything. Please.*

Life didn't work that way, though, and I knew it. There were no bargains possible. There was only reality.

Reality was Hope, changed into a short nightgown, a monitor strapped around her belly, her hand clasping mine, her voice soothing *me.* Telling me it would be fine, that this was why I'd brought a doctor, that I'd been right.

I didn't care about being right. I'd never cared less.

Reality was the pilot turning around and heading back to Auckland. Reality was being five hours out and forty thousand feet in the air. Reality was watching one movie after the next with Hope—Cinderella and her prince, Beauty and her beast—and not seeing a thing. Reality was Karen singing along to the songs on Hope's other side, being her sister's caretaker for once and knowing how to do it, because Hope had taught her.

Reality was time passing and labor progressing as labors did, until Hope wasn't watching the movie anymore, until she was closing her eyes and going inward during the ever-longer contractions. Until the TV was off and Melody was putting absorbent pads under my wife, getting her ready, because she didn't think we were going to make it in time.

Hope shifted uncomfortably against the pillows, grimaced, and said, "So thirsty." Karen fed her ice chips, and I said, "What would help? Massage your back some more?"

"Could you… get behind me?" Hope asked. "Please? Can I lean on you?"

I could see the tears in her eyes. My endlessly brave, impossibly fierce little warrior, who wasn't going to have to do this alone. Not this time.

I got back there, I held her, and it was better, until it wasn't. Until she was blowing out rapid breaths during every contraction and squeezing Karen's hand so hard, her fingernails left red crescents on Karen's skin.

"Transition," Melody said. "This is the maximum, Hope. Take them one at a time. You're giving your baby room to come out. You're doing great."

Hope was white, the beads of sweat forming on her forehead as fast as Karen could wipe them away. "Hemi," she said. "Please."

"What, love?" I asked. "Anything."

"Could you… sing?" she gasped. "Please? Please sing me a Maori song."

I did. Of course I did. I sang every Maori song I knew. Ballads and hymns, fighting songs and loving songs. There were enough, because there were enough Maori songs in the world to get through anything. Even this.

My voice got hoarse, and I didn't stop. Hope was calling out loud now, and it was killing me, but something was changing. We were starting our descent. I was almost sure of it. Thirty minutes.

"Almost there, love," I told Hope. "Soon be down, sweetheart. And our baby's going to get born."

"Is she… all right?" Hope asked desperately. "It doesn't feel like she can be all right."

"She's fine," Melody said. She reached inside Hope again, and Hope hauled in her breath and moaned. It hurt so much. I could feel it as if it were my own body.

"Good news," Melody said. "Time to push. Come on, Hope. Let's get this little girl born. Let's make the magic happen."

"Sing, Hemi," Hope begged. "Please sing."

I did. I sang my baby girl into the world. I sang her a lullaby during a lull, and I sang her a protest song, a strong song, when things were toughest. And when Melody said, "We've got a head coming," and Hope was nearly screaming, I started singing a song to be born by. *Pokarekare Ana*, the song every Maori knew. The song my daughter would sing.

I wove a net for the two of them with my voice, strand by strand of silver and gold. I sang my strength into Hope. I sang my daughter into life. I sang my girls home.

♡♡♡

Hope

It wasn't until the bedroom door opened and the paramedics came in that I realized we were on the ground. I hadn't even noticed the landing.

I couldn't stop shaking. My hands, my legs. Melody was working on me, sewing me up, and it hurt, but it was so much less than the pain I'd just gone through that I could barely pay attention to it.

Besides, I was looking at my baby. *Our* baby. Hemi was beside me on the bed with Aroha cradled in his arms, wiping her off gently with a towel as he murmured something soft and sweet to her. I could swear she knew her father, too, the way her rosebud mouth nuzzled against his chest. Her dark curls were still damp, and her skin was a golden color that made me want to cry. Or maybe I was crying anyway.

Our golden girl. She was here.

A paramedic started to take her away from Hemi, and I put out a hand—to touch her, or maybe to stop him—but Hemi said, "It's all right, baby. It's all right," and I realized he was talking to me.

"We're… down," I managed to say.

Karen said, "Holy *shit.* Hope. You had a baby in the *air.* You had your baby!" She was laughing and crying, both together. I reached out a hand and clutched hers, as I'd clutched it all along, and was so grateful for her.

Hemi got up and left me, and the paramedics were loading me onto a stretcher, which was good, because I'd be going with Aroha. I said, "Hemi."

"What, sweetheart?" he asked. His face was streaked with tears, and I couldn't even wonder at it.

"What happens to a baby who's born on… I mean, it's New Zealand, isn't it? Isn't that where we are?"

"Auckland airport," he said. "You can run, but you can't hide. Once a Kiwi . . ."

He was babbling. My big, strong, stoic Maori husband was completely over the edge. I managed to smile at him—at least, I thought it was a smile. "So what does that mean?"

"Oh," Karen said. "If you're born somewhere, you're a citizen. Right? Wow, how cool is that?"

"Yeh," Hemi said, taking my hand, smiling at me, loving me. "I reckon our girl's a Kiwi. Through and through."

acknowledgments

♡

Thank you to my amazing alpha read duo, Kathy Harward and Mary Guidry, for holding my virtual hand through FOUND and the previous two books as I navigated this new territory, and continually steering me right. Mary, the title is for you, and Kathy, the singing is for *you.*

Thanks to Carol Chappell and Bob Pryor for their feedback, and a special thank-you to Phalbe Henriksen, who volunteered to do a last proofread and found things I could have sworn weren't there!

Thanks to Mary Guidry for being the best assistant an author could possibly have.

Thanks to my husband, Rick Nolting, for his support and encouragement during an especially tough time while I wrote this book, and to Barbara Buchanan and Rick Dalessio for giving me space and time in their home to finish it when it didn't seem possible. I may write all my books in your house, especially if Rick keeps feeding the author like that.

And finally, thanks to my readers for going on this journey with me. I appreciate you.

Sign up for my mailing list at:
http://www.rosalindjames.com/mail-list
and receive a free book!

Find out what's new at http://www.rosalindjames.com
"Like" my Facebook page or follow me on Twitter
(RosalindJames5) to learn about giveaways, events, and more.

Want to tell me what you liked, or what I got wrong? I'd love to hear! You can email me at Rosalind@rosalindjames.com.

other books from rosalind james

The Escape to New Zealand series

Reka and Hemi's story: JUST FOR YOU
Hannah and Drew's story: JUST THIS ONCE
Kate and Koti's story: JUST GOOD FRIENDS
Jenna and Finn's story: JUST FOR NOW
Emma and Nic's story: JUST FOR FUN
Ally and Nate's/Kristen and Liam's stories: JUST MY LUCK
Josie and Hugh's story: JUST NOT MINE
Hannah & Drew's story again/Reunion: JUST ONCE MORE
Faith & Will's story: JUST IN TIME
Nina & Iain's story: JUST STOP ME

The Not Quite a Billionaire series (Hope & Hemi's story)

FIERCE
FRACTURED
FOUND

The Paradise, Idaho series (Montlake Romance)

Zoe & Cal's story: CARRY ME HOME
Kayla & Luke's story: HOLD ME CLOSE
Rochelle & Travis's story: TURN ME LOOSE
Hailie & Jim's story: TAKE ME BACK

The Kincaids series

Mira and Gabe's story: WELCOME TO PARADISE
Desiree and Alec's story: NOTHING PERSONAL
Alyssa and Joe's story: ASKING FOR TROUBLE

about the author

Rosalind James, a publishing industry veteran and former marketing executive, is an author of Contemporary Romance and Romantic Suspense novels published both independently and through Montlake Romance. She and her husband live in Berkeley, California with a Labrador Retriever named Charlie. Rosalind attributes her surprising success to the fact that "lots of people would like to escape to New Zealand! I know I did!"

35058583R00194

Made in the USA
Middletown, DE
17 September 2016